DEADLY MATCH

THE HIDDEN REALM
BOOK THREE

D.N. HOXA

Also by D.N. Hoxa

The Reign of Dragons Series (Completed)

King of Air

Guardian of Earth

Warden of Water

Queen of Fire

The Pixie Pink Series (Completed)

Werewolves Like Pink Too

Pixies Might Like Claws

Silly Sealed Fates

The New York Shade Series (Completed)

Magic Thief

Stolen Magic

Immoral Magic

Alpha Magic

The New Orleans Shade Series (Completed)

Pain Seeker

Death Spell

Twisted Fate

Battle of Light

The Dark Shade Series (Completed)

Shadow Born

Broken Magic

Dark Shade

Smoke & Ashes Series (Completed)

Firestorm

Ghost City

Witchy Business

Wings of Fire

Winter Wayne Series (Completed)

Bone Witch

Bone Coven

Bone Magic

Bone Spell

Bone Prison

Bone Fairy

Scarlet Jones Series (Completed)

Storm Witch

Storm Power

Storm Legacy

Storm Secrets

Storm Vengeance

Storm Dragon

Victoria Brigham Series (Completed)

Wolf Witch

Wolf Uncovered

Wolf Unleashed

Wolf's Rise

The Marked Series (Completed)

Blood and Fire

Deadly Secrets

Death Marked

Starlight Series (Completed)

Assassin

Villain

Sinner

Savior

Morta Fox Series (Completed)

Heartbeat

Reclaimed

Unchanged

This book is a work of fiction. Names, characters, businesses, organizations, places, events, and incidents either are the product of the author's imagination or are used fictitiously. Any resemblance to actual persons, living or dead, events, or locales is entirely coincidental.

Copyright © 2022 by D.N. Hoxa

This book is protected under the copyright laws of the United States of America. Any reproduction or other unauthorized use of the material or artwork herein is prohibited.

CHAPTER
ONE

Nikki Arella

It's strange how my body knows when the sun is up in the sky, even though layers of concrete separate me from it. Complete darkness in the room I slept in, yet the light of the sun still reached me. Stripped me of my energy. Made my limbs heavy. Tried so hard to shut down my mind—and it should have succeeded. It always did.

Except the screams in my head wouldn't let it. I don't know where they came from, just that I woke up to them turning my mind inside out, demanding all of my attention. I sat up on the bed, completely disoriented, blind to my surroundings still. The whispers in my head were always there, but they'd never been *screaming* so loud that they woke me up in the middle of the day like this before. My hand moved to my chest, to the silver pendant full of magic resting against my skin. It was still there. I could rely on it to keep the whispers at bay for the most part...so why wasn't it working now?

"*Just shut up,*" I hissed at the empty room, falling back on the bed, hoping to get back to the coma-like state that vampires called *sleep* during the day.

And the voices screamed louder.

My eyes popped open again, and I stared at the ceiling. I forced myself to be aware of every detail around me, inside the room, and outside of it, too. If there was something going on out there, anything that could have triggered these screams in my head, maybe if I acknowledged it, they'd calm down and leave me alone.

But my breath caught in my throat and my heart stood perfectly still when I heard the voices.

Just like I suspected, the screams in my head stopped abruptly, except going back to sleep was no longer an option.

"*You left us no choice...*"

"*It's the only way!*"

"*This has to end now before it gets even more out of hand...*"

I recognized them. Garret, Fallon, Ray. The sorcerer, the lizard girl, and Scar Face—all of them *touched* by Vein spirits, same as me. All of them living in Jacob Thorne's house, same as me.

But then came a voice I'd never heard before, and the three words vibrated throughout me.

"*Where is she?*"

I didn't need magic to tell me who they meant.

My instincts took over. The screams returned but not as loud as a minute ago. The spirit living inside me wasn't calm by any means, but it had done its job. It had warned me, woken me up, and now I was perfectly aware of the danger coming for me.

My fangs were already out by the time I opened the door to my room. The sunlight streaming in through the small windows in the hallway took away half my vision, but I still saw. I'd just been caught off guard, that's all. I could still function, fight, survive—daylight or not.

I slammed against the walls more times than I care to admit until I made it to the front doors. Nobody was in the house, but there were seven people outside, right behind the doors.

And...

"*I made a deal with her,*" Jacob Thorne said. His voice was pitched high. He was alarmed. He was *pissed*. "*I gave her my word* and *my blood!*"

With my hand on the handle of the door, I stopped, squeezing my eyes shut for a second. My body was so weak. Daylight sucked balls, but...

"*A mistake you knew better than to make, my boy. Now, where is she?!*"

The threat in the man's voice was evident. Whoever he was, he wasn't going to back away without a fight. He was here for me, and Jacob apparently couldn't stop him even if he wanted. The fact that he was here, arguing with him about it right in front of the door, proved as much.

But whoever this man was, he had no idea what he was up against. Because I was not only a vampire. I was so much worse than he could have imagined—and he was about to witness it firsthand.

Pulling the door open took effort. It was incredible how slow my movements became when the sun was up in the sky. But I stepped onto the threshold and forced a smile on my face, anyway.

And finally, I saw the face of the stranger.

He was just as tall as Jacob, the same blond hair, the same whiskey-colored eyes, but there was a sharpness to them that Jacob didn't have and there were far more wrinkles on his face. He had to be at least a decade older, if not more. He was lean, long limbs and big hands, and the smile on his face matched my own. He wasn't exactly surprised to see me, but he did look excited.

"Looking for me?" I said in a dry voice, fisting my hands until my fingernails dug into my palms. The pain felt good. It kept me focused.

"Aren't you an ugly thing," the man said, his big eyes scrolling down the length of me.

"I was just thinking the same thing," I said, but I failed to sound as cheerful as I'd have liked. I stepped outside, allowing my muscles to relax as I took in everyone else—the five touched sorcerers standing behind the new guy and Jacob at his side.

Jacob, who was looking at me like he was *sorry*.

"Nikki…" he said, but whether he couldn't think of what to say, or didn't want to say anything, was beyond me.

"Who the hell are you?" I asked the new guy while he analyzed every inch of me—the white pajama shorts that were made for men, and the large grey shirt I had on, also made for men. He was measuring me up—and I was doing the same. My instincts were sharp, even in daylight, and I knew there would be a fight here today. It scared me, but not as much as it used to.

Because as much as I hated it, the spirit was still inside me.

And now, after three weeks of controlling it almost every single night with Jacob, I was pretty confident that this guy would not live to see sundown.

"Will Thorne," the man said. "I'm actually excited to meet you, bloodsucker."

"Always a pleasure to meet Vein leeches like you," I said,

but my heart wasn't in it. Would he really attack me right here in front of the house?

The man laughed. It was rough—in a really bad way—and dry, so awful I couldn't keep from flinching if I tried. "*Vein leeches*? Is that the best you got?"

"Well..." I said, thinking about it. He'd gone for *bloodsucker*, which gave me second-hand embarrassment for him, but... "Casting cunts? Magiwhores?" Those sounded pretty accurate. "How about spell-shitters?"

He laughed some more. Glad to be entertaining him because my spirit wasn't the only one who wanted his head at this point. I could feel the aura of magic hanging about him, and it was strong. It was tense. It was much more powerful than even Jacob's.

"Here's what we're gonna do," he suddenly said and took a step closer to me. Every alarm in my head rang, especially when I noticed the terrified look on Jacob's face. And Will Thorne raised his hands toward me. "You're gonna stand still like a good little bloodsucker, and—"

That's as far as I was willing to let him talk. My movements weren't as fast as they would have been in nighttime, but I still jumped and landed right behind him before he noticed. I stilled reached my hands behind my back and grabbed his head, then pulled him in front of me. With a weak cry, the man hit the ground on his back in front of my feet. Dark red smoke buzzed around his fingers, and he didn't hesitate. I raised my leg to slam my heel on his nose, but I didn't make it.

The giant Ray was onto me—slamming onto my side and sending me tumbling to the ground.

"*Stop, Uncle! I will not let—*"

Jacob's voice came to me as if from far away, but my

mind was infused with screams again the moment I gave up all my control so I didn't hear all of it.

Time to come out and play, I thought to the Vein spirit. My mind was made up, my body ready for the transformation. Would daylight slow the spirit down, too? I'd never actually shifted when the sun was up, but I was curious to see.

The pain was immediate. It emptied my lungs completely, and my skin felt like there were a million needles driving into me all at once. I was blinded for a split second, but I still felt the hit on the side of my face just fine. Ray, or even the new Thorne guy, had probably kicked me with all his strength, so I fell back and hit the ground on my side. The pain was nothing compared to that of the shift, though. My bones rearranged, my skin became tighter, thicker, and my fingernails turned to claws. My toenails, too. They kept kicking me while I was down, but the warmth of their magic that slipped right inside my chest didn't hurt the way it usually did.

That's because I was the spirit now, and *it* handled magic much better than I ever could.

When I jumped to my feet, I saw better but not as well as usual when I turned into the monster. Right now, I didn't think about anything—the spirit had full control. It took us backward, moving on all fours, analyzing our surroundings, making calculations. Will Thorne was the biggest threat here. The spirit could feel the magic coming off him much better than I could, so I knew to plan accordingly. And with that necklace around my neck, I could control it. Not all the time, but maybe fifty percent—and that was more than enough for me right now.

When we moved, we were of the same mind. When we jumped and slammed our clawed feet onto the chest of Will

Thorne, we did so in complete agreement. And if there had been any doubt in me that this man was related to Jacob by blood, it was gone the moment my claws hit the invisible barrier of magic that protected his body, the same one that Jacob could activate for himself. *Family heirloom.*

Shit.

The sun was up in the sky, falling in my eyes, and even though I could still see better than when I was just a vampire, the heat did slow me down now, too. They were all coming for me—Fallon, Ray, Garret and Will. Jacob, Dylan and Ethan stayed back, hands at the ready, waiting for the right moment to intervene.

Against *whom*, I wondered? I didn't care about the other two, but for Jacob, I was actually curious. He prided himself in being the good guy. Did that count only when it was convenient for him, or was it the real truth? Because I had yet to make up my mind about him, even after all this time living under the same roof.

Except the magic with which Will Thorne hit me was no joke. It was more powerful than any other thing I'd ever felt, and even the spirit was starting to be very careful to move away from the red smoke constantly coming our way.

We moved back toward the fighting arenas. White sand against my bare feet. It served me well because I could throw fistfuls of it to Fallon, who was standing to my left, hissing and throwing her magic at me every second. It was green and it was vile, a different feel from that of Will, much more in tune with my spirit. Maybe that's why it didn't hurt much, but she did distract me from Will.

And once she was forced to back off, I had all the freedom in the world to go after him. The spirit moved much faster than me, but not as fast as it did at nighttime. Still, its claws made sparks fly every time they slammed against the magic protecting Will's body. And even though *I* knew that that thing was going to take a lot to break, the spirit didn't question it. However long it took. I had much better control of it now than ever before, but I still couldn't get it to walk away at this point, not when it wanted Will's head more than anything in the world.

But while the spirit's attention was on Will, I tried to focus on our surroundings, too—Jacob, Dylan and Ethan still standing a few feet away, watching, unable to make up their minds. Fallon, still throwing her green magic from my left. And...Garret and Ray.

I couldn't see them.

Panic rose in me faster than the fear. They were behind me—I could faintly hear their hearts beating.

And then...

"Now!" Will shouted at the top of his voice, before he slammed a fist covered in red smoke on the side of my face.

I fell back. Magic suffocated me instantly. The dome closed around me in a split second, and when I jumped to my feet, I was locked up in it. Trapped—except this time, it wasn't for training with Jacob.

Just magic, I thought to myself, as the spirit slammed my fists against the shield.

But it wasn't—at least not the same magic that Jacob used on me. This one burned my skin, threw me back against the sand, and the vibrations of it still remained inside me, shaking me to my core. They had drawn their symbols on the sand right behind me. They'd infused them with magic, too, and now that I was locked in, Will Thorne was adding his own brand to it, arms raised as he chanted furiously, bloodshot eyes on me.

The spirit slammed against the magic over and over again, hoping to break it, but it just kept pushing us back.

The pain was almost unbearable, setting every cell in my body on fire until I felt like I was burning for real. Behind Will, Jacob stood there and watched me, eyes glistening like he was about to start crying soon, but he didn't do anything.

And then Will unleashed his magic onto me—the biggest ball of smoke I'd ever seen gathered by a single sorcerer.

It hit me square in the face. There was no way to run from it, nowhere to go. Dark red smoke, like blood in a gas state, slipped into my mouth, my nostrils, into each one of my pores.

My legs shook and let go of me, and I fell on my back, eyes barely open, but the yellow shield of magic, and the sky over me that looked more green than blue, were clear enough. The sun was there, too, almost winking at me every time I blinked. I heard the shouts from the outside world, but they were all muffled to my ears. My body didn't move, frozen in place by the magic still wreaking havoc on my insides.

Funny how I always thought that once the monster was out, there was nothing out there that could stop me. Turns out, put a bunch of sorcerers together, have them ambush me in daylight, and the deed would be done.

But even knowing for a fact that death was staring me in the face right now, and there was no way I was ever getting out of this alive, I couldn't help but think of Ax. He was always there, more persistent in my mind than the voices, so it was easy to focus on him for a split second.

In the next, my mind gave up and unconsciousness took me.

CHAPTER TWO

My eyes opened when the sky was still a bit grey, the sun hidden behind the horizon to leave way for the darkness slowly crawling up the sky. My body felt like it had gone through the sewer. My limbs were heavier than when I awoke in daylight, and even the voices in my head were barely whispers. No screams. No anger. The spirit inside me was locked into a dark corner of my mind somewhere, licking its wounds. Because that magic had affected it, too. It had affected it just as much as me.

I moved, skin covered in goose bumps, all my insides threatening to come right out of my mouth at the mere effort of sitting up. The glowing yellow light of the dome they'd put me in was still there, buzzing with so much magic, I felt the heat of it clearly pressed against my skin. I raised my hand, mesmerized, to try to touch it with the tip of my fingers, but I was still at least five inches away from it when it burned my skin. It had burned me when the spirit had taken over, too. This was not the same magic that Jacob used to keep me contained when we trained. This was different. There was a layer to it, one the spirit inside me felt clearly, and it was designed to work against it. Way too powerful.

And now...

The doors of the house opened, and Will Thorne came out with a huge smile on his face, a cigar burning between his fingers as he led all the others toward me.

I wanted to stand. I wanted to give up control again, let the spirit take over, throw as many kicks as it could before they killed us. Killed *me*.

But what good was that going to do me now? It was already over, wasn't it? I didn't really care, to be honest, but there was one thing that hurt me so much more than these men ever could—Ax. I'd cut our time short on purpose. I'd been so sure that I was doing the right thing by trusting a sorcerer. I hadn't trusted *him* when I should have.

And now I was never going to see him again. It hurt so much my legs wouldn't even carry me if I tried to stand. So, I didn't.

My eyes were on Will Thorne's face, even though I wanted to look at Jacob. I wanted to tell him with my eyes what I never would with my words. I didn't exactly feel betrayed by him—he was a sorcerer. But I did feel betrayed by my own self for my choices.

"Good evening, bloodsucker," Will said, squatting in front of the magic shield that separated us. He brought his cigar to his mouth and sucked in the smoke deeply before he blew it my way. The smoke had no trouble getting through the magic. It reached all the way to me, and the smell was horrible, but I didn't move. Didn't flinch. Just watched him.

"Not much of a talker anymore, are we?" he said, laughing that awful laugh, and the others joined. Especially

Fallon. The way she hated me was incredible. I could see it written all over the unusual green of her eyes.

"Serves me," Will said, standing up again, as if he wanted to look down at me. As if he thought he could scare me if he did.

Nothing scared me anymore. It would just be wasted energy.

"Look at you. This tiny thing responsible for so much chaos," he told me, shaking his head. "Does she even know?"

"No, I don't think she does," Fallon said with a sneaky smile.

"It's a *guess*. We don't have proof that it's true," Jacob said from behind his uncle. I resisted the need to look at him.

"I have all the proof I need, boy," Will said, never taking his eyes off me or that smile from his face. "She's responsible for all of it." He squatted down again. "Do you even know how much trouble your existence has caused the world?"

"Not really," I said. "I don't really give a shit."

He forced himself to laugh. "You don't give a shit that the entire world might end because of you?"

My stomach twisted and turned for a second. His words took me off guard, and he must have noticed because his smile widened like he'd already won.

When he took something out of his pocket, I thought it would be a weapon. It was a phone instead, and on the screen was a map of some sorts, with different colors on it but not names. And the darkest red of all was in the middle. Will pointed at it.

"It's because of *you* that that Vein has come out to the

surface, bloodsucker. Your spirit has the same magic signature as that Vein."

My heart stopped beating for a long second.

"It was that spirit that lives inside you, breaking the barriers just to get to you, that allowed such a catastrophe to happen," he spit. "That must make the likes of you proud."

I could barely breathe, but I forced a smile on my face, anyway.

"Very," I choked, and in my mind I told myself, *not true*. What he was saying was absolutely not true. My spirit was just a spirit like any other—it couldn't have broken barriers or pulled Veins of magic onto the surface of the world. No fucking way. This guy was full of shit.

"I'm sure you are," Will said. "Imagine my surprise when these young ones called me. Out of all the people in the world, I expected at least ninety-nine percent of them to go behind my back when it was convenient—but not my own damn nephew. Never him."

He turned his head back to look at Jacob. The smile never left his face, but it was bitter now.

"I didn't go behind your back," Jacob spit, but Will pretended he hadn't spoken at all.

"I didn't raise *my* boys like that, that's for sure," he told me, like he was letting me in on a secret. "My brother, though... he was never as strict as he needed to be with his."

"I'm pretty sure you find that fascinating. Just the most interesting thing in the world," I forced myself to say. "And it's working. You're gonna fucking bore me to death if you keep talking."

His smile faltered. "You've got a mouth on you..."

"I don't give a shit why you're here or what anyone did.

If you're gonna kill me, do it. Stop talking. I would literally rather die than listen to you speak."

My heart thundered in my chest. I spoke the words but didn't feel them. It was just my automatic response to assholes like him.

Or maybe I was just hoping to piss him off sooner so that he'd get this over with. And he thought about it—oh, how he did. The fact that he *didn't* throw his magic at me, though, made me curious.

Leaning my head to the side, I forced a smile on my face next. "In fact, why haven't you yet? Why wait for me to wake up at all?" If he wanted me dead, I'd have been easy to kill while I was unconscious. Why wait?

"Oh, I will get to it, don't you worry your ugly little head about that," he spit, then stood up again. "Come here, boy." Jacob stepped to his side instantly, still looking like he was about to either pass out or explode into pieces any second. "You're gonna serve a purpose, at least. Once we banish your spirit, the Vein will have no power here anymore." He grinned proudly. "Your death is gonna leave this world a better place, bloodsucker. Tell me—does that piss you off?"

His every word rang true. I felt it in his heart, in the way his blood coursed in his veins calmly. I heard it in his unwavering voice. He *really* believed that. He really thought that I was responsible for that Vein.

My stomach twisted again so fast, I had to lower my head for a second just to make sure I didn't throw my guts out.

"So now, Jake here is gonna release you from your blood oath, and we'll get to my favorite part in no time," Will said.

I looked up then, and I met Jacob's eyes. They were wide, glossy still, and he was paler than I'd ever seen him before. His heart hammered in his chest worse than mine, and the way he gritted his teeth, you'd think *he* was about to die any second now.

But...the way he looked at me, the way he was sweating...it made me curious.

"Go on, now. Stand. Release each other from the oath. Enough time has been wasted," Will ordered.

I didn't move. Jacob didn't move. I could have sworn that for a split second there, he shook his head—only slightly, just a tiny movement, but it was there.

He was telling me *no*.

Words he'd said to me almost two months ago came back. When we made that blood oath, he said that we couldn't release one another from it unless we both agreed to it.

Was that what he meant now when he shook his head?

I turned to Will again, more confused by the second. "What's in it for me?"

Will smiled. "I don't think you realize what's happening here. This is not a choice. You're not going to benefit from this in any way."

I waited a heartbeat to see if he'd say more. If Jacob would give me another sign, but he didn't.

"Then I'm afraid it's a no."

I had no idea what the hell was happening, but my instincts insisted that this wasn't *it*. I couldn't be responsible for that Vein. He was just bullshitting me, trying to get me to feel guilty so that I'd submit to him. I wouldn't do it, not until I knew what the hell was going on.

Because...what if he was actually telling the truth?

The idea made me want to pull my own hair out.

Slowly, Will squatted in front of me again. "We can do

this the easy way or the hard way," he whispered, no longer smiling.

"And I'll pick hard every time," I said and forced myself to wink at him.

The way his cheeks flushed and his heart picked up the beating instantly was almost funny.

"I *will* break you, bloodsucker. Don't you doubt that for a second," he said, standing up. "I got time."

"Well, since you went there, I got *more* time than you."

He raised his brows. "Without food? Without blood?" He laughed. "How long do you think you're gonna last?"

The icy touch of fear crawled up my body instantly, but it didn't really last long. "Guess we're gonna have to wait and see."

His hatred grew the size of a mountain right there in front of my eyes. He despised me so much, I'd be dead right now if looks could kill.

But he didn't say anything else. He turned around, nodded his head back, and stormed toward the house. Jacob lingered for a couple of seconds longer, wide eyes full of *sorry*. Can't even say I hated him. I just...felt *nothing*. And if he saw that on my face, he didn't comment.

"Jacob!" Will called, and Jacob finally turned his back on me, too.

Ten seconds later, they all locked themselves inside the house.

I couldn't hear their heartbeats. Couldn't even smell them, which was for the best. My body reminded me of its weakness the moment I lay down on the sand again, staring at the sky through the magic. The whispers were there, but they were contained. My hand moved to the pendant on my chest, and I played with it as my mind wandered.

Strangely, I wasn't as afraid as I thought I would be. As I *should* have been. The sadness that was forcing the tears in my eyes had nothing to do with what was happening to me today. Maybe it was the shock, or maybe the disbelief, but ten minutes in, I couldn't bring myself to care about Will or Jacob or anyone.

All I could think about was that I was never going to see Ax again.

THE SUN WAS PEAKING in the horizon. The night was over, the lights in the houses were off, and I was all alone in the arena, wrapped up in so much magic it was making me sick. Holding my knees to my chest, I looked at everything around me, but I didn't really see anything.

"Should I try?" I whispered to the night. Should I let the spirit take over now and try to break the shield while they were all inside, sleeping? Will had locked himself in the small house, while the others remained in the big one.

I wanted to. I wanted to fight. I had reason, after all, now more than ever. What was it that Jones said to me once—that I'd fought myself every day all my life, even though nobody had ever asked me to?

Where had all that will to fight gone?

Had I lost it somewhere in the look in Ax's eyes in that cave, when I told him that I'd find him, and he told me not to bother? Had I lost it the moment I woke up yesterday and found out what a stupid mistake I'd made to come back here?

...did it even matter?

The door of the big house opened, making my heart skip a beat.

Jacob came out, head down, hands tucked in the pockets of his jeans as he came to me slowly. It made me smile. I knew he wouldn't be able to stay away for long—his complex wouldn't let him—but I thought he'd wait a couple days first. He was afraid of his uncle—that much was clear. That he even dared to come out here all alone made me wonder if I'd misinterpreted the situation. Maybe he and his uncle were on the same page, but he was keeping up the game to fool me because...*why* exactly?

He didn't say anything, didn't even look at me, just came to sit on the sand next to the shield. His heart was racing in his chest and his blood rushed. Sweat covered the palms of his hands, too. I studied his profile, seeing less and less of him the brighter the sky became. The need to lie down and just close my eyes, give up my mind was strong, but I was too curious to sleep right now. Too curious about what he had to say—*if* he'd say what I thought he would.

He took his time, but eventually, he whispered, "I'm sorry, Nikki."

I nodded at myself—it had been an easy guess.

"That's okay," I said, playing with the sand. "It's not your fault." Technically, it wasn't. He offered me a deal. I took it. That was my decision, even if he forced it on me. I could have chosen death then and spared myself all this trouble.

But then again, if I'd chosen death then, I'd have fewer memories with Ax. Those had been worth it, at least.

"Yes, it is," Jacob said in half a voice, still not daring to look at me. I sighed.

"I was always meant to get to this point, Jacob. I knew it since I was six years old." This was not news to me. Even though I hadn't realized it in the beginning, I always knew I was going to end up killed. It didn't really take a genius to figure it out.

"I can't stop him," Jacob told me. "He's too powerful."

"Oh, I saw that. Felt it all the way to my bones." That red smoke of Will was nothing to kid around with, but I was still curious. "Why did you want me to say no last night?"

"Because he'll kill you," Jacob said without hesitation.

"But if he's right and my spirit is the reason for that Vein...don't you think it's for the best?"

He shook his head. "He doesn't know that for sure—it's just a guess. Something he read and interpreted the way it was convenient—that's it. He's got his laptop, his signal markers planted all over the world, tied to fucking satellites, too. They measure the intensity of magic all over the States, and he's gotten it in his head that the same kind and same intensity of the magic that exists close to that Vein is the same as the magic that makes your spirit." Ugh, my head was already starting to hurt. Satellites? Seriously? "And even if it's true, we can still close that Vein when we take out your spirit."

I turned to him. "I'm pretty sure that's exactly what he's trying to do."

"No—he would kill you, too. He would never let you live."

"There's a ninety-percent chance I'll die in the process, though, remember?" He'd told me that himself.

"Yes—ninety. With Will, it's one hundred."

"So, why doesn't he just do it? Why does he need me to be released from that oath?"

That's when Jacob finally looked at me. "Because if he tries to extract the spirit from you, the oath would kill you. The magic of it would know that you're no longer capable of holding your word, and if your body dies, your spirit will be free for a second, possibly two. Two seconds is all it needs to disappear and make a home out of someone else's body."

I nodded. "Then you'd have to find it again."

"Which is how he's gonna do things if you don't cooperate," he said. Not really surprising.

"Then we'll do it. Let's release each other from the oath so we can get on with it." I'd get my wish, wouldn't I? I'd be free of the spirit once and for all.

"Didn't you hear me? He will kill you, even if you survive the extraction, and you'll be in no position to stop him. Nobody will," Jacob said, a dumbfounded smile on his face.

"That's okay. Like I said—I always knew I was doomed." But he shook his head.

"Bullshit. You've just given up," he told me.

It made me laugh a bit. "I didn't, actually. These past three weeks since you found me in that cave, I tried, didn't I? I tried every single night." He was right here with me.

"And it was working, Nikki," he said, as if that meant anything anymore.

"Yes, it was." I pulled the pendant from under my shirt. "Thanks for this. It gave me more hope than I ever had before. I really do appreciate your help, Jacob."

I never thought the spirit in me could be controlled, but Jacob made it possible with his sheer stubbornness—and with that pendant he gave me.

But the moment the words left my mouth, he burst out laughing.

I turned to him, surprised for once. That was funny? How was that funny?

"That thing isn't worth shit, Nikki!" he said, shaking his

head to himself. "It's just a piece of silver with a stupid spell to alter the color—that's it."

I must have heard him wrong. "Excuse me? Because I thought you said—"

"Yes—that's exactly what I said! I made that thing myself. It doesn't take root into your mind or give you control—*nothing* can do that!"

My lips parted, my heart beating like a drum in my ears. "You're lying, Thorne. I felt it." I felt the magic of the pendant. I felt the power of it, too, the way it slowed down the whispers and the way it gave me more control of the spirit every day...

"You felt *magic*—that's it," Jacob said, smiling like he was constipated or something

I shook my head. "I don't understand."

"All you needed was to believe that you can do it, Nikki. To believe in yourself. You were so sure that you were *never* going to control that spirit that you kept getting in your own way every single night we tried. So, I tricked you into thinking it's magic, but it was all you. You just needed to believe that it could be done, and then you did it."

My mouth opened and closed a couple times, but I had nothing to say. I wanted to laugh, but tears pricked the back of my eyes instead. It wasn't possible. He was a fucking liar —I'd felt the magic of it. I'd *relied* on it since that night he gave it to me!

I'd fucking fought Ax just to keep it on me, and now he was telling me it was all in my head?

But the sun was way too high in the sky now, and I just wanted to stop thinking. I lay down on the sand, still playing with the necklace. Feeling the warmth of the magic buzzing on it.

"Hold on, Nikki," Jacob said, and I felt the urgency of his words. "Just hold on, okay? Don't quit now."

If I'd had more energy, I'd have laughed. Hadn't I already?

"What are you going to do—turn against your own?" I asked in barely any voice. "You can't do that, Jacob. You're a *good guy.*"

He didn't say anything, just like I knew he wouldn't. And it was okay. I would never expect that from him.

Eventually, my eyes began to close.

"Ever heard of a sorceress named Alida…something?" I whispered, searching my brain for the last name. I was pretty sure Ax had told me, but I couldn't remember it. I was barely awake.

A moment later, Jacob said, "Alida Morgans?"

"Yes—Morgans. That's the one." When he mentioned it, the memory was crystal clear—not just of the name but of where I'd been when I heard it—lying on Ax's chest with his arms wrapped tightly around me.

My eyes closed and I went there again.

"Of course, I have," Jacob said. "She's the reason why the Hidden Realm was created. She was a very powerful sorceress and a seer. She saw the whole thing when she was just a little girl."

Wasn't that curious.

"She's in the Hidden Realm," I told him.

The second of silence stretched to eternity. I thought he'd left, and I was more than eager to let go, too, but…

"That's impossible. She died a long time ago," Jacob finally said.

Though my eyes were closed, I could imagine the confused look on his face just fine. It didn't surprise me that he'd say that—Marie had told Ax the same.

"Nope. She's alive, living in the Realm, in a room under the Sangria Castle. She's the one who sent us here after Marie," I whispered. "Do you think the reason was *me*?"

Because it kept nagging at my brain. It made so much more sense than anything else—she'd sent me here because she knew how I'd end up. If a seer could actually see the Hidden Realm before it even existed, she could probably see the Vein, too. She knew I was responsible for it.

Which is why I believed that Will Thorne was right. It just clicked into place the second he said those words. Our coming out of the Realm had nothing to do with Marie. Or Ax.

Just...*me*.

"I don't know. I don't think so," Jacob finally said.

"I do. Marie, she...she never had trouble controlling it."

"Her spirit?"

I think I nodded, but I wasn't sure. I was too far gone to coordinate my movements properly. I could barely speak as it was.

"She pulled out her fangs at will. She ran fast when she wanted. Jumped when she wanted. She never had any trouble with it. It didn't force her to do anything she didn't want to." And I used to think she was *lucky* because of that.

"That's...strange," Jacob whispered.

"It is. So, maybe...maybe it's just about me."

Maybe it always had been about me. Maybe I was to blame for everything.

Jacob took another long second to think about it, but he had no answer for me. "Just hold on," he finally whispered.

I was very happy to let go.

CHAPTER
THREE

Two weeks later

I could barely open my eyes, even though my instincts were screaming for me to do it. Night had fallen—I felt it all over my body. I felt the cold, and the dark, but I also knew what happened when I woke up.

I lost it, just like I'd been doing for the past three nights.

"Wakey, wakey, sunshine."

Will's voice pierced right through my ears. I barely managed to sit up, my limbs shaking, my fangs already extended, the vampire in me in full swing. I hadn't had blood in two weeks. I hadn't been fed in two weeks. All that energy I'd wasted the past week when I let the spirit out to try to break us free had caught up with me. It had spent me. It felt like I was fading away into nothing with every second. It made both kinds of monsters in me furious.

And there was still nothing they could do about it.

How much longer until I lost my mind for good?

Will Thorne came to me with a plastic bottle in his hand. The blood in it made my heart race. Every monster inside me screamed, and when he squatted in front of me, right behind the fucking magic that kept me trapped in the sand, he smiled wide.

"I can't even believe it, but you look worse than yesterday." He said it like it was the best thing he could have possibly imagined.

A growl ripped from my throat, the spirit in me starting to demand control. But if I let it out, he would just fill up this fucking dome with his magic until I passed out. Nowhere for me to go to escape it. No way I could reach him to stop him. And then I would be more spent than now, if that was even possible.

"I know you want this." He put the bottle of blood right in front of the magic shield. My stomach twisted and turned, my mind in chaos. "Just release yourself from the blood oath, and it's all yours. All I have to do is use this stick to push it all the way inside the shield."

He showed me a small stick he picked up from the ground. I growled louder like a fucking animal, unable to form words.

"You won't last much longer," Will said, his wide brown eyes disgusted at the sight of me. "I will give you another week—that's it. Then I'll kill you. You can't get away from this." He spoke slowly, like he wanted every word to make sense to me. He didn't really have to—he'd been saying the same things to me since day one. I knew what he was going to say every night he came out here.

And unfortunately for me, I could find no hint of a lie anywhere in his voice. His heart beat steadily. His smile was wide. He wasn't bluffing. A week was all I had.

My eyes squeezed shut. I didn't want to keep looking at him—or that blood. *Just hold on,* Jacob said.

But for what?

This was my end. I knew it. He knew it, too. I could stop the suffering at least if I just gave in right now. I could finally give up and be free for real.

"Will," Jacob called from somewhere close to the house. I didn't have it in me to even look at him. "I'm leaving."

"Go, boy," Will said, without bothering to even face him. "Be back soon."

Jacob didn't say anything else, but I heard his footsteps. I heard him when he got in his truck. When he drove it outside. *Free* to be anywhere in the world, like I never was. Like I never would be. And even though it made no difference whether he was here or not, I still felt a little bit more alone when the gates closed and I no longer heard his heart beating. Guess I was just used to the sound of it. Guess I still liked to fool myself into thinking it meant something.

I lay down on the sand again, and Will continued to tell me exactly what he was going to do to me. And eventually, the others came out of the house, too. They all came to watch me, like the sight of me wasting away entertained them. All except Ethan the werewolf. He tended to stay away from me, not even look my way when he was out of the house. He was probably more disgusted than the rest.

Even Jacob hadn't come back to talk to me again since that night. I thought he might, but he never did.

Maybe he'd already given up.

Maybe it was time I gave up, too.

Just...in a little bit. Because I did find a way to cope with the nights when I had to stay awake. I escaped inside my own mind, and I went to Ax, somewhere far away, somewhere where nothing and nobody else existed. It was just us. And in my mind, we fought, we laughed, we talked, we devoured each other. We *lived* for one another.

And I would hold onto that illusion because it was just too beautiful to give up right now. Maybe tomorrow.

CHAPTER FOUR

Ax Creed

The numbers swam before my eyes. No matter how hard I tried, I couldn't keep focus. None of it made any sense.

I dropped the folder on the kitchen table like it was on fire. The twins had made me promise to look at their plan last week, and I still couldn't bring myself to go over everything they brought me. A fucking restaurant in the Realm. As if it had any kind of importance.

When I heard the footsteps upstairs, chills rushed down the length of me. I wanted to get out. I wanted to be out there, somewhere, *anywhere* that wasn't here, but...where the fuck was I going to go? Anywhere I went, I'd just want to leave that place, too, and then the other, and the next...

"Hey, Ax," Marcus called as he came down the stairs with his sister. It's not that I had anything against them—they stayed in my house, and I made sure they were safe, fed, clothed. But something about the magic hanging in the air around them made my insides twist. It reminded me of everything I *never* wanted to think about if I'd only had as much control over my mind as I always thought I had.

Turned out, I was full of shit.

"Hey, kid. What's up?" I said, forcing myself to sound calm. It wasn't their fault that they were here. It wasn't their fault that I'd practically dragged them into a world that was designed to separate our kinds, keep us far away from each other—and with good reason.

"Nothing much. I was wondering if you wanted to play video games later?" He came to sit at the dining table, grabbed an apple from the bowl, completely at ease. "What's this?" he asked before I could reply, opening the folder that the twins had brought me with their plan about the new restaurant they wanted me to invest in.

"Nothing important," I said, half my focus on Marie, who sat down on the couch on the other side of the room, a book in her hands. "And I can't play tonight. I've got work to do."

Lie. I didn't have shit to do. And everything Robert came up with just pissed me off more. He'd noticed, at least. That's why he hadn't asked me to even go see him in the past four days.

"You always say that," Marcus said, eating the apple as his eyes scrolled down the sheet. It still amazed me how comfortable he was here. Like he was at home. They both wore the wooden circles that the old sorceress had made for them, but even that shouldn't have had them so relaxed. They couldn't care less that they were living in a house with a vampire—neither of them was ever scared.

Did they *really* trust me that much?

"It's always true," I told the kid, then turned for the stairs to go to my bedroom.

"No, it's not. I don't have to be a vampire to know when

you're lying. If you're afraid I'll beat you, just say so. No need to bother lying," Marcus called from the kitchen.

It actually made me smile. I wasn't used to people talking to me like that. It was a bit amusing.

I stepped back until I could see him again. "You know what? Let's play video games."

Maybe it would be a distraction. Maybe I could get lost in a different world for a little while. Maybe I could get myself to stop feeling like the end of the world was seconds away.

Marcus grinned mischievously. "If I win, I get an X-box."

I raised my brows. "I got you the damn Play Station."

"Yes, and I want the X-box, too." He stood up from the chair. "And if *you* win, which is not going to happen, I'll take a look at all these numbers for you and tell you if they're worth something." He pointed at the folder on the table.

Damn. Now he really backed me into a corner.

"Game on, kid," I said, feeling *slightly* better for a second, but...it didn't last.

I heard the car when it circled the castle. It didn't stop or turn for the garages, which were on the other side of where my house stood. Instead, it came in my direction.

Holding my breath, I waited...and the car parked right in front of my driveway.

The next second, I was in front of the window next to the entrance door. The black Aston Martin was polished to perfection, and the headlights remained on, even when the engine stopped purring and the driver's door opened.

Abraham Jones stepped out.

Every alarm in my head rang at the same time.

"Kids, get upstairs."

"Why, who is it?" Marie asked.

"Just a friend. Go," I said, and they immediately rushed to the stairs. My eyes stayed on Jones—the way he stopped in front of the house, hands in the pockets of his suit pants, analyzing every inch of the exterior, before his eyes met mine through the white curtain.

A million thoughts crossed my mind, but none gave me even the slightest clue as to why Abraham Jones would be in my driveway. Did he know this house belonged to me?

Of course, he did. Maybe he was here to accuse me of something else again?

Better to find out.

My instincts were sharp, my body ready, my mind empty the moment I opened the door. He moved fast and was right in front of me before I could even blink. It didn't scare me—on the contrary. I'd always loved taking advantage of the benefits that came with vampirism, unlike most of my kind. He seemed to be on the same page with me.

I expected a greeting. I expected him to attack. I even expected him to say, *sorry, wrong house.*

What I didn't expect at all was what he said...

"How much is she worth to you?"

My jaw was instantly uncomfortable, my fangs begging to come out because I knew who he was talking about. His black eyes held mine without ever blinking, and he wasn't even breathing as he focused completely on *my* lungs and my heart instead. Waiting for a reaction.

When I didn't give him any, he added, "Is she worth your life?"

His voice was crystal clear, ice-cold, tempting me.

I'd made a habit out of controlling my body a long time ago, and I didn't slip this time, either, no matter what the inside of my mind looked like. So, I turned my head to the side and just continued to look at him with a forced smile on my face.

What the hell was the meaning behind those questions? Why was he asking?

A second later, Jones smiled, too, so bitterly I could almost taste it on my tongue. Then, he stepped back. "Clearly I've misjudged the situation," he said, and turned around to leave. Just like that.

The curiosity in me roared like a monster. I gritted my teeth and fisted my hands for as long as I could, but in the end, it won.

I'd promised myself five weeks ago that I *never* wanted to even hear about Damsel again. I didn't need to. It was already done. She'd made her choice. I'd made mine, too.

But, fuck if my entire body didn't threaten to turn inside out if I didn't speak.

"Everything," I said, raising my head. Fuck it, I couldn't let him walk away without knowing why he was here first. Jones stopped walking. "Not just my life—she's worth everything." And as sad as it was, it was the most undeniable truth of my being. Even now, even after everything. I wanted to hate her for it so much, but I couldn't. Not yet.

Maybe one day.

Jones turned to face me again slowly, a real smile stretching his lips this time. And when he moved and popped right in front of me, I expected it. He took his hand out of his pocket and reached out to me. A small piece of paper was between his fingers.

"Jacob Thorne sends his regards," Jones said.

My blood rushed at the mentioning of that name. I reached out my hand, and he dropped the piece of paper in my palm.

Then he turned around again and was by his car in a blink.

"Did you send them after her?" I called before he could get it. We'd been attacked at that motel, Damsel and I, and a bunch of vampires had claimed there was a bounty on her head. Robert didn't know anything about it. I thought maybe Jones might.

He stopped again, the driver's door half open. "Who?"

"Vampires, about four weeks ago."

Jones shook his head, brows narrowed in confusion. "I would never send anybody after her."

His words rang true.

I stepped back inside and closed the door.

My eyes squeezed shut for a moment. I remembered the vampires who'd ambushed us in that motel, the same ones who'd been working with the sorcerers coming for my head. Damsel had thought it was Jones, but I'd had my doubts. Not anymore. Somebody else had sent them after her.

Did it even matter, though? As much as I wanted to know and kill the person responsible, it didn't. Not anymore.

Footsteps behind me. I opened the small piece of paper in my hand. An address in Minnesota was scribbled in it.

Was that where she was? *With* Jacob Thorne? Had he really given that address to Jones, or were they all just playing me?

Couldn't think of a reason why they would. Robert was happy to have me back. He'd let me have all the time in the world, too, so long as I didn't leave again.

Unless Jones was working behind his back?

What does it matter?

Closing my fist around the piece of paper, I went and

threw it in the trashcan in the kitchen. Even if that address was really where Damsel was, it didn't matter. She didn't want to be with me. She'd made her fucking choice over a month ago. And I would not go there only to have her say it to my face again.

No—it was *done*.

"Was he talking about Nikki?"

I turned around to see the siblings in the living room, both looking at me, eyes wide and heartbeats accelerated. I'd told them that Damsel was alive when I came back—they wouldn't shut up with the questions otherwise. I told everyone—it had never really been a secret, anyway. It didn't really surprise me that they spied on my conversation with Jones—especially with Marie's enhanced senses—and put two and two together.

"Yes." I turned for the stairs again. "How about that game you promised, kid?" It would be something to do, something that would keep me from thinking.

"Wait," Marie said, rushing closer to me. "He said *Jacob Thorne,* right? I heard it."

Just the mentioning of that name made my skin crawl. "Yes."

"That's the same guy who ambushed us that night," Marie said, her wide brown eyes glossy, like they were full of unshed tears.

"Yes—and the same guy Nikki chose to go with." My voice sounded strange, and it took all I had to stop myself from growling.

"Really?" She sounded surprised, even a bit skeptical. Though I'd told them that Damsel wasn't coming back, I hadn't exactly given them details.

"Yes, really. She *chose* with her own free will." Which

was something I needed to remember, too, for my own sake.

"So why—"

"I don't want to talk about it," I forced myself to say before I lost my shit.

But Marie had a way of getting into my head by saying things I couldn't fucking ignore if I tried.

"What if she needs you?"

My heart skipped a beat. I fisted my hands tightly.

"She doesn't need anyone. She can take care of herself." I started walking up the stairs.

"So why was Abraham Jones here?" the sorceress asked, making me stop mid-stride. "What did he give you?"

I thought about it for a second... "An address."

Jacob Thorne sends his regards.

The same Jacob Thorne who'd taken her from me. Who'd told her I was a monster. Who *didn't want* me near her.

Why would he send me his fucking regards—and an address?

Better yet—how would Jones know to come to me if Jacob fucking Thorne hadn't told him something? Robert knew, but I doubted he'd told Jones about me and Damsel. He'd have let me know if he did.

I turned to the siblings again, no longer really seeing anything in front of me. Was Damsel in trouble? Why the fuck would that man send me this address?

"You tracked your brother once," I said to Marie, putting my hand on her shoulder without really thinking about it. I saw her flinch at the contact, but at that point I didn't really give a shit. "You could tell that he was okay. That he was breathing."

"That's...that's because I had his blood. And he's my sibling," she whispered, suddenly terrified.

"Is there another way to track her?"

Her eyes widened. "I can't do anything without blood."

"Well, I don't have her blood," I spit. I had nothing—not even a hair from her head.

"I'm sorry," Marie whispered. "There are herbs and—"

"Alida."

Marcus was right by my side, and I hadn't even heard him moving. "Alida could probably do it. She's old, probably more experienced in spells and stuff. Plus, she has things in that room of hers, doesn't she? She made us these." And he touched the wooden circle hanging onto the leather tie around his neck.

Alida Morgans, the old sorceress who'd somehow *chosen* to live in the Hidden Realm.

By the time I was out the door, the siblings were right behind me.

"We're coming with," Marcus said.

"No, you're not."

"If we both do the spell, it will be more powerful," Marie insisted. "Trust me—I know how magic works."

I stopped and turned to them so fast, they both jumped back. "Why do you care?"

"She saved our lives, remember?" Marie said, shaking her head like my question insulted her. "And we're not fools, Ax. We know she's the only reason why you're keeping us here, in your house."

She was right. And despite my better judgment, I didn't have it in me to argue anymore. So, I turned to the door again.

"Stay close."

The siblings didn't make another sound.

DEADLY MATCH

I HADN'T SEEN the old sorceress in over a month. Couldn't say I missed her. Couldn't even say I hated her any less. She'd been the one to tell me that Damsel was alive the first time. She'd *heard* her heart beating.

But she'd also claimed she knew where my path would lead me, and look at me now.

"I understand," she said, when Marie explained to her why we were here in the first place, in Robert's wine cellar, under the castle.

Then, she looked at me. "You're worried she's dead?"

Every hair on my body stood at attention. Damsel, *dead*.

Fuck, I wanted to break something so badly.

"I just want to know if she's well," I said through gritted teeth.

"She saved our lives, Alida," Marie told her. "If we can do a tracking spell, maybe we can feel her."

"That would be very problematic, dear," the sorceress said, taking off her half-moon glasses. "We don't have her blood or her hair. We don't—"

"We can still try. Both of us. The spell will be more powerful that way," Marie insisted.

I watched Alida closely for a reaction. She looked worried. She looked *sorry* as she smiled at Marie.

"Okay. Sure, dear, we'll try it." She said it like she was just indulging us. Like she didn't really think it was going to work, but she would do it anyway, for Marie's sake.

My mind was in chaos. I hadn't been this confused in my entire life. Half of me wanted me to stop this fucking nonsense. Damsel could take care of herself, and if she really was in trouble, she could handle it. She'd *chosen* to handle it by herself. She didn't need my help for anything—

better yet, she didn't *want* my help. I'd come to terms with it. I'd accepted it. I'd let go.

But the other part of me, the mind of the man I had been when I'd went on a killing spree searching for her, demanded that I sit still and wait. See what the sorceress would say because if there was a chance that Damsel was really in trouble...if there was just a chance that she needed me...fuck if I could stop myself from breaking the world in half to find her again.

That's why I stayed by the door with Marcus while Marie and Alida prepared everything they needed, drew lines on the hardwood floor with their chalks and spread dry leaves all over in no apparent order—but what the fuck did I know about magic?

"What are you going to do if she's okay?" Marcus asked, while the women held hands together, sitting inside the chalk circle, whispering words with their eyes closed.

"Nothing," I said. That's what I would do—*not* a single damn thing.

"And if she's not?"

I looked at the kid, a million thoughts spinning in my head. But before I could pick one to stick to, Marie and Alida both opened their eyes with a sharp intake of breath. I lost sight of Marcus and was in front of them without even realizing I'd moved.

"What is it? Did you feel her?" I demanded, and Marie reached out to grab my arm, her wide eyes dark and terrified as she nodded.

"She's...she's barely breathing, Ax," she choked.

That's when I knew I was fucked.

CHAPTER
FIVE

Six hours until Minnesota. I put the address on that piece of paper in the GPS of my car and drove it right out the gates of the Hidden Realm. If I drove like I usually did, I'd get to the woods displaying in the screen of my car by three am.

I really hoped that nobody was unfortunate enough to stand in my way.

The phone I'd thrown on the passenger seat kept buzzing—Robert's name flashing on the screen. I'd texted him to tell him I was leaving, and now he probably wanted to know why. I wouldn't answer. I wouldn't tell him. *I couldn't* tell anyone anything until I saw it with my own eyes. Until I knew what the fuck was happening.

She's barely breathing.

The words circulated inside my mind, demanded my full attention. Good thing I'd taken the west gates, where most of the supply trucks came into the Realm. The road was made of asphalt and there was no traffic ahead, nothing in the way except the animals who heard me coming long before I got to them. The fucking car had to come, though I'd have preferred running.

But if I ran all the way there, I'd be too tired to fight. I'd need to rest—and I already knew I wouldn't. And if I ran all the way there, I couldn't take Damsel away in daylight. She couldn't stay awake when the sun was up. She'd have no choice but to sleep, so she could sleep in the back while I drove us away.

Slamming my fist on the steering wheel, I cursed out loud. What the hell was wrong with me? Did I forget so fast how we parted ways? Did I forget so fast that she'd chosen to walk away from me? Where the fuck would I even take her if she didn't want to go?

And she wouldn't. She'd made that pretty clear last time.

So why was I so eager to make an ass out of myself again, to have her look me in the eye and turn me away again, so I could come back here and break my entire fucking house with my own hands in hopes it would make it hurt a little less—*again*?

It wouldn't work. Nothing would work. It would be even worse than the first time.

But the idea of her being in pain, of someone hurting her while I didn't know about it...fuck, I lost reason completely. Nothing mattered, not even if she told me to go fuck myself. I had to see her. I had to know. I had to make sure she was okay, everything else be damned.

If she turned me away again, that would mean she would be okay enough to do it.

And no matter how fucked up it was, *that* was the only thing that mattered.

I MADE it to Minnesota by two-thirty. I drove like a maniac, hit three cars on the way, but I made it. I was here.

The woods stretched before me, full of animals, a million smells coming at me in waves. There was no house that I could see, no building. No people—human or sorcerer or vampire. Nothing but trees.

Half my mind was made up that this was a trap. Jones had brought me here for something. Maybe even Thorne had brought me here for something—but not because of Damsel. If I turned back now, I could rest somewhere for the day and be back home by nightfall. I could spare myself the fucking pain.

Still, I gritted my teeth and entered the woods with no idea where I was even going. All I knew was that I needed to see. Once I did, everything would be clear. Once I did, I could go back without this weight on my shoulders and start my hopeless attempt at forgetting about her all over again.

It took about half an hour of walking through the dark woods to catch the spicy scent of magic. It was just a little bit, but I recognized it way better now that I'd lived with two sorcerers brimming with it for five weeks. Following it wasn't hard, and it only took me a few more minutes to see the white wall in the distance, about eight feet tall. It didn't exactly convince me that this wasn't a trap yet, and if I'd had just a little less faith in myself, I'd have wanted to double check the entire woods before I went close to that wall. As it was, I made straight for it, and the closer to it I went, the more I felt the magic.

So much of it—*too* much. It didn't even let me hear anything inside. Breaking through it wasn't an issue—I could. But it would take time. It would take energy. It would let anybody inside those walls know that I was right there.

How the fuck was I supposed to get through without anybody knowing?

Maybe circling the entire place for a little while wasn't such a bad idea. After all, I was early.

The property surrounded by that wall and those wooden gates was huge. It went into a wide circle with no other entrance but the gates at the dirt road I'm missed when in the car. I could jump over the wall without an effort, if there only wasn't so much magic surrounding it.

But it was okay. There was a good chance that Damsel was in there. An even better chance that she'd flip out if she knew I was here and turn me away the second she saw my face.

Even so, I'd see for myself. So, I sat on the ground for a bit, just close to the gates, and I forced myself to think, to come up with a good plan. I was already here—might as well see this through.

If I drove the car through the road and slammed it into those gates, would the magic stop it, or would it go through? Objects could get through shields, but once the magic felt *me* inside the car? I wasn't sure.

How about if I broke the wood of the gates first with something else? A weapon…maybe a hammer or an axe or a fucking machine gun. Possible, but I'd need to find those weapons first.

If I tried to break the wood with my bare hands, on the other side…

Looking back, I spotted the tallest tree closest to the house. I would climb it, see what was inside if the magic allowed it, and then I would at least know how many people I'd be up against, but…

The sound of footsteps caught me a bit off guard. I couldn't really hear anything going on inside those walls through the magic, but someone must have been close. Very close to the gates, and the wood let out more sound than the concrete.

Moving slowly, I stood up and went closer. If someone was coming out, I would get in the moment they opened those gates. It would be easy. All I'd need would be five seconds.

But the footsteps stopped for a good long minute. I could faintly hear a heartbeat, too, but I couldn't smell anything through the magic.

And then...

"Are you there yet?"

My eyes closed. Even my heart stood perfectly still for a moment.

Jacob fucking Thorne.

He was there. He was *right* there. I recognized his voice, though he hadn't been loud. I recognized the way his fucking heart beat, too, even though I couldn't smell his scent. He was here, and...

A second later, I heard his footsteps as he moved away.

I had two options. I could sit out here and wait, see what more he would do, keep my presence unknown until I knew for sure what the fuck was going on.

Or...

I grabbed a rock from the ground and threw it over the wall within a second.

The magic shield didn't stop it. It went right through. Made me wonder if it would stop a bomb from going in, too.

But Jacob stopped walking for a second, and then he

turned back to the gates. I held my breath, straining my ears, ready to attack at the first sign of danger.

"You have ten seconds," he said, his voice barely reaching me.

And when I heard his footsteps retreating again, the magic that wrapped around these walls hissed.

Then, it released into the air like a heatwave, slamming against my face. I stepped back for a second, just to make sure that the heat wouldn't scorch me. And when it didn't, I jumped.

I didn't think. I didn't try to listen first. I just jumped and landed on top of the wall, and finally saw what was inside.

Two houses, one big, one small. A large space on their other side and a small woods at the end, separated from the rest behind it by the same wall I was standing on. I heard the heartbeats. I heard the voices—at least three of them.

The air began to heat up with magic. My ten seconds were already up.

I jumped as silently as I could on the other side of the wall. Five trucks were parked at the back of the houses—one of them red, the same truck that Jacob Thorne had been driving when he caught us in Albuquerque. I strained my ears as I moved closer to the houses, to the voices, as slowly as possible. I had no idea how much they could hear yet.

Seven heartbeats in total. It made sense—Damsel, Thorne, and the other five sorcerers he kept around here.

But...none of their hearts beat like Damsel's. Maybe I'd lost my fucking mind to think I knew the rhythm of it still, but I did. And none of it was hers.

The closer to the side of the house I got, the more I heard. The better I saw. There was a big area covered in white sand right before the trees began. A man was outside, talking about some magic spell to three others, while another three were somewhere inside the house, possibly sleeping. I pressed my back to the wall of the house and kept going, focused on my ears the most.

But the moment I could see *all* of the view in front of me, my mind was wiped completely clean.

My instincts failed me. Hiding no longer seemed like a necessity. I couldn't care less who saw because *I* couldn't believe what I was seeing, either.

Yellowish magic buzzed in the middle of the white sand, made into half a circle, and inside it was Damsel.

I walked ahead but didn't really feel it. I noticed that the voices stopped abruptly the second I stepped away from the house, but I couldn't tear my eyes off that magic, off Damsel sitting in the sand inside it, hugging her knees to her chest.

Her eyes were lifeless, the bags under them a deep blue, her cheeks hollow. There was a grey tint to her skin, too, which I recognized perfectly. It happened when vampires didn't drink blood for at least a couple of weeks. I'd seen it countless times on my prisoners in the past.

But on Damsel…I just couldn't believe it. It didn't make sense.

Who in the world would dare to do *that* to her?

Her eyes were on me, but she didn't react. She just put her chin on her knee and watched me, like she couldn't even see me standing there. Like she *wasn't* there herself.

What had they done to her? *Who* had done this?

As if awakening from a dream, I turned to the front of the house, to the people who'd been talking until I showed up, and I found them all facing me, arms raised, fingers sparkling with magic.

Jacob Thorne stood to the far left, sweat covering his

forehead as he looked at me. Next to him was a man with a face full of scars I'd seen before. And next to him was another, an older version of Jacob, taller, better built, with sharper eyes and a sneaky smile on his face. And the last was a skinny guy with long hair, who looked like he really wanted to be anywhere else but here.

These people had put Damsel in that thing. They'd starved her. I could see it—even the clothes on her body were torn, dirty. How long had they kept her in there?

My mind was no longer my own. I was perfectly calm—not angry in the least. Even my heartbeat was steady. I surrendered myself to the monster completely. My fangs were extended, and my lips stretched into a smile.

"Who touched her?" I asked them because I wanted to know who died first. I *needed* to be extra careful and extra slow when I took their lives.

None of them said anything, so I took a step closer.

"C'mon, you can tell me. I won't be mad." And I really wouldn't. "Tell me who put her there."

"Sonovabitch," the older guy muttered, just before blood-red smoke gathered between his hands, lightning fast.

Bingo.

He threw his magic at me. I jumped.

CHAPTER
SIX

NIKKI ARELLA

I'D DREAMED about him so many times now that I was seeing him even with my eyes open.

That's why he was there right now, walking from the side of the house slowly as he took me in. In my imagination, he didn't look disgusted at the sight of me, though he probably would have in real life. I hadn't showered in almost three weeks. I'd had to pee twice in the fucking sand, but luckily I hadn't eaten anything in a couple days before I got locked in here. My clothes were a smelly mess. My hair...ugh, I didn't even want to think about it.

I *was* disgusting to look at, but Ax of my imagination didn't think so. He didn't flinch. He didn't even look at me for long.

He just turned to Will, Ray, Jacob and Dylan, drinking beer and hanging out in front of the house, because Will wanted to wait for sunrise so he could offer me his stupid bottle of blood again and hope I'd be too weak to turn him down so close to dawn.

I was *this* close to caving.

But the moment Ax's fangs started to come out, I got a bit more curious. I hadn't imagined his fangs at all since I'd been locked up here.

And then he spoke, too.

"*Who touched her?*"

My gods, his voice sounded *exactly* like it did in real life. I'd fantasized about him a million times by now, but I'd never gotten it so right before.

Nobody said a single word, so he smiled wider.

"*C'mon, you can tell me. I won't be mad. Tell me who put her there.*"

And the others…my gods, the others could *see* him, too. In fact, they had their hands raised toward him, sparkling with magic, and Will was even smiling.

"Sonovabitch," he said as he gathered his red smoke and threw it at Ax before I could blink.

"*Ax!*" I shouted at the top of my voice, standing on shaking legs as he jumped on the roof of the house.

Everything happened so fast, I had no chance of keeping up with it. My mind was numb, only one thought making sense in the chaos: Ax was really here. He had come for me.

And then he jumped again.

Seeing it all through a screen of magic made it almost impossible to believe. The voices in my head were screaming as Ax jumped down to the ground again, landing right behind Dylan before anybody could even see him. He grabbed Dylan by the head and threw him back without looking. The sorcerer flew in the air a few feet before landing on the ground on his face.

Will had already turned around, his magic fast but not fast enough. By the time he threw it at Ax, he'd already jumped again, and the magic hit the corner of the house, shaking it to its core. Ax landed right on Will's side, slamming his fists on his head and face too fast for the eye to see, but other than making Will fall back a bit, he couldn't hurt him. He had the same family heirloom spell that protected Jacob around his body. It was the reason why I hadn't been able to hurt him at all, either, before he locked me in here.

But Ray was on Ax before he could get to Will again, a monstrous roar coming out of him, his eyes *red* now that whatever spirit he had in him had come out to play. Mine wanted to do the same. Ax moved, jumped and kicked and took Ray's feet from under him before Ray could even touch him, but Jacob was on Ax, too.

And...he moved, but he moved extra slowly. It's the one movement of Ax that was slow enough for me to see in detail. He turned, eyes on Jacob, who had his back to me. He stopped only for a split second before he slammed his fist on Jacob's chest and threw him back, flying.

Jacob spun in the air three times before he landed with his face in the sand at the beginning of the arena, just as red magic came toward Ax again. This time, it touched his shoulder. He growled and jumped back, putting some distance between himself and the sorcerers, and the door of the house opened. Ethan, Garret and Fallon came out, their eyes on Ax as they slowly moved closer to Will. Even Dylan had come to his senses, cracking his neck to the sides as his eyes zeroed in on Ax.

My heart skipped a long beat. All of them against Ax. They were going to kill him.

The monster in me roared. I gave up control instantly,

even knowing that I could never get out of this fucking magic. But maybe now that they were distracted, they wouldn't stop me. Maybe the spirit could actually crack the shield and get us out. Maybe...

"*Nikki.*"

My eyes moved to Jacob, as colorful smoke came at Ax from all sides. His eyes were open. He was looking right at me, but he wasn't moving.

It took me a second to realize what he was doing.

"*I release you from your oath, Nicole Arella. You are no longer bound to me,*" he whispered, just loud enough for me to hear. And his right hand moved on the sand, drawing something the way he usually did with a stick.

I shook my head. What was he doing? Why would he release me now?

"Nikki, *now*," he hissed, and I swallowed hard, a million questions filling my head.

What if it didn't work? What if I was still stuck here? What if they actually killed Ax?

What if, what if, what if...

"I release you from your oath, Jacob Thorne. You are no longer bound to me," I said, digging my fingernails in my palms as the spirit in me thrashed, demanding control.

And Jacob began to whisper words I didn't understand, as magic released from the sand where he drew his symbols. I felt the heat of them on my skin even through the magic shield. It pressed on me, and though it didn't hurt, it was very uncomfortable, just like sunlight. I released a long breath when it lifted off me again, and the energy it took out of me made my legs even weaker. I hit the sand on my knees, squeezing my eyes shut. A cry ripped from me when the spirit took over my body and mind completely.

When the shifting started, I blacked out for a moment. I still felt the pain in my bones, in my muscles, on my skin as my body rearranged itself to better fit the image of whatever spirit was inside me. And when I came to again, all I saw were sparks. My spirit was clawing at the magic shield surrounding us, and nobody was coming to knock us out.

They were all still going after Ax.

Out of all of them, only Garret was able to keep up with his movements. His spirit, whatever it was, made him fast. Not as fast as a vampire, but close. Even so, Ax was unstoppable. With the spirit enhancing my senses, I could hear his movements better, see him perfectly even through the sparks and the magic, and he was a true savage. His heart beat steady. His blood didn't rush. He had complete control over his body, and his aim was true every time. Fallon, Ray, Garret and Dylan hit the ground every few seconds, and only Will stayed on his feet, chasing Ax with his colorful magic, whispering the words of his spells out loud to give them more power.

And then a loud howl reached my ears. Ethan had shifted, too.

My spirit heard it and began to slam my fists and claws on the magic even faster. It knew that out of all of them, Ethan was the most powerful. Not as powerful as *us* right now, but powerful—and *big*—enough to hurt Ax.

When I heard the magic cracking, Ax had already been hit by at least half a dozen spells. Though he still stood, his movements had become slower, and with Ethan slowly walking around all of them, waiting for the perfect opportunity to strike, I had no doubt that he was in for a lot of pain.

And it was going to take me *hours* to get through that magic.

My heart all but beat out of my chest. If they killed him…my gods, if they killed him, I would skin them alive. I'd take my time with them. I'd fucking break them to pieces with my bare hands.

But…

I felt the magic releasing in the air a second before I heard Jacob's voice. His hands were full of white smoke as he raised them toward Ax, but those words…they weren't aimed at Ax.

They were aimed at me.

At the shield that was keeping me trapped in this place.

It only took seconds for the magic to begin to fade.

My spirit went nuts. I moved too fast for even *me* to realize it. Sparks flew, claws slammed onto the magic. *Crack, crack, crack,* and it gave. I felt it the moment the outside air filled my nostrils, so light, so scentless, so free of magic.

I didn't have the time to feel glad. I didn't have a single second to even make a plan. My spirit moved, and I only saw it when my clawed feet slammed on the back of Will Thorne, taking him to the ground. My energy was minimal, and when Will turned to me, eyes bloodshot and magic ready, I saw the magic coming for me. But before it reached me, everything went dark. I blacked out again.

Even in unconsciousness, the fear didn't leave me. It was right there, ringing all the alarms in my head until I had no choice but to come to again.

But I hadn't fallen. I was on the other side of the yard, slamming my claws on Fallon's chest now, and behind her, Ax, Will and Jacob were dancing around each other. The spirit was in complete control of my body, and even when my mind gave up again and again, it was there. It still fought. It still kept going.

I'd never been more thankful for its existence than I was that night.

The fifth time I came back to consciousness, I felt the pain on my back. Two knives were buried inside me deep, and Fallon was still standing, Ray and Dylan at my back. Garret was on the ground near the house, not moving. Jacob was on his back on the other side, eyes closed, though he was breathing. And Will and Ethan were still going at it with Ax.

It felt like it lasted a lifetime before the spirit grabbed Fallon by the hair and pulled her down, her claws read to stab her chest. The sorceress screamed in pain, and I had no hopes of controlling the spirit in the state I was in, but it let Fallon go all on its own because Ray was right behind us, trying to stab us for the third time. His spirit made him physically strong, and he could take anything thrown his way—magic or weapons—but he wasn't fast. My spirit was.

I jumped behind him, running my claws on his back, making a mess out of his shirt, but I knew it wouldn't be enough damage. And Dylan was there, too, trying to get to me with a katana, moving like a fucking ninja as he pushed himself away from my claws and tried to cut my head off.

That's why I didn't see the magic coming for me until it hit me on the back.

I fell forward, and the blade of Dylan's katana buried in my gut all the way to the handle. My breath was cut off, and the pain fried my nerve endings completely.

Dylan smiled, sweat coating his skin, as he put his hand right on my face. Nowhere to go. The magic that came from his palm was an orange red, and it slipped right inside my nostrils, my eyes, my mouth, sending me back again, flying.

I hit something hard before I slammed on the ground,

barely even breathing. I blacked out again, and this time, the pain stayed with me, too. Too much. I was losing complete control of myself. And the spirit was losing control of my body, too. Not because I was trying to stop it, but because my body didn't have the energy to support it anymore.

But my eyes opened anyway. Big, blue ones in front of me. *"Hold on!"*

Ax's words barely reached me. He wanted me to hold on, but for what? We were already dead because I couldn't get my body to move. The spirit tried—oh, how it tried just to get my arm to raise, but it couldn't. I was spent. The next time unconsciousness took me, it didn't let go of me for a good long while. I heard the sounds of the fight, and I prayed harder than I ever had in my life for the only thing that truly mattered to me: *please, let him survive.*

CHAPTER
SEVEN

The sun was shining, though I could have very well been dreaming. The way my mind shut down and came to again what felt like every few seconds couldn't really be trusted. A blink, and I was lying on something soft, something that smelled like leather, the sun streaming through a window at my head—which made absolutely no sense.

Another, and strong arms were around me, large green leaves over me, orange sunlight slipping through them. That made no sense, either.

And then the smell of wood and fire filled my nose. A wooden ceiling, loud footsteps falling on creaking wood, and...something even softer under me.

My eyes closed, my energy at its limits, as the voices in my head grew louder now that there was no sun in the sky. I felt it, even though I didn't see it. It wasn't just the spirit anymore—it was the vampire in me, too. That's why my jaw was so uncomfortable—my fangs were out, the craving for blood stronger than I'd ever felt it before. If my body had had just a tiny bit more energy, I'd have been up and searching for someone to bite. *Anything* with blood in it.

As it was, my eyes closed again. The cracking of the fire somewhere nearby took me under. I didn't come to again for what felt like a long time.

My eyes popped open and every monster that lived inside me roared. The scent of blood somewhere close made my heart trip all over itself, and I sat up, limbs shaking, lids so heavy I could barely keep them open. There was a window across from the bed I was lying on, and the sky had turned grey outside it with new light. Had I been knocked out the entire night?

Didn't matter—because there was a small dresser in front of the window, and on top of it was a metal bowl filled with blood.

I didn't even remember how I got to it, how I got my legs to carry me, but the bowl was in my hands and the cold animal blood was in my mouth, going down my throat, spilling out my lips and down my chin, but I didn't care. It was blood. It was *everything*. Even the taste of it didn't disgust me. I drank every last drop, then licked the bowl clean, then scooped every drop that had dripped down to my chin and neck on my finger, and licked that, too.

The first ray of sunlight fell on my face, and I hissed at it, finding myself on my knees in front of the window. The bowl was empty. The voices in my head stopped somewhat, and my heartbeat slowed down, too. But my muscles still ached. Even my bones hurt. I held onto the dresser, trying to sit up, see where I was, where Ax was…had he made it? Had he brought me here?

Gods, please…

I fell on the floor, the metal bowl slipping from my hands.

"Ax," I think I whispered, but I wasn't sure. The sun was up. My body was still a mess. How much blood had I really lost? How much did I even have in me at that fight?

I'd find out. I just needed a few minutes to rest right there on the cold wood. It felt great against my cheek. I just needed a few minutes…

My mind shut down again.

CHAPTER
EIGHT

I SMELLED *CLEAN*, WHICH WAS STRANGE. I'D NEVER SMELLED worse than when I was trapped inside that magic shield for two weeks straight, not even after a full day's sparring with other vampires back home. So, how could I be clean now, after everything?

The same wooden ceiling was over me, except I wasn't lying on the cold wooden floor near the dresser anymore. I was on the same bed I'd woken up in last time.

I sat up with a jolt, my body actually functional. My limbs weren't shaking. My muscles didn't ache. The whispers in my head were barely there.

The room I was in wasn't big. It was a cabin made entirely out of wood. There was a fireplace to my left, a low fire burning in it, and to its side was a wall, behind which I could barely make out wooden cabinets. A door to my right, and the main one was right across from the bed, next to the window, the dresser, and a tall, narrow shelf full of books. There was no more blood in the room, but there was food nearby. I could smell the steak and the vegetables perfectly as my stomach growled with hunger.

I stood up from the bed, straining my ears, hoping to hear something outside. Some*one*.

Where the hell was he?

I had no doubt in my mind that Ax had brought me here—wherever *here* was. And if he did, that meant he was okay. He hadn't died. Hadn't been hurt.

He was okay.

And despite everything, I closed my eyes and smiled, just soaking in the relief for a second.

Then, I looked down at the clean white shirt and pajama shorts I was wearing. They smelled brand new. My skin was clean, too. No dirt or sand under my fingernails. My hair was no longer greasy but soft, like it was just washed hours ago. Still a bit wet at the roots on the back of my head. The minty scent that hung about me proved that I'd been scrubbed with shampoo.

"Ax," I said to the empty room, though I couldn't hear a heartbeat anywhere around me. My legs carried me forward, and I went behind the wall of the fireplace to find a narrow kitchen with light wooden cabinets on both sides. On the small countertop, I found a plate covered in foil, and on it was a thick piece of steak to the side of some roasted potatoes.

I dove in and ate like a mad woman. I hadn't tasted food in over two weeks, and I *never* wanted to stop eating.

But I hadn't even finished half the steak when my stomach began to complain. Too much. Too soon. I had to leave it and eat later. And my gut hurt, too.

Pulling up the shirt, I found a raw red scar where Dylan had stabbed me with his katana. It was still tender to the touch. I hissed when I ran my finger over it, but it wasn't bleeding anymore. I'd had so little blood in me that it hadn't healed yet, but it would. I was full—of blood and food, and I'd heal in no time.

I just needed to find Ax.

Going back to the main room, I grabbed the handle of the wooden door and pulled it open. The trees and the birds and the animals outside hit me like a slap to the face. Rocks in front of the door, and then the ground fell at least twenty feet, before the large pine trees began. There were no lights outside or *inside* other than the fire, and I could see everything perfectly. There just wasn't anything to see except the dark sky, the rocks surrounding me, the trees and the animals watching me from a distance. No human heartbeat.

"Ax!" I called at the top of my voice, heartbeat already tripled at the idea of seeing his face.

But he didn't come.

A few more times of screaming my guts out, and I realized just how tired I truly still was. Just how little energy I had in my body, despite the blood and despite the food. I needed time, too. I wasn't going to just snap back, not after two weeks of that fucking hell.

And just the thought of it made my stomach twist and turn.

I sat on the threshold, enjoying the cold air, hoping to gather enough energy to get out there, start running, start searching for him. If he just left me here and went away, I swore to all gods that I was going to murder him with my own hands. I swore I was going to fucking burn him to a crisp.

Fuck, I needed him so much, I couldn't stand it. I didn't dare even *think* about anything at all, not where I'd been, not what had happened, because I was scared shitless. So fucking afraid, my hands were shaking, and I just needed to see him for a second so I could deal with reality.

Just for a second.

The pendant Jacob had given me still rested on my chest. I'd relied so much on that thing that a part of me still didn't believe what he said—that it was nothing, the magic on it meant to only change its color. I'd never really needed it, just like Ax said.

All I'd really needed was him. He always took care of me.

Taking the chain off me was hard—there was a part of me that had deeply connected to it, but I did it anyway. I trusted him with my everything. I trusted him more than any magic in the world. So, I put it down there on the threshold, wrapped my arms around my legs, and I waited.

It must have been at least twenty minutes before I finally heard the sound of a heartbeat. I still didn't have the strength to start running, but I did make it to my feet, breath held and heart beating like a drum in my ears. I waited and sniffed the air, and I looked west to where the sound was coming from.

It got closer and closer until I was a hundred percent convinced that it was him. I knew how his heart beat. I knew the scent of him. I knew the rhythm of his steps, too.

And when he finally stepped away from the rocks at the side of the cabin, a scream left me before I ran. I didn't care if I'd fall or if my body would just collapse—I ran and I jumped in his arms, feeling completely reborn. My arms locked around his neck, and my legs locked around his hips. I smelled his skin, felt his warmth, heard his heart beating, and I didn't let go until every part of me was convinced that he was *here*. That he was alive. He was okay for real.

Maybe that's why I didn't notice how he didn't hold me

tightly to him the way he always did. Maybe that's why I didn't notice how he let me go the second I moved back. I didn't notice how *distant* his touch was until I looked into his eyes—dark, troubled, like the sea during a thunderstorm. Not alive. Not happy. Just…cold.

"How are you feeling?" he asked, and the sound of his voice was fucking *freezing*. My flesh broke in goose bumps instantly as I stepped away from him, my own smile gone.

"I'm fine," I said, so confused, so hurt for a second that I didn't even remember the cave. I didn't remember what had happened to us last time, or what I'd said.

What *he'd* said.

"Did you eat?" He stepped to the side and moved to the open door of the cabin. His heart didn't even skip a beat.

"Yeah," I forced myself to say, my voice dry. "Thank you."

"No problem." He stepped inside the cabin, then opened another door, and locked himself inside it.

Just like that.

Tears spilled from my eyes, and I only realized it when I felt them on my cheeks.

What the fuck was happening? He couldn't even fucking look at me? He just…*didn't care*?

No, that wasn't it. I just needed to talk to him, that was all. I just needed to know what he was thinking so that I could explain. He'd understand. He had to.

So, I wiped my tears and walked back inside the cabin, closing the door. He was in the bathroom because I could hear the water running. And I had about a minute to gather my thoughts, think about what I was going to say, before he walked out.

But at the sight of him, my breath caught again.

Gods, I'd missed him so much. He looked so good! His

stubble had grown, his skin was clean, even his hair was a bit longer than I remembered. He wore jeans and a black shirt, topped with a leather jacket. Same old Ax, except for the eyes. Still as dark. Still as cold. No hint of amusement in them. No hint of *anything* good in the way he looked at me.

"Ax," I whispered, every thought I had slipping from my mind. I didn't know how to talk to him like this. I just needed to be close to him. If I could touch him, it would be easier. It would all make a little more sense.

So, I made to get close to him again, but he stepped back.

My body froze in place, too. I shook my head. "You're killing me here." My voice broke as I fisted my hands so he wouldn't see them shaking.

But the smile he gave me was so full of pain, it broke me to pieces. "You killed me first."

In that moment, I knew exactly how much damage I'd caused to us. I knew that no matter what I said to him right now, I wouldn't get through to him. Just the way he watched me, you'd think he was looking at his rival, his enemy—exactly what we were supposed to be from the beginning, and then weren't.

I couldn't fucking stand that look. I couldn't breathe when he told me so much with it.

"Can we just talk?" I asked, needing a second to make a plan. To understand what to expect. To make sense of the fact that Ax was right there, in front of me, and he *didn't want me*.

"Sure," he said, then stepped to the side to rest against the dresser by the window. I had never been caught more off guard in my life.

But I took in a deep breath and I tried to calm my racing

heart. *Just talk,* my mind told me. If we just talked, we'd get to the bottom of this. I could fix it. I could make it right.

"How...how did you find me?" I asked the first question that popped into my head. Not that it mattered.

"Your sorcerer called Jones," he said. "Jones came to me."

Your sorcerer. He meant Jacob, and it fucking made me sick.

"He's not *mine*," I spit, shaking so badly I had no hopes of hiding it. "*You're* mine!" That's what he said, wasn't it? He said it himself, he was, but...

"Not anymore," he told me, crossing his arms in front of his chest. "You gave that up, remember?" And he was completely calm about it, too.

"I didn't!" I said, incredulous. How could he even think that?! "I would never—"

"Yes, you did," he cut me off. "It was your choice. You made it. And that's all we really need to talk about." He moved away from the dresser, toward the door, and he opened it. "Eat your food. Rest."

I burst out laughing as tears streamed from my eyes. "Where the fuck are you going?!" We weren't done, were we? We were not fucking done!

But his response was to slam the door shut on his way out before he started running. By the time I opened it and walked outside, he'd already disappeared. I could no longer even hear his heartbeat anymore.

Still laughing at myself, still crying, I found the stupid pendant right there on the threshold where I left it. I picked it up again, so starved for something familiar to hold onto, and I just held it in my hands when I walked back inside the house. I sat down on the floor next to the fireplace. The fire in it was already fading. But I watched the small flames and

I tried to take strength from them. And when that didn't work, I tried lying to myself, telling myself that it was going to be okay. We'd make it. He was pissed, I'd hurt him, but we'd make it.

And when that didn't work, either, I slipped away into my daydreams just like I did when I was under that magic ward, feeling more trapped now than I ever did then.

Ax didn't come back until the sun was up in the sky.

I knew because I was awake. As much as my body craved unconsciousness, my mind somehow refused to shut down still.

I couldn't really keep my eyes open, but I was aware. I could hear. When the door opened, my heart didn't skip a beat. I recognized his scent. Another was added to it—that of fur. And he had blood with him this time.

It didn't even awaken my craving. I held onto the sheets, hoping he'd get into bed with me. It was the only one in the room, and it wasn't big, but we'd fit. We always fit anywhere.

But Ax didn't come to lie down with me.

Instead, he took off his jacket, put pieces of wood in the fireplace, and lit a fire. I didn't get why—we didn't need heat. We were fine with the cold, but I loved the sound of it. It soothed me somewhat. And when the flames started to crackle, he sat down on the floor next to it.

I could feel his eyes on my face. Half of me wanted to open my eyes and see him, but I was afraid he'd walk away. Even being in the same room with him right now was enough.

Here I was, still conscious even though the sun was up

on the other side of whatever mountain we were on, the sky an icy blue outside the window, just begging any god who would listen that we weren't beyond repair. Everything else had faded from my mind—my spirit, *the* spirits in the Vein in Arizona, Jacob, Will, the Hidden Realm—everything. He'd gotten all that power over me while I hadn't even noticed, but here we were.

Eventually, he lay down on the floor. I heard his movements, smelled his scent, and I no longer felt his eyes on my face.

So, I forced mine open to see that he'd closed his.

Ax didn't sleep, but he'd slept that one time in the motel, when I'd been by his side. Maybe he needed to sleep today, too. The gods knew I needed it. My body, my mind was craving it. And if I lay beside him, I would. I'd sleep in seconds.

So, I gathered every bit of strength left in my body to get out of that bed.

Ax didn't move. He pretended he couldn't even hear me. I walked to him on shaking legs, sat down next to him, then put my head on his shoulder. My eyes closed instantly, and though he didn't even move at first, I wrapped my arm around his waist, pressed my body flush against his, and finally...his heartbeat doubled.

Gods, how I'd missed the sound of that. I'd had no idea just how much I'd been used to it. How much I craved to know how he responded to me.

And a second later, he moved his own arm underneath me, and pulled me closer. I could have fucking cried from how good it felt. Fuck, I'd missed him so much. I hid my face under his chin, and though I was desperate to kiss him, I couldn't. Wrapped up in his arms like that, my mind was already a goner. So damn comfortable. I wanted to stay right here for the rest of eternity.

Unconsciousness pulled at me so hard that I barely heard his voice.

"I should have never trusted you," Ax whispered. I couldn't move, couldn't talk if I tried. I couldn't even get my eyes to open. "I should have known you wouldn't stay. I should have known you would only ever care about yourself."

My gods, I was breaking on the inside, but my heartbeat stayed exactly the same, my body too far gone to react. *Please, please, please...*I begged, and I didn't even know what for.

"Guess I should say *congratulations*," he whispered. "You killed the savage when nobody else ever could." And he kissed the top of my head.

I had never felt weaker in my life.

CHAPTER NINE

I KNEW HE WOULDN'T BE THERE WHEN NIGHT FELL AND MY EYES opened. I didn't bother to strain my ears to search for a heartbeat. He'd put me in the bed again, gods knew when. The fire had gone out in the fireplace. There was blood in a bowl in the kitchen, and food, too—pizza, by the smell of it. Which meant there was civilization somewhere close by.

That was good enough for me.

I walked into the bathroom, the words he said to me last night spinning in my head. Weighing down my shoulders. Breaking me with every new breath I took.

"*Congratulations*," I told my reflection in the small mirror over the sink. I looked like a fucking ghost. Pale skin, paler hair, eyes so lifeless they could be considered white. I'd have no trouble scaring people away from me even without my black eyeshadow, which made me smile for whatever reason.

There was a tub in the bathroom. I didn't bother cleaning myself up—I was clean enough. I just washed my face, used the toilet, and I walked out again.

"No need to hurry," I whispered to the room. He wasn't

going to be back anytime soon. I didn't touch the blood—I could fucking get my own. I didn't touch the food, either. I just grabbed one of the books on the shelf and managed to find a pen in there, too.

Then I sat down and wrote him a note on a blank page at the end of the book.

When it was done, I left the book on top of the drawer so that he'd see it. If he wanted to read it, he could. If not... the fireplace was right there. He could burn the whole book to a crisp.

I left the pendant over it, too. He could do with it whatever he wanted. I never thought I'd actually say this—or believe it—but the spirit didn't fucking scare me anymore. Not when there was *this* weighing down my shoulders.

There were clothes in the drawers that hadn't been there the night before. I smelled them, but I didn't even open them. I'd get my own as soon as I was away from here.

And with that thought in mind, I made it out of the cabin.

Walking barefoot on rocks was no joke, but it didn't last forever. I jumped when I could, then landed on the soft ground of the woods, finally seeing the small mountain where the cabin was constructed—right in a hole carved in the rocks. It looked so big from down here, but on the inside, it had suffocated me. Maybe it had just been the guilt and the pain and the fear I'd felt since I woke up in it.

I gave myself a second to breathe, taking in the trees, smelling the animals around me, searching for his heartbeat without really meaning to, but it was okay because he wasn't there. I already knew he wouldn't be.

And there was no point in staying here anymore, in keeping him here with me. I knew he'd stay as long as I did, and as tempting as that was, I also knew that every time I saw him, it would only break me further. He didn't have to stay here and babysit me when he obviously couldn't stand to even look at me. He'd be free to go wherever he needed to go.

Meanwhile, I was finally going home.

I was just tired of it. So sick and tired of running, of hiding, of *trying to do the right fucking thing*. I was done. I just wanted to go home.

If Jones wanted to end me then, good. If not, I'd tell him everything—about the sorcerers, about the Vein in Arizona, and he could decide what he wanted to do from there. After all, he was the ruler of our coven, wasn't he? He could make much better decisions about it than me.

And in time, I'd heal. Probably. If I didn't, I'd exist. I'd still exist.

For now, I just kept on walking, not really sure where the fuck I was going, dressed in a white shirt and pajama shorts that were too big for me, but I didn't mind. I could steal clothes. Food. Blood.

I could even steal a car.

I'd just take it one step at a time.

CHAPTER TEN

AX CREED

THE MOMENT I went close to the cabin and didn't hear her heartbeat, I knew something was wrong, but I convinced myself that it was okay. She was out for a walk. She didn't need to stay inside the cabin all day, anyway. She still needed to rest, to heal, to be fed properly—her arms were way too skinny—but she also needed to stretch her legs.

It was fine.

The small mountain where I'd built this cabin was in Colorado. It had served me perfectly in my first years as a vampire, when the outside world got too loud, the cravings too powerful, when my own self had slipped away from my fingers. I'd come out here and regroup. Rethink. Establish control over my mind once again.

I hadn't been back here in almost five years now, but it was exactly as I'd left it. I'd built it so far up the mountain for that purpose—no human would see it, or just happen to walk that way to get curious about it. Only animals.

I don't even know why I brought her here—this was *my* place, where I came to get my shit together. To hide. To work on myself. Two days ago, it had seemed like the perfect place, but now that I'd been here, running from her, walking around the mountain, analyzing the fucking woods, I hadn't gotten anywhere—just become more miserable with every second that I had to force myself to stay away from her. To stop myself from taking her in my arms. Kissing her. Ripping those fucking clothes off her body. Making her mine the way she yearned. The way we both yearned.

But no.

Because she'd made her choice. And I'd be damned if I let myself be in a position where she *wouldn't* choose me again.

It wouldn't be long now. A few more days and she'd be back to herself. Then, she could decide where she wanted to go. I'd take her, then...what?

We'd say goodbye, and that's that?

The idea of it fucking turned my mind inside out. I couldn't stand it.

And she was still not back in the cabin.

I went a bit closer, sure she'd be close by, close enough for me to hear her heartbeat. But I jumped and landed right in front of where the cabin was up the mountain, and I still got nothing.

Forcing myself to stay calm, I climbed and jumped in front of the door. Closed. I could smell her scent—she'd been out here not too long ago, but she wasn't here anymore.

The first wave of panic hit me when I pushed the door open, and I smelled the blood of the rabbit I'd caught hours ago, still there in the bowl like I'd left it. The pizza, too. The box wasn't touched at all.

My fangs began to come out as I searched the kitchen and the bathroom, even though my ears were working just fine.

Where the fuck did she go?

I sat on the edge of the bed, forcing myself to breathe. She'd be back in no time. We were in the middle of nowhere —she'd just gone out for a walk. She'd be back.

And then I saw the book on the drawer. That hadn't been there before—and neither had that fucking pendant she carried around her neck that reeked of Jacob Thorne.

Here they both were.

I grabbed the pendant and smelled it—magic and Thorne, the worst combination in history.

I picked up the book, too. That one only smelled like her. Had she read it?

But the second I pulled open the back cover, I saw the blue ink.

She'd written me a fucking note.

Hey, asshole,

You probably won't read this at all, but that's fine. You hate my guts right now, and that's fine, too. I deserve it.

You never gave me the chance to say thank you for saving me. I don't mean from that house or that magic shield. But you were right—I made my choice. I chose to do whatever it takes so I can be with you. So I can be someone you'd want by your side every second because I can't fucking get enough of you. Right now, I can't do that. Not with this thing inside me. I want to be free, Ax. I just want to be free to be yours. I know you don't understand it, but maybe someday, you will.

I'm leaving now, and I'll be back. If you think you're gonna get rid of me at any point in your life, you're a fucking fool. I'll sleep in front of your door for years if I have to. I'll have all the time in the world. I know you don't trust me, but I promise you: you can trust that.

You are the reason that finally explains this ridiculous idea of my existence. So have fun while you can, Savage. Because I'm coming for you.

Your Damsel

I TORE the page off the book and stuffed it in my pocket. The door almost flew off its hinges when I pulled it open. I jumped off the rocks without closing it.

The smell of her blood on the ground reached me before I started running at full speed. Her fucking feet were bleeding—and where the hell did she think she was going? If she thought she could write those words then walk away, *she* was the fucking fool, not me.

My heart almost beat out of my fucking chest as I ran, stopping every few seconds to find drops of her blood. It drove me fucking nuts. I left her shoes in the damn drawer—why did she have to be so goddamn stubborn?

So goddamn perfect.

It took me another five minutes of running and stopping, until my ears picked up her heartbeat.

There were plenty of animals around us, but I could recognize her among any kinds of creatures. I knew her scent and her heartbeat, the way the blood in her veins rushed. Giving myself a second, I stopped and closed my eyes, willing myself to just calm down. She was here. She hadn't left.

She wasn't fucking going anywhere.

I started running again, no longer needing to stop and smell her blood to make sure I was going in the right direction. I could see her now, see the white shirt I'd put on her after bathing her. She hadn't even put proper clothes on, and I'd left everything in the drawers for her!

Never mind. She wouldn't need clothes now.

She heard me when I was barely ten feet away. She turned.

I didn't stop running. I grabbed her in my arms and took us a little farther away, then pressed her against a tree trunk. She held onto me, arms and legs locked around me tightly, just like she'd done when she first saw me. It had taken everything I had to keep myself in control then, to keep my heartbeat from slipping, to keep my fucking hands off her.

Not anymore. I grabbed a fistful of her hair and pulled her head back so I could see her beautiful face. She resisted, not wanting to move away from me, but she had no choice.

"Where the fuck do you think you're going?" I said, growling like an animal, on the brink of losing my shit for real. Her pale face, those pale eyes that came alive for me, were the most perfect thing the gods have created.

"Why didn't you put your shoes on?! You're fucking bleeding, Damsel." I grabbed her cheek between my teeth, biting hard, but she didn't make a sound. Fuck, I'd missed her so much I was going to burst. I'd missed her flesh between my teeth, her body flush against mine. I'd missed the way her breath caught for me, the way her heartbeat tripled, the way her whole body exploded into fireworks for me.

"I'm leaving," she whispered, holding onto the back of my head so I didn't let go of her.

"No, you're not." She wasn't going anywhere.

"It's okay, Ax," she said, kissing my jaw. "I know you're mad. I know I fucked up. You need the time. I hurt you, and—"

"You think I care?" I said, pressing onto her harder until she moaned. The sound of her filled my head. "Keep fucking hurting me, Damsel. Hurt me every day for the rest of your life—but don't walk away from me!"

Couldn't she see by now that that's *all* I cared about? We could fight. We could argue. We could disagree on *everything*, but we could work it out if we were together. If she just stuck with me. I didn't fucking know how to do this without her anymore—how did she not get that?!

I grabbed her face in my hand and pushed her back once more. She cried out in complaint, but I didn't care. She needed to understand. I would make her. I would spell it all out for her until she did.

"Fight me. Argue with me. Fucking *force* me to do whatever the fuck you want. Don't turn your back on me, damn it! Don't walk away!"

Warm tears slipped from her eyes, touching my hand. "I'm sorry," she whispered, so fucking broken it hurt me worse than anything in the world. "I didn't think you'd agree to come with me."

"So, you just gave up?"

But she shook her head, squeezing her eyes until new tears rushed down her cheeks. I kissed them off her skin, feeling every ounce of her pain.

"I didn't. I swear it, I didn't. Not for a second," she said. "I didn't want to hurt you."

"You did," I hissed, biting on her lip. "You fucking killed me, Damsel."

"I know," she said. "I killed me, too."

"You're going to make it up to me," I warned because she needed to know.

"I will," she said without hesitation.

"How are you gonna do that?" It would take a lot. She'd fucked me up so bad, it was going to take a whole fucking lot to make up for it.

But...

"I'll never walk away again. Not ever. No matter what."

Fuck. She made up for it, just like that.

I devoured her mouth like a starved man. She didn't belong anywhere else in the world but here, with me, in my arms, her body pressed to mine, coming to life for me. I smelled her desire, smelled everything she felt for me, and I'd be damned if it didn't rival all that *I* felt, too. Mate or no mate, we were one already.

"I need you," she whispered against my lips. "I need you right now." She unlocked her legs from around me and reached for the button of my jeans.

Thank the gods. I'd never needed her more than I did right now, either.

"These damn clothes," I growled, pulling her pajama shorts to the sides until they tore in half. She cried out, her pleasure turning up, and she finally got my cock out of my jeans. Fuck, to feel her small hands wrapped around it like that was everything. She stroked me hard and fast, desperate, her tongue in my mouth, her pussy dripping for me. I grabbed her perfect ass in my hands and squeezed tightly before slapping her so hard, the whole fucking woods heard. She moaned into my mouth, almost making me come at the sound of her pleasure alone.

I slipped my finger down her ass and to her pussy. She was soaking wet for me, just like always. Nothing had changed between us. We were still starved for one another. She pushed her ass back while she stroked me, and I teased her with my fingertips. I wanted to make it last, but fuck, I needed to be buried inside her more. So, I grabbed her and pulled her up, and her legs locked around me again. I held her by the ass with one hand and positioned my cock at her entrance with the other.

"Scream for me, baby," I said, then pulled her down.

The sound that left her ripped right from her soul. That, together with the feel of her warm, tight pussy was a heaven designed only for me.

"Good girl," I whispered, holding her down while I rose on my tiptoes.

She didn't stop screaming for a good long while. My name on her lips intoxicated me. I slammed into her with all my strength, knowing she liked it hard. Knowing she *needed* it hard, needed to feel my cock on every inch of her until she breathed only for me.

"Ax, I need to..." I pounded into her hard enough, so she finished that sentence with another delicious scream.

"A little more, baby," I said, biting her neck. "You're doing so good. Just a little more." Her pussy clenched around my cock so well, making me see stars, but we weren't done yet. I need a bit more. "Almost there. You got it?" I didn't want her undone just yet.

"Yes," she choked. "I got it, baby. As long as you need."

Fuck, she was going to end me for real.

And I need the rest of eternity.

But I barely lasted another minute before my legs threatened to give. The pleasure she gave me was unlike anything I'd ever felt in my life. It was never just sex with her. It was two fucking souls merging together.

"Come for me, beautiful. Let the world hear it," I said as I thrust into her deep, holding her hips down.

And when she let go with a gut-wrenching scream, I let go, too.

We weren't done yet, not even close. But I knew from that second on, that if we got through this, we could get through anything. She could spin me around her little finger any way she pleased, and I'd be happy. So long as she was with me.

Chapter
ELEVEN

Nikki Arella

The door of the cabin was open. Ax held me in his arms as he ran and jumped and took us back, and since he wasn't afraid that somebody had broken in, I wasn't either. I didn't even try to hear anything—that's how much I trusted him.

He slammed the door closed behind us and threw me on the bed. I hadn't even blinked yet before he had the shirt off me, and I was completely naked, my pussy still dripping with his cum and mine. Exactly how it should be.

I watched him take his own clothes off, revealing to me every inch of his body, every muscle and every scar on him. I was an emotional wreck today because I saw him, and I just wanted to fucking cry. Stupid tears. He was just so damn perfect.

And he hadn't let me leave.

He'd read the stupid note and he'd stopped me. He'd made me understand—and I did.

By the gods, I fucking got it—*finally*. He hadn't been

kidding around. Since the first time he told me he would burn the Realm to the ground as long as I was with him, he'd meant it completely. I just didn't get *all* of it. I didn't get that he would do *anything* in the world if I was with him. He'd have even come with me to Jacob's if I'd asked him to.

Which was plain stupid of me, considering he'd *never* left my side, not ever, only when I forced him. But it didn't matter anymore, did it? Because he hadn't let me leave. I hadn't even dared to hope or expect it, but he hadn't.

And I would *never* try that again.

He climbed on the bed with me, settled between my legs, wrapping his arms around me. The feel of his skin on mine, his warmth slipping inside me, was what I'd started to live for without really realizing it. Sometimes, I didn't pay attention to what was happening around me as much as I should.

And sometimes, it was absolutely worth it.

"I missed you so much, you prick," I said, holding onto him with all my strength. Fuck, I never wanted to let go.

He planted kisses on the side of my neck slowly. Gently. Just like I needed.

"I know, Damsel. I was there with you."

"I can't believe you didn't hug me when I first woke up," I said in wonder. "That must have been hard."

He squeezed me even tighter until I could barely breathe. "It was fucking torture."

I smiled, kissing his shoulder. "You deserved it, asshole." He absolutely didn't.

He chuckled. "Totally worth it. You should have seen your face."

I slapped his back, then dug my fingernails in his skin.

"What face? I didn't even care. I knew you'd cave eventually. You're so easy, it's pathetic."

He pressed his hips down, drawing a moan out of me.

"I would have believed you if I hadn't read that note," he said. "I don't know what's more pathetic—you coming to lie with me on the floor yesterday or actually writing me a fucking note."

"I think we can both agree that you running after me like that is as pathetic as it gets. It takes the cake, hands down."

He laughed, shaking me and the entire bed with it. My toes curled all the way. I fucking loved the sound of his laugh.

And when he raised his head a little bit to look at me, I saw his eyes. I saw the brilliant blue in them. Not dark. Not cold. Just full of life.

Damn those stupid tears that stabbed the back of my eyes again. Ugh, I couldn't stand how emotional I was these days.

"Don't you get it, baby? I felt *sorry* for you," he teased.

I took his bottom lip between my teeth, sucking hard as he squeezed his eyes shut, then slammed his hips down on me again. Fuck, he was already hard. I felt his cock on my thigh perfectly, and suddenly, I was starved for it. The best part? By now I was pretty sure that was *never* going to change.

"You're feeling sorry for me now, too," I said, just like he'd said to me before…gods, it felt like a lifetime ago already.

"I'm always sorry for you," he said, licking my cheek. "Can you handle it, though? You seem pretty weak. You've lost weight, too."

"*Please,*" I said. "You think I can't keep up with you?"

"I don't know—can you?" he teased, making me push him back.

"Not only can I, but if I wanted, *you* couldn't keep up with me."

His eyes sparkled as if he were suddenly challenged. "Oh, Damsel. I could fuck you all day, every day. In daylight, too. I don't need to sleep. I don't need to feed. I just need to be inside you because every time I am, I want more."

His words made the fire in my stomach burned brighter. "Maybe we should put that to a test."

"We will," he said without hesitation. "We've got time."

My smile faltered. "How much time exactly before someone finds us?"

He brought his lips to mine but didn't kiss me. "You're worried. Stop worrying," he whispered.

"I just—"

"If anybody finds us, they're not gonna like what they find here." He was dead serious.

"I know that."

"If anybody finds us, it will serve as a reminder to everybody else why they *don't* want to come find us." He grinned mischievously.

"You're a cocky bastard." And I kissed the hell out of him.

"Why wouldn't I be?" he said, licking my lips.

I laughed. "No reason whatsoever." He could absolutely back it up. "Did you...did you kill them?" I asked. And I was really hoping he'd gotten to Will Thorne.

"No, I couldn't," he said, closing his eyes. I kissed his jaw, his cheeks, his lips, as he talked. I thought it helped him the way it helped me. "You weren't waking up. I called your name a few times and saw that you were out of it. So, I walked away."

I smiled, my heart swelling in my chest even though I'd been so sure I'd want to hear something else.

"You walked away from a fight? Are you even Savage Ax?" I teased.

"I'd walk away from every fight in the world for you, Damsel," he said. "Whatever it takes."

Damn him. "Whatever it takes," I breathed, then slammed my lips to his, serving him my whole being in that kiss.

He eagerly took it, and for a little while, we got lost like we always did. There was no cabin, no woods, no world around. It was just us, and it was perfect.

But I still needed to know more.

"How did you get out?" I said breathlessly, my voice completely dry. He squeezed his eyes shut again as he tried to clear his head, his hard cock poking my thigh. It wasn't going anywhere, though. That's how I managed to keep from pulling him to me. I just needed to know first.

"Jacob put the wards down for me. They were all wounded, so they were happy to see me go, I guess," he said, his own voice dry, hoarse, better than anything my ears had ever heard.

"Will Thorne will not just let it go. He'll be looking for me."

"I'm hoping he does," he said with a growl.

"Me, too." I wanted his head so badly, it hurt.

"Why did he put you there, baby? Why did you let him?" he whispered, and I could feel all his pain in those words.

"I couldn't help it. He came in daylight. Ambushed me," I said with a flinch.

"And what the fuck did Jacob do?"

"He helped. He knew he couldn't best Will in a fight, so he pretended."

"That fucking—"

"No, that was actually smart. Much smarter than I thought he would be. He knows his limits. There's power in that." And the fact that I was still alive, still here, proved it. "He told me to hold on, and I did."

He sighed, like he was trying to let go of the anger. "I can't believe I owe *him* my life." And he sounded disgusted.

"You do?" I asked, a bit surprised.

"Yeah. He called Jones to get to me, to save you."

"So, *I* owe him my life."

"You *are* my life," he whispered, so low I barely heard it. I smiled, so warm on the inside I was afraid I would melt soon.

"My, my, Savage," I whispered, kissing his lips. "And I thought I was the only one fucked up in the head here."

He grinned. "I keep telling you I'm way worse than you think."

I pushed him to the side until he lay on his back, so I could climb on top of him. He made himself comfortable on the tiny bed, and there was more than enough space on his chest for me. I stretched my body as he ran his hands up and down my back, slapping my ass.

"Jacob released me from the oath," I told him, and at the mentioning of his name, he flinched. "C'mon—you owe the guy your life. You can stand to hear his name. Or would you rather I call him *my sorcerer*?"

The look in his wide eyes was priceless when he grabbed me and spun me around again, digging his fingers in my ass, biting the side of my neck so hard it hurt, but it also tickled. I couldn't hold back a laugh if I tried.

It was actually fucking amazing. Just an hour ago, I felt

like I was *never* going to laugh again in my life. So hopeless. So fucking alone.

Look at me now.

Sometimes it scared me how much power this man had over me.

"You want me to fucking murder him, baby? Call him *yours* again and I will." It wasn't even a joke, but I laughed harder, and he sank his teeth in my jaw. "Laugh all you like. I fucking mean it."

"I'm just saying what *you* said," I reminded him. *Your sorcerer*—that's what he'd said to me two nights ago, the asshole.

"Well, I was pissed."

"And jealous."

"And losing my fucking mind because I couldn't touch you," he finished with a whisper, making my stomach turn up in knots.

"He's not mine, baby. Nobody is, except you." I would swear it on everything I had if he wanted.

"Maybe," he teased, running his hot tongue up my neck.

"Not *maybe*. You are," I said, and when he tried to kiss my lips, I pushed him off. "Say it. You're mine."

"You know that already," he said with a grin.

"But I wanna hear you say it."

"You—" I pushed him to the side again and climbed on top of him, straddling him and moving lower until his hard cock was right between my soaked folds. *Fuck*. What was I saying again?

"Say it," I demanded in a shaky whisper. "Say you're mine."

"Or what?" he teased, eyes wide and vivid as he looked up at me.

I slowly moved up and down his length for a second,

and he moaned. "Or I won't let you touch me at all when I ride you."

It was the best I had. No way was I going to threaten him with *not* fucking me, when we both knew it wasn't gonna happen.

"But you love my hands on you," he said, pushing up his hips, making my eyes roll in their sockets. I swear, the orgasm was *this* close. I wasn't going to last ten seconds.

"I do," I breathed. "So don't make me go without them, baby." I batted my lashes at him and pouted, knowing exactly how much it affected him.

And...

"I'm yours, Damsel. You fucking own all of me."

I smiled. "Good boy."

He growled, and when I sat up, his hungry eyes roamed down my naked body. I was going to take my time with it, but then his cock was in my hands and I became possessed, so I played with him a little bit, pressing his tip to my clit as I rolled my hips, just to see the helpless look on his face. And then I sat on him, taking him in all the way.

Fuck ten seconds—I came right away. My back arched as soon as he filled me, and the orgasm burned every cell in my body to a crisp until I was free, light as air.

"Damsel? You there yet?"

My eyes opened lazily to his beautiful grin that had my heart tripping all over itself. And he heard it perfectly—that's why his smile widened.

"Yes," I breathed as my senses came back to me.

"Good. Cuz I need you to ride my cock until you get there again," he said, raising his hips while he pulled mine down.

"With pleasure," I said, my body buzzing with energy still, but I moved. And every time I took him in all the way, it became easier to keep up the rhythm. Natural—like breathing.

I soaked up all his warmth, his moans, the sight of him like that, completely at my mercy as I rode him. The pleasure came back twice as strong, and when I rolled my hips with him inside me, every muscle on his chest and stomach contracted as he held himself back.

"That's it, baby," I told him, picking up the speed, ready to come with him again. "Don't let go yet."

"Lay on me," he whispered, and I did so eagerly. I put my hands on the bedpost over his head and closed my eyes as his hands moved down my body, squeezing my thighs. Every time I moved, my clit rubbed against his pelvis, making me cry out.

"Scream, baby. Shake the entire fucking mountain," he told me, and fuck if his words weren't my undoing.

I let go, screaming until my throat was raw, and he held my hips down while he pushed his up and came with me.

"Open your eyes," he breathed, and I looked down at him, saw everything I felt reflected in his gorgeous eyes, just like he saw everything in mine. His fangs extended in perfect sync with mine. Every ounce of me lived for him, breathed for him, and I wanted to be his for real so badly, the pain blinded me for a moment.

He slammed me to his chest, and we were face to face, breathing heavily, burning with a need different from the one we had seconds ago. And to know that I couldn't soothe his or mine yet killed me a little.

"I don't care," he whispered, as if he could read my mind.

I kissed his lips slowly. "I do."

I expected him to try to convince me again, to give me

all the reasons why we should do it, bite each other, mate. Become one for real.

But he didn't. "I know, Damsel," he whispered. "I know." And I saw in his eyes that he understood.

I knew exactly what he wanted. And he knew exactly what I wanted, too.

That's how he broke down the last of my defenses. I was finally, completely bare before him, in body, mind and soul.

CHAPTER
TWELVE

Sleep left me while the sky was still a bit grey with sunlight, which happened rarely. I was so weak these days, still healing, that I thought I'd sleep way past nighttime, but here I was. It's like my mind knew what I'd find when I woke up—Ax, in bed with me, his warm body flush against mine, and it couldn't wait to get there already.

But Ax wasn't in the bed with me.

Instead, he was sitting on the floor next to the fireplace...reading. He had a knee up, hand resting on it as he held a piece of paper, his eyes moving slowly with the letters he was reading.

My note. He was reading my note. He'd torn the page from the book and he was reading it now as the sun slowly set. My heart squeezed so tightly, I had no chance of trying to control it.

And Ax heard it. That's why he looked up and saw that my eyes were open. The smile he gave me made my toes curl.

"What are you reading there?" I teased in barely a whisper, and by the time I finished speaking, he was already in front of me, kneeling next to the bed.

"Just this pathetic little note I got yesterday," he said, bringing his lips to mine. I didn't want to fucking move an inch, just let him kiss me until I withered away into nothing.

"Who is it from?" I mumbled, and he smiled again.

"This chick who's crazy about me. She's telling me she'll sleep in front of my door for years. It's frankly a bit disturbing," he said, making me laugh. I pulled my arms from under the covers and wrapped them around his neck.

"You know what? I get it. I get her," I said, nodding. "I'm not judging."

"She also said I should have my fun while I can because she's coming for me," he mumbled, planting kisses all over my face.

"Sounds like a real nut job."

"She's kinda perfect, actually."

Warmth spilled all over me. "There's no such thing." At least that's what I'd believed before him.

"You wouldn't think that if you read that note," he said, chuckling.

"You liked that." He'd *loved* the note. Fuck, if I'd known that's how I would get through to him, I'd have written it before I even saw him here.

"I did, Damsel," he said, breathing in my scent as he buried his face under my neck. "I've never *seen* you so clearly before."

My poor heart. "Then I'll write you a whole damn book." I'd write him a hundred.

"And I'll read every word," he promised.

"It's gonna be spicy," I warned him. "It's gonna be really, *really* spicy."

His shoulders shook with laughter. "You can just leave those parts out."

I pushed him back. "But those are the best parts! How am I gonna write about *you* without spice? That's just...it's *absurd!*" He was just that kind of guy. It was part of who he was.

He laughed out loud. "Fine. Add the spice. I'll just skip it."

"Trust me—you won't." And I knew that for a fact.

Pushing the cover off me as he shook his head, he pulled me in his arms. "What are you doing?"

"Taking you to the bathroom." And he kicked the door open.

"I can walk, you know." But I'd be damned if I didn't enjoy being carried by him.

"I know. You just don't have to." And he sat me down on the toilet. Since I was completely naked, it worked perfectly fine. But...

I raised a brow. "You're just gonna stand there while I pee?"

"Yep," he said, then opened a cabinet over the sink. "Then I'm gonna brush your teeth. Shave your legs. Bathe you. Do your hair. Get you dressed. And take you out."

"Are you serious?" Because he really sounded like he was.

"Mhmm. There's a really shitty diner about thirty minutes from here. You're gonna love it."

I shook my head. "I can get ready myself." I was more than capable.

And he grinned again. "I know. You just don't have to," he repeated.

So, we started. He literally brushed my teeth, which was fucking ridiculous, but okay. I indulged him. Then he shaved my legs with a brand-new razor, which meant he cut me in at least twenty places. Okay again. Then he combed my hair—or *tried* to before he finally had enough of my calling him names every time he ran the brush down. Still okay.

And when he put me in the small tub and filled it with lukewarm water to bathe me, he gave me a little *extra* something.

I'd never enjoyed a bath more in my life, but I'm pretty sure it had nothing to do with the bath itself, just with his fingers inside me. I rested my head on his shoulder as he played with me under the water, and his mouth was right next to my ear, licking and biting and kissing, saying things so dirty they made me blush afterward. At least I lasted almost a minute, which was saying something with him. Being finger fucked in a bathtub by Ax was definitely at the top of my favorite-things-to-do list now.

About an hour later, we stopped on the highway and looked at the three buildings on the other side—a gas station with a convenience store, a gross-looking motel, and a roadside diner with possibly the dirtiest windows I'd ever seen.

"I love it already," I told Ax with a grin.

"Wait till you try the pizza," he said, and holding my hand in his, our fingers intertwined, we walked to the diner together, like we weren't basically wanted by the whole world. Like we had no cares, we were in no rush, we had no troubles—just a couple going out to eat in the middle of fucking nowhere.

I wouldn't have it any other way.

Just to walk with him hand in hand like that without actually fearing someone would attack us was enough. So far, we couldn't see anything, hear anything, which didn't mean we were safe, but I was choosing to enjoy the night rather than panic right now. If something came, we'd hear it. If something came, we'd deal with it.

The diner wasn't half as bad as I feared. Red booths, white and red tiles on the floor, way too many neon signs hanging on the walls, but the counter was clean. Only about four people were in there, each by themselves, which was a relief. I'd drank rabbit blood Ax had gotten me, but there was something about hearing human hearts beating so close to me that kept me a bit on edge. And the woman behind the counter wasn't half bad, either. She had that smile about her that I usually found irritating, but… strangely not tonight.

It was probably just Ax.

We chose a booth at the very end of the bar, opposite from the toilets, kind of hidden from the rest. That's because we knew we wouldn't be able to keep our hands off each other, and who could really blame us? I didn't.

"I've got bad news, and I've got good news. Which one do you want first?" I asked him as we waited for the pizzas to arrive.

He raised a brow, putting his hand on my lap, reaching for mine. I grabbed it, then pulled up the skirt he got for me, so I could feel his hand on my naked thigh. It just made me feel better, and it was an added bonus that he loved it, too.

"Bad news," he finally decided.

"You sure?"

"Yep. I wanna get it out of the way sooner," he said, pushing his hand a bit farther up my thigh with a sneaky grin.

The way he looked just now, one arm propped over the seat, his white shirt melting onto his torso, showing me just enough of the curves of his muscles to get me hot and bothered, shoulders completely relaxed...it took my breath away, the prick. There was still an edge to his face. It was in his aura. It hung in the air about him. It made it clear to anyone near him that he was a predator. He didn't fuck around. And maybe it was only me, but it just added a lot to his appeal. It suited him. He wore his energy about him, not the other way around. He wasn't a slave to it at all. He was in complete control of himself.

He just didn't want to be often.

"Breathe, baby," he whispered, barely moving his lips when I forgot to speak for a couple seconds.

Asshole. I forced myself to roll my eyes. "You're not even that hot."

Suddenly, he leaned close to my ear. "Is that your insides melting?" he said. "Or are you just wet for me?"

Chuckling, I pushed him back. "Bad news coming, remember?"

"I don't give a shit," he said, adjusting his cock that had started to get hard already. Yum.

"Well, you should," I said, trying to focus on what I wanted to say. "Because it's *bad*."

He raised his brows. "What is it?"

"Turns out, I just might be the reason for that den of spirits we found in Arizona," I whispered. Nobody would be able to hear me but him. The humans were far enough away so that I could barely hear their blood rushing if I was focused on Ax—which I was.

"How in the fuck is that possible?" he said, shaking his head.

"Turns out, that's an actual *Vein*. A Ley line that broke the earth's surface, and that fucker Will Thorne thinks that the spirit that lives in me sort of brought it up here. He also thinks that by banishing my spirit, he's going to close the

Vein and send it back to the depths of the planet where it belongs."

The more I spoke, the heavier the fear in me. Fuck, when I said it out loud, it just seemed so real. And the reminder wasn't doing me any favors.

"That sounds impossible," Ax whispered after a while.

"Actually, not that much. I've been thinking. Remember the way the Vein kind of *sucked* me back when I was in there?" His hold on my hand tightened and even his heart skipped a beat. "I think that's why. It was sucking back my spirit. Not *me* specifically."

"Fuck," he muttered.

"Yeah, but that's not *all* the bad news." I smiled the sweetest smile I had because I was about to piss him off right now.

And he knew it. That's why his whole face fell. "What did you do?" he asked in that hoarse voice of his.

"Jacob offered to release me from the deal when I went back, and I refused. I stayed and I trained for three weeks before Will came."

No reaction yet. "Why?"

"Because I wanted Jacob to get this thing out of me," I said. "And because if I don't help him close that Vein, those spirits are gonna break out of that shield eventually. Then it's bye bye, world."

The waitress came with our steaming hot pizzas. It gave us both a moment to process what I said.

And when we were alone again, Ax turned to me. "So, now you think it's your responsibility."

Bull's eye. "It *is* my responsibility."

He raised his brows. "So, you *chose* that spirit? You forced it to get inside you, to mess with your head all your life?"

"No, you know that's not it."

"Then how are you responsible?"

I swallowed hard. "Maybe not responsible for *causing* it, but I am responsible for closing it."

"No, you're not."

"Yes, I am. If I don't, eventually, those spirits will break out. The world will be in danger—the *whole* world." And now I sounded like a *good guy*. Ugh.

"Not your problem," he insisted.

"Except *you* live in this world, Ax," I said with a sigh. "Anya lives in this world. Jones lives in this world. *I* fucking live here, too."

"No—we live in the Hidden Realm. That's separate."

"You can't be serious." How was I going to live in the Hidden Realm, *even if* spirits couldn't get through to it, knowing that the world outside was in ruins?

I couldn't. I *wouldn't*...

Shit—I was *really* starting to sound like a good guy here! It was freaking me out a little bit.

"What other choice do we have? Because you're not going into that place again." And he was dead serious about *that,* at least.

"Baby, don't be a dick," I whispered and kissed his cheek. "All I'm saying is, right now, I don't have to go anywhere. Jacob released me from the oath so that he wouldn't be able to track me. Or *Will* wouldn't be able to track me through him. Just that...I can't just forget about it, you know."

"And the good?"

I blinked at him. "What?"

"The good news," he said.

"Oh!" I did have one of those, too. "I can actually control my spirit about fifty percent of the time now. I even shifted back to vampire without losing consciousness once." I smiled proudly.

He kissed my lips so fast, I barely even felt it. "Is that why you took that thing off?"

I flinched. "About that." Shit—I'd forgotten about the pendant completely. "Yeah, it didn't actually give me any control or anything. Turns out, Jacob spelled it to alter the color, and he just made me think that it could help me. Said I needed to *believe* that I could do it, and that the necklace had nothing to do with it. I kept it on me anyway until I came here. Then I took it off because we had a deal, remember?" We'd made the deal on that rooftop that I would take off that necklace the moment I trusted him completely.

I did.

He remembered, too. That's why he smiled and squeezed my fingers. I thought he was going to say *I told you so* or something, but...

"I hate that guy so much, it's making me sick."

I burst out laughing. "You're a goddamn idiot." I grabbed his neck and kissed him, not really caring who could see. And he didn't hesitate. He wrapped an arm around my waist and pulled me until I almost sat on his lap. Good thing we were in a diner because I would have straddled him right now otherwise.

As it was, I had to move back a little bit, just so we could both breathe. It wasn't helping that his eyes were bloodshot, his dick rock hard. I *felt* it even without seeing it. It's like it was sending me invisible signals.

So, I turned to the pizza. It should be cold enough by now.

"The whispers are barely there, too," I said, biting into a slice. It wasn't all bad. Not the best I'd ever had, though.

"Oh?" Ax said, raising his brows as he watched me eat.

"Yep. I mean, that came as a bonus when I actually started to get through to the spirit. But they aren't as relentless now as they used to be," I said, then looked at his pizza. "Aren't you gonna eat?"

"Yes, but not now. Not this," he told me.

Blood rushed to my cheeks instantly. "Then what are you going to eat?"

I knew the fucking answer, but I just wanted to hear it from his lips.

"You, Damsel. Eat up. You're gonna need the energy," he said, nodding at the pizza.

Suddenly, I wasn't hungry anymore, either. Not for pizza, anyway.

"You can't just say that and expect me to—"

"Eat," he cut me off, running his hand on my naked thigh, sending electricity jolts up and down my body. I couldn't tear my eyes off his face, his bloodshot eyes, but he was right. I needed the energy. I hated how easily spent I was last night. So, I ate. And the way he watched me bite that pizza, and chew, then swallow, you'd think I was giving him a fucking lap dance.

"What else happened while you were gone?" he said, and I barely swallowed the bite.

Because there was one other thing... "Nothing." Which I didn't plan to share with him tonight.

Or ever.

Except...his fingers dug into my thigh. "Damsel, don't lie to me."

"I'm not lying." And I was perfectly aware that he could hear my heartbeat. He could smell it on my skin, too.

"Baby, you can tell me anything."

"Except this." It was...too much. I already knew what he was going to say. I didn't want to argue with him.

But he moved closer to me in the booth, put his hand on my cheek and turned my head to him slowly. "It's fine, Damsel. Whatever it is, we'll handle it. You can tell me."

Fuck—how could I say no? His eyes were open, honest, a brilliant blue that I could get lost in every second. I had no chance of holding back.

"Jacob said there's a ninety-percent chance that I'll die when he takes the spirit out of me."

The second the words left my lips, Ax's face changed immediately. He moved back to his place, looking like...

My jaw hit the floor.

"Did you just *manipulate* me into telling you that?" Is that why he became so open and earnest all of a sudden? *Baby, you can tell me anything*?

Oh gods—and I fell for it!

He grinned wide. "You're a great teacher, Damsel."

The asshole! I'd done it when we were in bed. I manipulated him into *fucking* me, not telling me his secrets.

Fuck.

"And you're also *never* getting that spirit out of you in your life."

I dropped the pizza. "Not your decision to make."

"Yes, it is."

"No, it's not! Besides, I would have done it and you wouldn't even know about it if Will fucking Thorne hadn't locked me in that magic." And now I was pissed.

But he didn't give a shit. "*I'm yours*—remember that? That's what you said. What—did you think that wouldn't mean anything?"

"I—" but he didn't even let me speak.

"It means what happens to you, what happens to *me*, we both get a say in it. It's both our decision. That's what *I'm yours* means."

Damn him. "I can't keep this thing inside me forever."

"Sure, you can. You're already controlling it."

"That's not the point! The Vein could pop any second!"

"I would trust Jacob Thorne to handle it," he said calmly.

"Ax, it's not that simple. He isn't touched."

"He has plenty of touched people around him."

"Yes—with spirits other than the one who pulled that Vein up from its place!" I said, exasperated. "Can you imagine all that power? This thing inside me is way too much for me."

"It isn't," he said, still as calm which pissed me off even more. "It's powerful, yes. I saw it with my own eyes. But you can handle it, baby. You've *been* handling it all your life already."

And he believed every word.

"What if I just don't want to?"

"You want to be free?"

I nodded. I wanted that so much it knocked the breath out of me.

"Good—then be free. Free means to be alive, not dead. And you are free, baby. I promise you that. You can be anywhere you want to be. Just be alive."

"There's a ten percent chance I'll make it." That had to count for something.

"Even if there was a ninety-nine percent chance of you making it, I would never risk it. I won't risk your life, even for this entire fucked up world, Damsel."

I sighed. "That's disturbing, baby."

"But you know what's more disturbing?" He grinned. "You, wanting to save the fucking world—*for me*."

I shook my head. "Of course, I would lose my head after you," I mumbled, running my fingers along his stubble. He was the most senseless man I'd ever met, and somehow, it just fit my already fucked up life. "Let's make a deal, okay? We don't have to decide anything right now. We can take our time. We can *live*. We can do whatever you want. And then after a few years, we'll talk about it again."

"The outcome will be the same," he told me.

"I have faith." I had more faith in us than in anything else in the world. No magic, no spirit, no nothing.

He smiled. "You're way too tame, Damsel." And he kissed me.

"Somebody has to balance you out." Because he was way too wild.

"I'm wilder than you know," he whispered, running his fingertips up my thigh.

Shaking my head, I turned to the pizza. I really needed to eat at least half of that to be able to keep up with him tonight. And tomorrow.

"How long are we staying here?" I wondered, then bit into the pizza, and his fingers slipped under my skirt. I looked down at my lap, then at him. "What are you doing?" I said with my mouth half full.

"Eat, baby," he whispered, fingers moving up until he reached my panties.

"We're in a diner," I hissed, but I didn't push his hand away. How could I when he felt like that? I swear, he touched me and my own body turned against me without hesitation.

"I know. Keep eating," he said and came a little closer. "And spread those legs."

"Ax," I begged. I couldn't eat. I could't *think*. I couldn't do shit when he touched me like that.

"You think you can keep quiet for me this time?" And he

slipped two fingers under my panties. My eyes squeezed shut.

"I can't..." I grabbed his hand over my skirt when he pressed a finger into my wet folds, growling.

"Look at you, already dripping," he whispered, then pushed his hand lower. I watched, fascinated by my own self as I let go and moved my legs farther apart. Something was definitely wrong with me.

Fuck it, if he wanted to play with me, it was fine. I could handle it, damn it. He wasn't going to make me come—we were just playing.

"Take what you need from me, Savage," I whispered to him. "And then it will be my turn."

He was hard, too. I could see the bulge in his jeans, but for now, I put my elbows over the table and closed my eyes, focusing on not making a sound.

"There's my good little girl," he growled, moving his fingers deeper, lower, until his fingertips teased my entrance.

I rested back on the booth, eyes squeezed shut, tongue between my teeth. And once I gave him access, he moved much more freely. His fingers pressed onto my clit and he circled it slowly. My hips moved on their own accord in rhythm with him, and it was a couple seconds before I even realized it.

"That's enough, Ax," I begged. "There's people back there."

But he pressed his fingers onto my clit harder, making me whimper. "So, keep quiet," he whispered, eyes almost completely red as he continued to torture me. And my hips started moving again. Fuck, he felt so good. He knew exactly how to touch me, and the orgasm was building in me so fast, I feared the whole fucking world would hear it when it ripped me open.

But the heartbeat that was getting louder in my head made me pause for a second.

I gripped his hand tightly from over my skirt and moved forward, putting my arms over the table again, just as the waitress stopped in front of us with a bright smile on her round face.

"Is everything okay with you two?" she chirped.

Oh, gods. "Yes!" I breathed, and Ax continued to circle my clit.

Fuck, she was *right there*! What if she could see us?

"Everything is perfect, actually," he told her. "We're having a great time. Right, baby?"

Biting my tongue until I tasted blood, I forced a smile on my face. "Yes, baby," I choked, and the fucker moved toward the table, too, just so he could reach deeper, then slipped his middle finger halfway inside me.

"So happy to hear that!" the waitress said with a laugh. "You two are so lucky."

Just leave already!

Ax pumped his finger in and out of me slowly...

"Oh, *I'm* definitely the luckier one here," the asshole said with a grin, knowing exactly that the waitress was *begging* for a reason to drag this on.

And she laughed again. "Oh, Lord! You're so charming," she said, waving him off. "I wish there were more men like you in the world."

He thrust a second finger inside me, too, slowly, so he didn't move me an inch. And I could do nothing but take it, bite my tongue and keep a probably terrifying smile on my face as I looked at the woman but didn't actually see her.

My gods, that felt so good. Shit, I was going to come in seconds.

"Thank you, Deborah. That's very kind of you," the asshole said, and she all but melted.

He was fucking keeping her there on purpose to torture me!

I don't know how I convinced myself to speak, but I said, "Do you mind, though? He was just telling me something very...sensitive about himself."

"Oh!"

"Yeah—he *cried* all day today, and he just needs to let out the words, too," I whispered, and her cheeks flushed brighter while Ax began to pump his fingers inside me faster.

Holding back the orgasm felt like trying to push back a freight train. Every inch of me was shaking.

"Oh, how very brave of you! You don't find many men who cry these days," the woman cooed. "But okay—I'll leave you to it," she said, walking backward, her eyes still on us. "Just let me know if you need anything!"

"My greedy little slut," Ax said, grinning as he full on fucked me raw with his fingers now. And I moved on the leather of the booth like I was riding his cock.

"You fucking prick," I said breathlessly, then bit my lip hard.

His eyes moved to it and he let go of a long breath. "Let go, baby. Let me see you come without making a sound."

"Don't," I begged. "I can't...just stop, please."

"Stop moving those hips and I'll stop, too," he said instead.

That's how I knew I was doomed.

"I'm imagining what your ass looks like, baby. I'm

imagining how your tits are bouncing," he kept going. "Stop moving, Damsel."

Yeah, fuck no. That wasn't going to happen. Instead, I spread my legs a bit farther, and I prayed with all my heart that nobody saw. Then I moved to the edge of the seat so he could thrust his fingers all the way inside me, bringing the heel of his hand right on my clit.

"Good girl," he breathed against my ear. "C'mon, baby. Come all over my fingers."

And I was done for.

Squeezing my eyes shut, I brought my hand to my mouth and bit my skin so hard, I drew blood. Not a sound left me on the outside, but on the inside, I could hear how he fucking broke me to pieces, then put me back together again.

And when I finally opened my eyes, completely spent for a moment, he held them while he brought his fingers to his lips and licked them clean. He enjoyed it, too. He fucking loved the taste of me just as much as I loved the taste of him.

"Better than pizza?" I said breathlessly, still unable to sit straight properly.

"Better than fucking blood," he said, eyes dark and bloodshot.

I grinned. "My turn."

As much as I'd have liked to see the look on his face when he came and wasn't allowed to make a single sound, I couldn't. I had to move a lot, and I didn't give a shit about people, but even I had my limits of what I let myself be seen doing.

So, we took it outside.

We barely made it to the back of the diner before he grabbed me, took my bottom lip between his teeth and bit hard, then tried to reach for my skirt.

I wasn't having it, so I slapped his hand away.

"You're not allowed to touch me yet," I told him, then slammed him against the back of the diner before I fell to my knees. He growled when I freed his cock from his pants and ran my hands up and down the length of him, drooling. He was so big, I had to remind myself that I'd taken him in my mouth before because right now my mouth felt *tiny* compared to it.

"Quit playing, Damsel," he said, grunting and growling as I moved my hands faster, squeezing him harder.

"You don't like being played?" I said, licking his tip just a little to give him—and myself—a taste. Fucking delicious.

"Fuck," he breathed, pushing his hips forward, and I let him press against my lips but didn't open them yet. He looked possessed already.

"Maybe I should get Deborah out here so she can keep you company while I do this," I said and took his tip in my mouth, sucking hard. The sounds he let out could be mistaken for an animal—a very hungry animal.

"Damsel," he warned, and I would have ignored it, except my tongue craved him so bad. I was wet again, which didn't surprise me in the least, so I opened my mouth and took him in all the way until he was pressed against my throat.

The feel of his smooth skin on my tongue had me feeling possessed, too. I'd really meant what I wrote on that note—I couldn't get enough of him. I picked up the pace, sucking and grazing him with my teeth as I went, and he had no complaints. With both hands on the back of my neck, he thrust himself inside my mouth violently, just like I liked.

Ten seconds in, and I was gasping for air. Tears streamed from my eyes and I was so ready to come, I'd be done if I so much as nudged my clit a little bit. But instead, I licked the length of him, sucked until my jaw turned completely numb.

I was so lost to the feel of him that I barely heard the footsteps coming closer to us. I stopped moving, letting his cock out of my mouth for a second, just to make sure I'd heard right.

"Who's there?!" a man called.

Oh, shit.

Biting back laughter, I jumped to my feet. Ax was grinning ear-to-ear, too, and he grabbed me by the hand and led us toward the trees that started about half a mile behind the diner.

The second we reached the first tree, he slammed me with my chest on the trunk, just as the man came behind the diner, a flashlight in his hand as he searched the darkness.

And Ax ripped my panties off.

"I'm not done yet!" I complained in a whisper, but the feel of his cock pressed against my folds made me jut my ass out. He growled, slapping my ass hard, and the sound of it reached the man still searching behind the diner. He turned the flashlight toward us, but I wasn't worried. We were too far for him to see us.

"Hello?!" he called at the darkness.

Ax thrust his cock inside me all the way.

Fuck, the feel of him. I bit my forearm to keep from screaming out as he held me by the hips tightly and kept himself buried inside me for a second. He rested his forehead on my shoulder, breathing as heavily as me.

"Ax," I whispered, hoping he wouldn't move until that man was gone because I needed to be able to moan and scream.

But the asshole didn't care. He pushed himself back and slammed into me again, twice as hard. I saw stars when I squeezed my eyes shut, and the low growls he let out filled my head in an instant. He fucked me against the tree like he was in a rush, and when his hand moved to my front and his fingers began to circle my clit while he pounded into me, I was a goner.

The orgasm ripped through me and my back arched all the way, taking him even deeper. He let go of my clit and wrapped his hand around my neck, squeezing just enough to make it hard for me to breathe, and the orgasm was twice as powerful. It lasted twice as long, too.

When he came, too, he slammed me against the trunk so hard I thought my ribs would break. The way he needed me, so desperately, so violently, made every ounce of pain welcome.

By the time he pulled himself out, I could barely stand.

He spun me around and hugged me to his chest, keeping me on my feet. The man was gone, no lights around us, no humans close enough. Not even animals. It was just us.

"You're gonna pay for that," I whispered against his neck, barely breathing.

"I couldn't help it," he said, biting my earlobe as his hands moved under my shirt, his warm palms pressing against my naked skin.

"I'm gonna tie you up tonight. I'm gonna make you come three times in a row before you can touch me."

He growled, squeezing me to his chest harder. "I'll fucking lose my mind before you're done," he warned.

"You won't. You'll lie there and take it like the good boy that you are," I teased, licking his jaw. "And when I'm done, you can have your way with me, too."

He grabbed my face in his hands and pulled me back so he could look in my eyes. "Are you sure you can handle it, though?"

Oh, the fucking asshole. My grin mirrored his. "*Six* times," I told him. "And you better start running, Savage."

I'd be damned if I didn't keep my word.

CHAPTER
THIRTEEN

Eight days later

I FELT his eyes on my face as I pretended to be focused ahead.

"What do I get if I win?" I asked.

"You're *not* going to win, Damsel."

I rolled my eyes. "Suck it, asshole."

Ax was suddenly right behind me, whispering in my ear, "But you're so much better at sucking."

Shivers ran down my back. "I am," I whispered, turning my head to the side. "It's a talent."

He bit my cheek, growling. "Then that's what you'll do *when* I win."

"I'll do that for free." I winked. "You can ask for anything else—*if* you win." Which *wasn't* going to happen.

"What's better than your lips wrapped around my cock?"

Tingles went straight to my pussy. "Not much, really." I

leaned back onto his chest. His hand snaked round my waist, under my shirt, pressing to my stomach.

"Fuck, Damsel," he said, licking my cheek. "If we keep this up, there will be no race."

Shit, he was right.

I forced myself to step away from him, shaking my head to clear my mind. "No—we're doing this. We have to."

"Not really." He ran his fingers down my arm.

I slapped his hand away. "We do! C'mon, we got this. We can keep our hands to ourselves for five fucking minutes!"

We always did this. We'd plan to go hiking up the mountains surrounding us and end up fucking the whole night instead. We'd plan to go shopping in the closest town, almost an hour and a half away, but we'd start talking, and end up fucking the whole night—again. We'd plan to go back to that diner to eat every night, but the reminder of what he'd done to me and what I'd done to him last time got us naked, and once we were naked, there was no putting clothes on us again for the rest of the night.

It had been eight days! We needed to do something *else*, too. Didn't matter that we didn't want to—we had to. It just felt important.

"Except I *really* can't," he said, wrapping his hands around my waist, emptying my lungs. "I don't want to."

"And I know why," I teased. "It's because you know I'll win."

He threw his head back, laughing. "You'll *never* win this, baby."

"There's a way to find out. We just need to agree on what the winner gets." It was just a race—we would run to the edge of the woods, all the way to the first tree, and whoever touched it first, won. It wasn't anything *big*. We could do it, damn it! We were capable of doing more than just mind-blowing sex.

"Okay," he finally said, stepping away from me. "Okay, fine. What do you want if you win?"

Now, that was a hard question. What could I want when I had *everything*? I had Ax. I had blood. I had a roof over my head, and a tiny place to screw his brains out every time I pleased.

There *really* wasn't anything else I wanted or needed to live and be happy.

"I want you to cook something for me. Steak. And rice—I want rice. And also desert. Something with a lot of chocolate in it. Preferably chocolate chip cupcakes." I smiled.

"Deal," he said without hesitation.

I raised a brow. "*Can* you cook, though?"

"I'll figure it out," he said, not worried in the least. "But *when* I win, you're coming with me." He came closer to me again, but he didn't touch me. The weight of his gaze on my lips was more than enough, though. "We're getting in the car and we're leaving this place behind. We can go anywhere you want—Rome, Paris, Amsterdam...everywhere in the world."

I flinched. "Where there's humans. And sorcerers." And Vein spirits, too.

"We'll be careful," he whispered.

"But we don't need to go anywhere else. This is perfect." We'd agreed to stay here for now, hadn't we? I didn't want anything else, just this.

"You deserve so much more, Damsel. I want to give it all to you. I want to fuck you in every continent, every county, every city on earth, too." Every hair on my body rose. "Just come see the world with me. I'll make it worth it." He brought his lips to mine but didn't kiss me.

Every instinct in my body demanded that I say *no*. There were humans out there tempting me with their heartbeats and the fresh blood rushing through their veins. There were sorcerers out there who were probably looking for the both of us right now. It wasn't safe.

No place was ever safe for me.

The fear had my hands shaking already, and…that was *it*. I'd been a prisoner of that fear my whole life. I'd confined myself inside it, stuck in my comfort zone for so long, it had become the only way I knew how to live.

What would happen if I just *stopped* being afraid for a second? What would I say if I just put that fear aside and focused on what *he* wanted first?

"Yes," I said breathlessly. *That* was my answer. "Fuck, yes, let's do it." I wanted to see the world, too. I wanted to fuck him in every city, too. Anywhere was fine as long as we were together.

His lips stretched into one of my favorite smiles—the one that was proud and happy and completely genuine. No hint of mischief, no nothing. Just a smile.

"Good girl," he whispered, then kissed me softly. "I'll keep you safe, Damsel. You don't have to worry about anything."

"I don't," I promised, fisting his shirt as I raised on my tiptoes to kiss him, too.

But he stepped back. "The race," he said, his voice already hoarse. "Let's get to it because we need to get ready."

"*If* you win." Though there was a good chance that he would. He was faster than me, the asshole, but I hadn't given up yet. "See you on the other side, Savage." I said and started running. He was right beside me.

It was a four-minute run all the way to the edge of the

woods and the highway, but I wasn't planning on playing fair. If he expected that from me, he was a damn fool.

But he didn't. That's why, when I jumped and grabbed a branch, then threw myself forward lightning fast, he was right there with me.

And he landed on the ground before I did.

No problem. I jumped again and landed on his back, taking him down. We rolled on the ground a couple of times, and I waited for the right moment until I could put my feet on his back and push him, while pushing myself forward.

When I started running again, he was ten feet behind me. The cold wind blowing on my face, the dark of the night, the thrill of the chase had me smiling so wide my cheeks hurt. Fuck, this was *freedom*. This was what I'd always craved. The voices in my head calm. The world for me to explore. A man who adored me and was just as hungry for me as I was for him at my back...

When he went past me, the asshole, he pushed me to the side. Since I was running, I lost balance instantly and landed with one knee on the ground before I could fall.

Cursing under my breath, I made it back to my feet. He was way ahead of me now.

But I wasn't done yet.

I ran until my muscles screamed, and the moment I felt I was close enough to him, I jumped on the nearest branch, then to the next tree, and the next, until I got to his other side. He looked behind, curious to see what I was doing, and he really shouldn't have done that. Because I jumped to the next tree, wrapped an arm around the trunk, and the momentum sent me to him lightning fast. I locked my legs so that when I slammed my feet on his shoulder, he literally *flew* at least ten feet before he hit a tree trunk with the back of his head.

"*Woohoo!*" I shouted to the night and started running again, now a hundred percent sure that he wouldn't be able to stop me.

Thirty seconds later, my eyes zeroed in on the last tree in the line, barely fifteen feet away from the highway. The lights of the cars passing by, and those of the diner, gas station and motel blinded me momentarily. But the tree was right there, and I was smiling, arms outstretched to touch the trunk, except...

My fingertips were an inch away from it when he slammed onto me from the side, wrapped his arm around me and took us to the ground, rolling.

"I win!" I shouted breathlessly as we rolled a few more times, before finally stopping with me on my back and him on top of me. There was blood on the corner of his lips, and dirt in his hair, too, but his eyes were wide, sparkling with mischief as he grinned.

"No, you didn't," he said, keeping my arms pinned to my sides. "You didn't touch it."

"I would have if you hadn't slammed onto me, asshole!"

"But you *didn't*," he said. "That's not winning."

"It's—"

"It isn't." He nudged my face to the side and licked my neck right under my earlobe, where he knew I was the most ticklish. Laughter bubbled out of me instantly and my body began to thrash, but he was way too strong, way too heavy.

"Stop!" I said, unable to breathe already, but he didn't give a shit. Just kept licking and grazing my skin with his teeth just enough to make me feel like I might die of laughter if he didn't stop it *right now!*

"*Stop it!*"

"Not until you admit you didn't win," he said, and no matter how hard I tried to push his head away with mine, he was just stronger. And I couldn't properly coordinate my movements when I laughed like a fucking maniac like that.

"Admit it, Damsel. You're a sore loser. You cheated, too. That wasn't very nice of you," he teased, licking and biting until I literally couldn't breathe for real.

"Never," I choked, but then...

He was lying right on top of me, so I felt it the second his muscles clenched and his body went rigid.

He stopped tickling me, too. The laughter died on my lips.

"We're not alone," Ax whispered, and my heart skipped a long beat when I turned my head to the side...and saw.

Jacob Thorne was standing at the edge of the highway, hands on his hips, watching us.

CHAPTER FOURTEEN

Ax stood and pulled me up by the hands within a second. The whispers in my head began to get restless the way they hadn't done in over a week. Glad to find I hadn't missed them at all.

Jacob started walking toward us slowly.

I grabbed Ax's hand in mine. "Don't attack."

"But he's right there," he whispered, and I could hear the grin in his voice.

"Don't you dare," I said through gritted teeth, squeezing his fingers tightly.

Two seconds later, Jacob stopped in front of us. I kept my eyes on him, on the highway behind him, the red truck he always drove around parked in front of the diner. Was he alone? Because I couldn't hear anybody else or see anything other than him.

"What are you doing here, Jacob?" I said, my instincts on high alert because I didn't know for sure he was the only one here. Sorcerers had magic. Magic could keep the sound of everything away from you.

"I need to talk to you," he said, his eyes moving from me to Ax, lightning fast.

"Are you alone?"

"Yes," he said without missing a beat. And he was telling the truth. "I just need five minutes. Can we go somewhere to talk?"

Ax squeezed his fingers around mine. I squeezed, too. He knew what that meant.

Letting go of a long breath, I nodded. If Jacob was here, chances were he really needed to talk to me. I hadn't forgotten that he'd been the one to get Ax to his house. I hadn't forgotten that he'd released me from my oath, too, and had broken the shield for me to get out.

If he wanted to talk, I could at least hear him out.

"Sure thing. Follow us," I said and pushed Ax deeper into the woods. He moved, but I had to practically drag him by force.

"What the fuck does he want?" he said after a minute, while Jacob walked behind us slowly.

"I don't know but I want to hear him out."

"Why?"

"Because. He saved me, remember? He got you to me."

"Damsel..."

"Let's just hear him out. Don't be rude, Ax. Just let him talk."

He sighed, shaking his head. "Okay, Damsel. I'll let him talk."

And he did.

When we reached the rocks that would lead us to the cabin, Ax hadn't even looked back at Jacob once. Not that he needed to—we could hear his every movement perfectly, but still. I trusted him to keep his shit together for now.

"There's a small cabin about halfway up this mountain.

Think you can climb up there, sorcerer?" I teased, pointing up the mountain. "Or do I need to carry you on my back?"

Jacob shook his head with a smile. "I'll climb, thanks."

"Suit yourself."

I jumped on the rocks and Ax followed me. We reached the cabin in thirty seconds, but it was going to take Jacob a bit longer than that.

And it was for the best because I needed a moment to gather my own shit. It was okay that Jacob was here. So what that he found me? It didn't mean anything. It didn't mean that other people would be here, too, or that my life was going to drastically change—again—all of a sudden. This was not *it*. It couldn't be it. Gods, how long did I get—*eight days*? That wasn't enough. Not even close.

"Look at me," Ax said, grabbing my face in his hands while we waited in front of the cabin for Jacob.

"I'm fine," I told him, but he knew me too well to buy it.

"There's nothing anybody can make you do when you don't want to. Not Thorne, not anyone. Got it?" He looked into my eyes and held them, never even blinking.

Despite everything, I smiled. "I know."

"Besides—we're leaving here tonight."

"Except you *didn't* win," I reminded him. Not that it mattered—I *would* go with him anywhere he wanted.

"Yes, I did," he said with a wide grin. "I touched the tree with my fingertips before I wrapped my arms around you."

"No, you didn't." Did he?

"Yes, I did. I won, Damsel. Fair and square."

"Asshole! That *wasn't* fair!" I said, slamming my fists on his chest, which only made him laugh.

"I'll carry you on my back if I have to," he told me.

"What if I scream and kick and thrash?"

"Then I'll love it even more," he said, pulling my lips into his mouth.

"And what if I don't play fair, either?" I asked in a breath, my mind already consumed with the feel of him, the idea of him inside me...

But before he could answer, we heard Jacob's heartbeat, which meant he was close. Ten seconds later, he climbed the top rock and finally pushed himself up to his feet.

He breathed a bit heavier as he took in the cabin built into the carved rocks of the mountain. He even looked a little impressed.

"How'd you find me, Jacob?" I asked, curious to know exactly how long we had before anybody else found us.

"I saved a bit of your blood," he said, and when he saw the look on my face, he added, "For emergencies only!"

I raised a brow. "This is an emergency?"

He sighed, lowering his head for a second. "I think so."

Well, shit.

"Why did you call Jones, Jacob?" I asked before I could stop myself. The question had been bugging me since Ax told me about it. I knew Jacob prided himself on being the *good guy*, but that had been too much, even for him.

"Because I didn't know how else to get to Ax. I could only find Jones's phone number." He said it simply, like it hadn't meant the difference between life and death for me.

I took a step closer to him. "But *why*?"

He held my eyes for a second. "Because you didn't deserve what was being done to you."

I laughed, unable to help myself, and when I went a bit closer, he looked wary. Like he actually thought I might attack him or something.

"You're a piece of work, you know that?" I told him "Thanks, dickhead. You saved my life."

At that, he gave me a relieved smile. "You wouldn't have needed saving if it wasn't for me."

I laughed again. "You're such a good guy, Jacob Thorne."

At that, he flinched. "Well, I turned against my own, so...I don't know about *good*."

"Are they alive?"

"Garret didn't make it," Jacob said.

"That's too bad." Not really.

"I've sent them all away," he said. "I released them from their oaths...except Ethan."

"Oh, c'mon. You shouldn't have done that." They were his team. His pride and joy.

"They turned against me. Went behind my back when they contacted my uncle. It was obvious that I couldn't trust them anymore," he said, and he didn't seem happy about it.

I nodded. "I'm sorry." I really was. He worked hard with those people. With *us*. I appreciated it more than he knew.

"Don't be. It's for the best, anyway."

"But what about the Vein?"

"I'll handle the Vein," he said, but he didn't sound so sure.

How was he going to handle the Vein on his own? Was that why he'd come to find me?

"Right now, something else has come up, something I found." His eyes kept moving behind me, to where Ax was. And every time he saw his face, he flinched a bit. I could see why when I looked back and saw Ax's face, the murderous look in his eyes. So, I stepped closer to him again and elbowed him in the gut.

"Stop acting like a dick, baby," I whispered, but if he heard me, he didn't care.

"Remember the sorceress you told me about?" Jacob said, making me narrow my brows.

"The one that lives in the Hidden Realm?"

"Yes, that one. You said her name is Alida Morgans."

"I think so." I turned to Ax. "That was her name, right?" I could have easily remembered wrong.

He nodded. "Yes."

"And you saw her?" Jacob asked him.

"I did. Why?" Even his voice was completely transformed into that of a mad man. Low and rough and so damn sexy, I had to remind myself to focus on Jacob instead.

"Because I've done some research," Jacob said. "And Alida Morgans and Marie Graham's grandmother were cousins."

I blinked at him. "What?"

"They grew up together. They were the same age. Their mothers were sisters," Jacob said, and his every word rang true.

I shook my head. "That's...no, that can't be."

"She didn't know her," Ax said. "I was there when they met—Marie didn't know that woman."

But Jacob shrugged. "Whether she did or not doesn't really matter. What bugs me is that Alida Morgans sent your covens chasing after Marie. What are the odds that she *didn't* know who Marie was all along?"

I had no answer to that, but Ax did.

"None," he said without hesitation. "She knew Damsel was alive. She knew what I was planning to do, too. If Marie is really related to her, I don't see how she *wouldn't* have known."

Holy fuck. "I just need a second," I said, closing my eyes. The image of Marie and Marcus were right in the back of my lids. So *innocent*. The way she'd cried. The way she'd been afraid, so panicked for her little brother.

The way she hadn't hesitated, not even a little bit, when we told her we would take her to the Hidden Realm.

Chills rushed down my spine.

"How sure are you that they're actually family?" I asked Jacob in half a voice.

"A hundred percent. I found all their birth records when I was digging into Alida Morgans."

"But...*why*?" Why would that woman even have us bring Marie to her?

Why would anyone choose to live under a castle in the Hidden Realm?

"I don't know why, but I think it's very important to find out," Jacob said, taking in a deep breath as he looked at me. "Which is why I'm here. I need to get into the Hidden Realm, Nikki. And I can't do that on my own."

You've got to be shitting me.

I sat on the threshold, staring at nothing and just thinking. Trying to make sense of what Jacob was saying. Wanting to both laugh and cry at the absurdity of the situation.

"It doesn't make any sense," Ax said from where he was standing, leaning against the wall of the cabin.

"Unless...she was trying to keep Marie safe? And she knew she could do that within the Realm?" I guessed, but that wasn't it.

"I don't think it really matters," Jacob said. "Whatever reason she had, we won't find out until we talk to her." He waited for me to say something, and when I didn't... "So, how about it, Nikki? Think you can help a good guy out?"

Shaking my head, I laughed. Of course, I would help him—if that sorceress was in *my* home, and she'd somehow tricked me into bringing Marie and Marcus to her, then I needed to know why. I had to see her for myself, talk to her, just...*understand*.

I stood up, but before I could speak, Ax beat me to it.

"You're not going anywhere with him."

I turned to look at him, not half as surprised at this point.

Grabbing my hips, I raised my chin. "Not only that, but *you're* coming with me."

He grinned like a mad man. "Fuck that, baby. You're not going anywhere."

I laughed. "You think you can *stop* me?" Really? Had he forgotten what we already talked about? "Try me, big guy."

His eyes sparkled, and I'd be damned if I didn't want to stick my tongue in his throat.

And he felt it, too. That's why his smile widened a touch more. "Are you challenging me, Damsel? Because we both know where that leads."

"I am, Savage. C'mon—what are you waiting for?" I raised my brows and bit my lip, and the way his eyes heated up at the sight of it made me wet between my legs. I didn't think it was possible, but the more I had him, the more I wanted him. He just knew how to turn me on, and I didn't think he was even *trying*.

And when he strode to me slowly, watching me like a predator does his prey, I was all out of breath.

"I'll tie you to the fucking mountain. I'll starve you of the thing you want most," he growled.

My lips parted. "You wouldn't."

"Try me."

"You'd have to starve yourself, too." Because he was

talking about his cock, and we both knew that was *never* going to happen. Just empty threats.

"On the contrary. I'll be full all the time. It's just you who'll suffer."

I grabbed a fistful of his shirt, and my imagination ran away with me. I could picture it perfectly in an instant—the way he'd tie me up, completely naked, feed me and bathe me himself, torture me for *days* without ever giving me release. He'd just keep me there and use me for his own pleasure.

Fuck.

"I'll bring the fucking mountain down on your head," I hissed, already dripping between my thighs.

He leaned closer until the tips our noses almost touched. "You. Are. *Not*. Going."

"Fuck you, Savage. You're not the boss of me."

His eyes brightened up. "So, disobey me," he challenged.

Fuck, it was hot out here.

And it just pissed me off as much as it turned me on. "You can't fucking stop me."

"Damsel," he warned with a growl, grabbing my chin in his hand, squeezing hard. The slight pain somehow converted into pleasure within a second, until—

"Are you about to start fighting?"

I turned to find Jacob staring at me wide-eyed, and I was almost surprised to find him there.

Shit, he was still here.

"What?" I whispered, a bit disoriented.

He looked at me, then at Ax. "I said, are you about to start fighting?"

Fighting?

I smiled. "Yes, actually. That's exactly what's gonna

happen," I said breathlessly. "He just needs to come to his senses, that's all. So, we're just gonna, erm...fight. And it's gonna be bloody." I pushed Ax back toward the door of the cabin. "So, just...stay here for a while, okay? Don't come inside. Just stay right there."

Jacob had his brows raised and his mouth wide open as he watched us moving inside the cabin. He must have seen Ax's hands on my hips, the way he buried his face in my hair, growling. I'm pretty sure he knew we *weren't* going to fight by now, even before Ax closed the door, took me in his arms and sat me down on the narrow kitchen isle, devouring my mouth with his tongue.

Fuck, I was so turned on, it was completely senseless. There was just something about the way he looked when he *ordered* me. Something about that spark in his eyes that had drawn me in from day one. I couldn't resist it. I didn't *want* to resist it. So, I stuck my hands under his shirt and scratched the hell out of his back to give him a taste of his own delicious medicine.

He pushed me back a bit on the counter, his hands under my skirt, and when he found that I was naked underneath, he growled, breaking the kiss.

"No panties to tear?"

"I literally only have one pair left." He'd torn all of them in half, the prick. I'd learned my lesson.

He bit my jaw hard. "I'm tearing those, too," he warned, and he meant it.

"You'd have to catch them on me first," I said, struggling to undo his button until his thick cock was in my hands. *Yes.* I could breathe a little easier now.

"We're not going," Ax said as he spread my thighs apart until it hurt, and I positioned him at my entrance.

"Come inside me, baby," I whispered, pulling his hips.

He growled and moved fast, burying inside me so deep I saw stars. Fuck, he felt incredible.

I closed my eyes for a second and just breathed.

He dug his fingers on the backs of my thighs and barely gave me any time before he moved back and thrust himself inside me again. I leaned back on my elbows, and he pressed his chest onto me, never letting an inch of space between us as he fucked me on the counter.

"Slower," I breathed, wanting it to last just a tiny bit longer.

He buried inside me deep and stayed there while I moaned. I was *trying* to keep it down, but I wasn't really sure if it was working, especially when he invaded every inch of my body like that.

"Clench around my cock, Damsel," he ordered, and I did as I rolled my hips up and down, desperate to take him even deeper.

"We're going," I whispered, and he opened his eyes.

"No," he growled.

"Yes, baby. We have to."

He moved back just a bit and slammed into me with all his strength, making me cry out.

"My gods," I breathed. "Fuck, Ax."

"We're going to Europe, remember?" he told me, biting my lips as he stayed inside me like that. "Thorne isn't fucking invited."

"He helped me when I needed him. He can't get to the Hidden Realm on his own," I said, panting. "And I want to know about Marie. Don't you?"

He squeezed his eyes shut because he didn't want to admit that he did. "Damn it, Damsel."

"It's the Hidden Realm. It's home. All we have to do is talk to that sorceress, that's all." And I would talk to Anya, too. Maybe even Jones, just for some closure. "Then we can leave. We can do anything you want."

He touched his cheek to mine. "I don't trust him."

"That's okay. You can trust me."

He dug his fingers deeper into my skin, then thrust himself inside me one more time. My eyes rolled in my skull.

"And if I say no?"

It wasn't a hard question. I took his face in my hands and raised his head. "Then I'll try to force you, and if I fail, we stay."

He knew I meant it. He could hear it in my voice. I hadn't been kidding when I made him that promise. I really was never going to leave his side. Not ever.

And he knew it. He understood.

"Okay, Damsel. We'll go back home," he said, making me smile. "But after that, you're all mine."

"I'm already all yours."

"All mine to do with whatever I please," he said, moving in and out of me again, picking up the pace. "All mine to take wherever I want." I threw my head back and he bit the side of my neck, making me scream. "All mine, Damsel."

"Yes!" I cried out, the orgasm about to rip me open as he pounded into me faster by the second. Gods, he felt so good, it was no wonder that I constantly craved him.

And when I came, he let go with me. We held each other, face to face, lips touching but not kissing. I was lost to the feeling, to the look in his eyes, to the warmth of his skin. We both expected it when our fangs came out—they always did lately, at least once a day. But it was easy to push back the need to bite him now when we were both on the same page about it. We understood.

Mated or not, we were really, truly *one*.

And when we left the cabin again, we found Jacob sitting at the edge of the rock, looking ahead at the dark woods.

"That was *painful*," he whispered as soon as we closed the door.

Ah, shit. I hadn't been as quiet as I thought.

I bit my tongue to keep from laughing, then cleared my throat. "Right, so. We talked, and, um…we're gonna take you to the Realm, no problem."

Jacob jumped to his feet, looked properly shocked like he really hadn't expected that.

"You are?"

"Yep. We'll take you." I stepped to the side. "All I need is for you two to shake hands on it."

It was Ax's turn to look shocked. So shocked he couldn't even think of anything to say.

"C'mon, big guy," I said, nudging his arm.

Jacob already had his hand outstretched. He must *really* want this if he was willing to make peace with *Ax* about it.

Ax raised a brow at me in question. *Are you serious?* it said.

I absolutely was. It was the perfect opportunity to see him squirm—how could I resist?

"Do it, Savage. Shake his hand like the *good boy* that you are." I winked at him.

He grinned widely, shoulders shaking with laughter. "You're the fucking devil."

And he shook Jacob's hand.

CHAPTER
FIFTEEN

FOR A SECOND THERE, I CONSIDERED I MIGHT NOT HATE CARS anymore, especially since this one was *really* nice to look at, and it belonged to Ax. But nope—the leather of the seats, the million blue lights on the dashboard, and even Ax's hand on my thigh didn't make me feel any safer. Just that, every time I was in cars, something bad seemed to happen.

"If you keep this up, he'll lose us," I warned. Jacob was supposed to be behind us in his truck, but I hadn't seen him in at least fifteen minutes. Ax was probably doing it on purpose.

"We're on a highway. There's literally nowhere else he can go." He dug his fingers in my skin, and when I didn't turn, he said, "Hey—look at me."

"I just don't like cars," I said before he could tell me to calm down.

"No, you're just nervous to go back home," he said. Fuck, he was absolutely right. "Why?"

My instinct was to lie about it, just like always. But the past week had changed everything for me. It had literally changed my life. So much so that I felt like a brand-new person. And it had everything to do with *him*, the asshole.

Even though I'd always say I *hated* it, I was so glad to not have to carry everything on my own shoulders. So fucking glad to be able to share everything knowing he wouldn't judge me, that he'd understand and be on my side no matter what.

"It's Jones," I said, grabbed his hand with both mine. I just needed to hold onto him for a bit.

"He didn't send those vampires after you."

I turned to look at him, confused. "How would you know?"

"Because I asked. That night when he came to give me the address, I asked him. He said he didn't send anyone after you." And he meant every word.

My mouth opened and closed a few times before I was even able to say anything. "Then *who*?" Because if not Jones...who else would want my head, and why?

"I don't think it's Robert, either, but the other covens are all fair game. Any one of them could have hired those vampires," Ax said, and he didn't sound too happy about it. "I'll find out as soon as we get back. I would have known by now, but I didn't really have time to, erm...*interrogate* anyone before leaving."

And by *interrogate* he probably meant *torture*.

I shook my head. "There's no need to interrogate anyone. We'll figure it out eventually."

"Of course we will," he said, squeezing my fingers. Just that small gesture and it somehow made breathing a bit easier. I loved that he knew how to speak to me so well.

"I just...don't get *why*." And it bugged me. What the hell had I done to *anyone* in the Realm when I hadn't even been there for almost three months?

"Does it matter?" Ax said, pulling my arm. "Stop thinking about it. We'll be fine."

"We won't if you don't stop driving like a fucking maniac, Savage," I teased. I had no trouble with how fast he went whatsoever, but it did make me worry that Jacob wouldn't be able to keep up.

And Ax laughed. "You think *this* is bad?"

"Um…yep." Anybody would. He was going over a hundred and fifty. It was a highway, sure, but still.

But Ax suddenly moved.

One second I was sitting comfortably on the passenger seat, seatbelt on, and the next, he had his arm around my waist and was pulling me on his lap.

"What the hell are you doing?!" I said, so shocked I could do nothing but watch as he pulled my legs over his and made me comfortable on his fucking lap—*while* he drove the car.

"I'm gonna show you what *bad* really looks like. I'm gonna show you just how incredible *bad* feels." He grabbed my hands and put them on the steering wheel lightning fast. "You think you can keep us alive for a little while, Damsel?"

"Ax, I—" His hands were already under my clothes, one squeezing my breast, the other playing with my clit.

He was fucking *impossible*.

"Eyes open," he warned when I cried out, gripping the steering wheel tightly. Everything about him was so damn intense. So *fast*. So surprising, even though he kept on surprising me over and over again. He could still be unpredictable.

But the one thing I could always predict with perfect accuracy was how good he'd play my body. How incredible he'd feel. And he had yet to disappoint in that area.

He played with my nipple between his fingers, teased my entrance with his fingertips, while raising up his hips, pressing his cock against my ass. Fuck, he was so hard for me, and I couldn't even focus on that because I had to see the road ahead. There were cars driving by our sides, too, and Ax's foot was still on the gas.

"Slow down," I breathed, my hips moving on their own already, trying to take his fingers inside me.

"You got it, baby," he whispered and pressed on the gas harder, taking us forward faster.

Cursing under my breath, I forced my eyes to stay open and on the road as he growled and bit my shoulder, pressed his cock against my ass while he tortured my tits and played with my clit.

Damn him and the way I loved how he played with me.

"Ax, please," I begged, even though I wanted nothing more than to tell him to just hit the brakes, stop the car, fuck me properly.

But I needed the release more.

"Keep your eyes on the road, Damsel," he said, sliding his fingertips down my soaking wet folds slowly. My hips moved, my body desperate to feel him inside me. "Fuck, the way you move," he whispered against my neck. "Keep moving those hips, baby." I did so eagerly, and the more I moved, the deeper inside me his fingers went.

"We're gonna crash," I said breathlessly as he pumped his fingers in and out of me and pressed his hard cock against my ass harder each time. I couldn't even see what the fuck was ahead of me, just some lights.

"If we do, it'll be worth it," the psycho said and kept thrusting his fingers deeper inside me, faster. And he finally took his hand from under my shirt, then pushed me forward until my chest almost pressed to the steering wheel. I cried out, so fucking ready to explode I could hardly breathe.

But he pulled my skirt up around my waist and kept fucking me with his fingers, pushing me up and down with his hips.

"Look at your ass, baby. Fuck," he muttered, completely in awe. "That's a good girl. Keep fucking my hand."

"Ax!" I cried out, desperate to come, but terrified to let go because I was holding the fucking steering wheel in my hands!

"Come for me, baby. Imagine it's my cock inside you. Squeeze around it tightly," he whispered, pushing his fingers as deep as they would go, and pressing the heel of his hand to my clit. The next time he pushed me up with his hips, I had no hopes of holding on.

"Fuck yes, Damsel," he whispered, keeping his fingers inside me while the orgasm clenched every muscle in my body, setting me on fire. I didn't see anything for a long second, just bright stars in my vision, and somebody up there must have been watching over us because we somehow didn't crash.

And when I was finally able to control my body, I leaned back on his chest, and he took his fingers out of me.

"You're fucking sick," I said, barely breathing, smiling so wide my cheeks hurt.

And he had one hand on the steering wheel now, while he licked my juices clean off the other. I watched him, fucking mesmerized at the sight of his lips. His eyes were on the windshield because I couldn't bring myself to even *try* to focus right now. My body felt like jelly in the best possible way, and the way he licked his fingers and looked so fucking *happy*...I wanted to lick them, too. See what the fuss was all about.

So, I took his hand, brought his fingers to my mouth, and ran my tongue over them. Barely any taste was left on them other than his, and when I sucked, he moaned the most delicious sound I'd ever heard.

"That's it, baby," he told me, thrusting his fingers deep until he touched my throat. "Suck them hard."

And just like that, I was getting turned on again.

Damn it, he was impossible.

And I was even worse because I kept making out with his fingers, and the asshole kept on pressing down the gas harder, and all I could think about was his cock in my mouth, his cum all over me, warm and delicious and—

Before I knew it, I moved and sat back on the passenger seat. My hands tugged at his jeans, shaking badly, and I just couldn't get the damn zipper to move down fast enough.

"Damsel, stop," he said and dared to put a hand over mine, too.

I growled like a fucking animal. "Don't you fucking dare. Eyes on the road," I said, and he immediately moved his hand to the steering wheel.

"Baby, I'm fucking driving," he said, but I could hear the grin in his voice.

"And I'm giving you a blow job. Your point?" Finally, I pushed his jeans to the sides, and his boxers, then leaned down to his smooth pink tip that my tongue adored. I took him until he pressed against my throat and kept him there until I gagged.

He pushed up his hips hard, trying to fucking suffocate me for real, and I loved it. He grabbed my hair and kept me there while he thrust himself inside me fast, but I wouldn't have it. I wanted to torture him the way he did me. See how much he liked it when he had to keep the steering wheel in his hands while I had my way with him.

Yeah, probably just as much as I did.

"Fuck, Damsel," he whispered when I pushed his hips down so he wouldn't move. I loved that every time I took him in faster, he moaned a bit louder. "That's it, baby. Take it all the way. I want to hear you gag."

And I let him hear me, but when he lost control and pumped into my mouth faster, I slowed my pace again and pushed him down. He growled and hissed and grunted in protest, but I didn't give in. I took my time with him, licked and grazed him and sucked until my jaw was numb. I was so wet, but there was just no space for me to spread my legs and touch myself, too, the way I wanted.

"We're about to get off the highway," Ax warned, and I knew it was time to let him let go. It wasn't that I was worried about *us*—we'd be hurt if we crashed, but nothing we couldn't heal from within the hour. But if we hit someone else, that would be a big problem. I couldn't let that happen.

So, I took him in again until I gagged, and this time when he moved his hips up, I didn't stop him. Didn't move back. He came five seconds later, his cum filling up my mouth, salty and creamy as it slipped down my throat and dripped out of my mouth, too. The taste of him was intoxicating. I couldn't get enough.

But he grabbed me by the hair and pulled me up, biting my lip hard while he kept his eyes on the road ahead.

"That should be fucking illegal, Damsel," he growled.

"I'm pretty sure it is." I stuck my tongue in his mouth, touching the tips of his growing fangs in the process. We'd been through this a dozen times by now—we both got the urge to mate every time we especially loved what we were doing to one another, and we could hold ourselves back from it just fine, too.

"Let's fucking do it again."

I laughed. "Don't tempt me, Savage. I'm so wet still."

That's all he needed to hear to push me back on the passenger seat, then stick his hand under my skirt. But I caught it by the wrist and pushed it back because he was already taking the exit.

"All you can do is watch me," I whispered, putting my boots on the fancy dashboard. "This okay?" I asked because I knew guys liked their cars.

He looked at me for a second like I'd spoken a foreign language. "Of course, it is. Don't ever ask me that again. You can do whatever you want with what is yours."

"Except it's not my car."

"Everything I am, everything I own is yours. Don't ever forget that, Damsel. Now spread those legs," he whispered, looking at my naked thighs.

"Yes, sir."

I pulled my legs to the sides, made myself comfortable. Then I slipped my hand under my skirt and let him watch me finger-fucking myself as I screamed out his name.

CHAPTER
SIXTEEN

Ax Creed

Daylight was slowly becoming the best part of my day. Go figure. Just something about the way she lay in my arms, completely surrendered, asleep, and I could hold her, I could kiss every little inch of her, take my time to explore her, just lay down with her and soak up her scent, her warmth. Listen to her heartbeat.

I'd heard about this a million times before, and I'd always thought it was pathetic. Who would even want to mate, to lose sight of their own self, to fucking live for another being and be so infatuated with them every second of every day?

Now, I'd become the people I used to make fun of. And I couldn't have cared less.

The sun had another hour to set, but Jacob Thorne had been up for hours now. I could hear his heartbeat. I heard him when he left the motel, then came back, ate, showered, all of it. Not that I didn't want to sleep with Damsel—I did. And I would be able to, I had no doubt about that. But we were still not safe out here. I would not risk being caught asleep.

We were already in Newcastle, on our way home. As much as I hated to have to bring Jacob Thorne—of all people—with us, I was also excited about it. Because Damsel would be in my house. In my room. In my bed.

And in there, I would sleep with her, too.

Pulling my arms from around her was painful. The moment when she first opened her eyes at nightfall was something I looked forward to the whole day, but there was still time. Thorne's heart beat in my head, and I just wanted to get out there, see him, talk to him alone so I knew exactly what he was expecting out of this. Damsel trusted him, and I understood. But I didn't. At least not yet.

So, I put on my clothes and kissed her soft, warm lips for a little bit. I'd be back in time when she opened her eyes.

Walking out of the room, I stretched my limbs and focused on his heartbeat, until I heard it beating from outside. He was in the parking lot, sitting alone on the trunk, a notebook in his hands as he drew and wrote symbols I didn't understand. I moved fast, wanting to mess with him for a bit. I was in a good mood—a *great* fucking mood lately—so why the hell not? So, I ran and I jumped and I landed on the trunk right next to him before he even realized I was there.

"Whatcha doing?"

He didn't scream, but only because his vocal cords must have been cut off by the shock. He moved back, slamming against the trunk, pencil and notebook slipping from his hands.

"What the hell," he muttered to himself, breathing heavily, looking up at the blue sky as if he was making sure that it was still daylight.

It was. The sun shone west, the warmth of it like needles against my skin. Nothing I couldn't handle. In fact, with the right mindset, I could actually *enjoy* it, too. Except I didn't really want to enjoy anything other than Damsel anymore, so I didn't bother.

"Didn't mean to scare ya, Thorne," I said with a grin, and he knew damn well that was bullshit.

"You didn't. I was just...surprised." And *I* knew damn well that was bullshit, too. "Is Nikki up?"

"No, she's sleeping." I could hear her perfectly from down there. I was very in tune with the sound of her lately. I was pretty sure I could hear her from over two miles away, which was fucking amazing. I could smell her scent perfectly, could tell exactly what she was feeling through it, too. And I knew exactly when she needed blood, food, *anything* at all just by reading the look in her eyes.

I was *really* starting to understand what everybody meant when they talked about mating with so much fucking wonder.

"Why aren't you? I'm not gonna kill you while you sleep," Jacob Thorne said, and I laughed. He was a funny guy.

"You couldn't if you tried, sorcerer. But I don't sleep."

He adjusted his cowboy hat on his head as he squinted his eyes at me. "What do you mean?"

"I mean I don't sleep *ever*. I've only ever slept a handful of times since I was turned." One of them had been beside Damsel. And I couldn't wait to sleep with her again when we got home.

I couldn't wait for my house to be hers. For her scent to hang on the walls. For my sheets to smell like her. For her things to be all over our bedroom.

Fuck—I could hardly recognize myself. How in the world had this happened to me—and *when* had I started to want those things so badly? Because I couldn't fucking remember.

"So how do you recharge?" Thorne asked, more curious than I thought he would be.

"I lie down. I stay in one place during sunlight, mostly. I just don't lose consciousness."

He shook his head. "You can stand in the sun just fine. The sunlight is falling on your face….can you see me?"

I raised my brows. "Yes, Thorne. I can fucking see you." I was looking right at him.

"I had no idea vampires could do that," he muttered, and he suddenly looked very concerned. "Nikki could never stay awake in daylight. Not willingly."

"Why the fuck did you let that man put her in that magic trap?" I asked because I couldn't help myself. The moment he reminded me of the fact that *he knew* what Damsel was like, how she lived, when she slept, a new kind of a monster crawled its way up to the center of my mind.

Jacob flinched, and I heard his heartbeat perfectly as it accelerated. "I couldn't stop him if I tried," he said. His voice was strained, too, and he refused to look at me. I heard the truth in his words, though. I heard how much *he* hated it, too.

And the monster inside me only roared louder. He cared about Damsel. He cared about her much more than he let on, and I'd be damned if I didn't want to fucking rip his heart out with my own hands because of it.

"I want to ask if you've ever put a hand on her, Thorne... but I'm fucking terrified of the answer." Because if he lied, I'd know. And if he told me the truth...how would I fucking stop myself?

Jacob looked up at me, confused for a moment. But when he realized what I meant, he...

Smiled. "She'd have broken my arm herself if I ever did."

I held my breath, waiting for a hint that he was lying. That he was playing with me. Teasing. Anything other than the truth.

But that's what it was—the truth. He *hadn't* tried, but he also knew for a fact that she'd have stopped him if he did.

And I'd fucking *doubted* her. For a little while there, when she refused to take off that stupid necklace, I'd thought *maybe* she'd done something that was going to fucking bury me alive.

"I owe you my life, Thorne. I'll protect you with mine. You can ask anything of me, and if I'm capable of it, consider it done," I told him, and though the words cost me, they were also *my* truth, and he needed to hear them.

"I'll be damned," he said with a flinch. "I don't need you to protect me, Axel. I don't need anything from you. I haven't forgotten who you are."

"Good—and you never should. But if there's any other reason why you found us, why you're making us take you to the Realm..." I leaned a bit closer until I could see the brown of his eyes clearer. "If what you're trying to do here hurts her in any way, I *will* kill you."

He wasn't afraid, but he believed me. He stayed silent for a little while as he watched me, like he couldn't quite make up his mind about what to think of me yet.

"You know, if you care about her so much—" he started, but I had to cut him off.

"I don't simply *care* about her. I live for her."

That surprised him even more. He opened his mouth but found nothing to say for a good long minute, which was beyond me. I'd never hidden what I felt—I never would. I thought he had that clear since he met me.

"You've done...unspeakable things," he finally whispered, shaking his head. "Sooner or later, somebody will come for you. They will make you pay."

That made me laugh again. "I've done things that would make you shiver if you heard of them, even when I didn't really have a good reason to be alive. Imagine what else I could do now..." I let that sink in for a second.

When it did, Thorne flinched again. "I know you think—"

"You *don't* know what I think." And the sooner he accepted that, the better off he'd be.

But he must have thought I was joking because... "I've met men like you before, Ax."

I'd be damned if I ever heard anything funnier in my life. "Except I am no man, Thorne," I whispered—I'll admit, just to spook him a bit. Couldn't fucking help it. "I'm not even a monster. I'm something much more twisted than that." I leaned closer to him again, and the way his heart skipped a beat was fucking hilarious, too. "Believe me when I tell you—don't you worry your little mind about me. Not even a little bit."

He knew I meant it. That's why he was so fucking disgusted that he leaned back for a bit.

It suited me perfectly.

"Tell me why you're really trying to get to the Realm."

Marie was a good reason and all, but did I really believe that it was *the only* reason?

"Because it doesn't sit well with me. It can't be a coincidence," he finally said.

And unfortunately, I agreed.

"Marie and her brother have been living in my house since I took them to the Realm," I told him. "And something did strike me as odd." It had since the beginning.

"What's that?" Jacob asked, squinting his eyes at me as if he wasn't sure whether I was being serious.

I was. "They became way too comfortable, way too soon," I said in wonder. "How many sorcerers do you know who would be perfectly fine with coming to the Hidden Realm and perfectly fine with living in a city full of vampires?"

Jacob didn't need to think about it. "None."

"It's strange, isn't it?" I assumed that *I* was the reason why Marie and her brother were so comfortable in my home, but then...I wasn't there for a whole month. And when I went back, they'd looked...okay. Perfectly relaxed. Not the least bit relieved that I'd made it back, which they should have been if they were truly relying on me to protect them.

And now that Jacob came to us with that story...

"But why?" he whispered after a few minutes. "Why? It makes no sense."

It made no sense to me, either, but the sun was about to set, and I wanted to be in bed with Damsel. I had just enough time to read her note and be there when she woke up. So, I jumped to the ground again.

"Guess we'll figure it out when we get there."

"Ax," Jacob called when I made my way toward the motel again. I turned. "Don't let her try to take that spirit out of her." My stomach twisted instantly. "She won't survive it."

I had nothing to say. The truth was that I would try to stop Damsel no matter how long it took. I would, but if that was what she truly wanted, I'd stand by her. I'd be against it, would never risk her life, not for any reason, but I wanted her to have everything she needed, too. If her freedom was worth it, then we'd try. Jacob Thorne didn't know her at all. That's why he had no clue what the fuck he was talking about.

Because my Damsel could survive anything.

She slept so peacefully, hadn't moved an inch since I was there. So, I took my jacket and my jeans off, and got in the bed with her. There were a few more minutes left till nightfall, but I still held her tight to my chest as I read the note she'd written for me on that book. I don't know what it was about it that filled me up. I swear, it was like magic. It felt like I was taking a glimpse at the inside of her head for a second, and I could never get enough of it.

When the sun retreated completely, I put the piece of paper under the pillow and waited for her to open her eyes. My favorite fucking moment in the day.

She opened her eyes and I felt *seen*. I felt alive. Every breath I took filled me differently.

"Evening, baby," I whispered, claiming her lips. And she pushed herself closer to me, her naked body pressing against mine, melting onto me.

And then she shivered so hard, every inch of her skin was covered in goose bumps within a second.

Pulling back, I looked at her face. "What?"

"Nothing," she mumbled and tried to hide her face under my chin.

I didn't let her. "What were you thinking just now?" Because she was thinking *something* that made her shiver.

"Nothing," she insisted, wrapping her arm around my waist. "Just let me—"

"Damsel," I warned. "Tell me, baby. What is it?" Was she afraid? Was she worried again?

Because she really, *really* didn't need to be.

But she sighed.

"Fuck you, you prick," she suddenly spit, and...I knew.

I knew exactly why she had shivered like that. I was smiling even before she told me. "I was thinking that I fucking *missed* you while I was asleep. How pathetic is that?" She snapped. "It's all your damn fault."

Laughing, I pulled her to lie on my chest. "Pathetic," I muttered, kissing her soft cheek. "Really, really pathetic." Especially since she figured it out *tonight* and I had known it since I fucking met her.

"Hmm," she said, eyes closed as she moved her head to wherever she needed me to kiss her. It was incredible how much she loved my touch. "You're already sorry for me."

"I'm always sorry for you, baby." I pushed up my hips so she felt all of my hard cock against her thigh. It was enough to see her eyes, to hear her voice, to kiss her, and my whole being just focused on her.

"Is Jacob gone yet?" she asked, moving her hands down my sides, pulling herself up for a bit so she could grab my cock. Fuck, it was incredible how much *I* loved her touch, too.

"No," I said, biting her jaw as she positioned her knees on either side of me. I ran my hand down her ass, then slipped a finger in her folds, to find her just as wet as ever.

"Is Will Thorne on us yet?" she asked, bringing the tip of my cock to her clit as she moved slowly.

I moaned into her mouth. "Damsel," I warned. She knew I needed her right away when she woke up. The rest of the night, we could play. We could make each other wait as long as we wanted. But I'd gone the whole fucking day without being inside her. I needed it right away.

And she grinned, knowing that the answer to her question was *no*. If it were yes, I'd have said so.

"Don't tell me you missed me, too," she teased, bringing my cock to her entrance. I dug my fingers in her hips and pulled her down.

Fuck.

I kept her there, held her to me for a second, and just breathed. I didn't think there'd ever come a time when doing this with her would feel *normal*. Less than completely mind-fucking-blowing.

"I need you to ride me the way only you know how, Damsel," I told her, eyes closed, hands all over her, just like we both liked. "Don't hold back, baby. Take everything you need from me."

She licked my earlobe and grazed my neck with her teeth before she sat up on me. The sight of her drove me fucking nuts. Her face, her hair all over the place, just as wild as the look in her eyes, her beautiful tits bouncing a bit as she moved, her tiny waist and those fucking hips that were made for my hands...

"I need *all* of it," she whispered, throwing her head back. Her hands moved up her stomach and to her tits, and she squeezed them as she rode me. I got fucking jealous of her hands. It should be my mouth around her nipples instead. "Fuck, Ax. Don't let go!"

"I won't, baby. As long as you need." Holding her hips, I felt the way she moved them, slowly, so fucking seductively, that if my control slipped for just a second, I'd come right away.

But she needed more. She needed all of it. And her wish was my fucking command. So, I held on and didn't let go until she let me.

I'd be damned if I wasn't the luckiest man in the universe.

CHAPTER SEVENTEEN

NIKKI ARELLA

How was it possible that my life kept getting stranger by the week? I was on my way to the Hidden Realm with Ax *and* Jacob Thorne. Together. As in, we ate together, we planned together. We rode together, too, though in different cars. It just seemed so absurd because Ax and Jacob were *not* trying to kill each other, and I still expected them to attack any second.

"You know what I wanna know?" I asked when I finished the delicious burger we got at an overcrowded shithole that barely fit ten people inside. But Jacob said he'd had their food before and it was delicious, so we stopped to eat and stretch our legs for a little bit. We'd been on the road for two hours already.

"What's that?" Ax asked as the three of us walked down the sidewalk to where we parked the cars. Like I said —*absurd.*

"Where Will Thorne is." I looked at Jacob just in time to see him flinch. "Where did *you* tell him you were going?"

Because we were in Spearfish, surrounded by humans, and though a part of me was permanently focused on their heartbeats and the blood rushing through their veins, a bigger part was constantly expecting something to happen—for Ax and Jacob to start fighting or for Will Thorne to pop up in front of me and start throwing his nasty magic my way.

"I don't know where he is. After he almost killed me that day, he left, probably to go search for you," Jacob said. "I didn't hear from him again."

"It was bad, huh," I mumbled, looking at his face, at his body, with new interest. No wounds on him. No blood. No bruises that I could see. He'd probably done spells on himself to heal, or maybe Will hadn't been as hard on him as he'd been on me.

But Jacob shrugged. "I survived."

"He didn't try to make you tell him where I was? Or do a tracking spell on me or something?" Because that would have been expected of him.

"He did. And we tried. But after he put all that magic in me, he expected me to be weak, so when I used my magic to alter his spell to reveal several locations at once, he just assumed that it was your spirit. That it was interfering with the spell, and it wouldn't let him see where you were," Jacob said, and he sounded a hundred percent sure of his words.

And though I believed him, it just didn't sit well with me. I didn't know Will Thorne by any means, but he'd seemed dead set on killing me and closing that Vein. I doubted he was going to just let it go.

"What happens if he tries to track her again *without* you

there to alter the spell?" Ax asked, and my stomach turned in knots.

"I doubt it will be useful. He'd have to be close to track anything accurately without blood, and he has no reason to suspect you're here—or that we're on our way to the Hidden Realm," Jacob said. To his credit, he didn't sound worried, but I still wasn't convinced.

"And how much blood of hers did you save exactly?" Ax asked, squinting his eyes at Jacob.

"Just a drop when it fell on the sand while you were training."

I raised my brows at him. "C'mon. How much did you *really* save?" Had he actually taken my blood in daylight while I was sleeping?

But, no, I'd have felt it.

"I swear, that's it," Jacob insisted, and he wasn't lying. "All I had was that tiny bit. I don't have more."

Yeah, he was definitely telling the truth. Even Ax believed him. That's why he looked ahead, pointing at a large building in the distance the next second. "Look at that."

"What's that?"

"Mall," he said, grinning. "You did say you needed stuff."

"We don't have time to stop by the mall," Jacob said, and he was right. The cars were right across the street from us, and if we hoped to make it to the Realm by dawn, we had to go *right now*.

But Ax didn't even look at him. "I'll have us back in fifteen minutes. How about that? We're gonna need...*stuff*." Stuff—as in sexy lingerie that he could put on me then tear off again. "We'll be locked inside for a while when we get home, so we might as well take advantage of this."

Just like that, I was sold. There was only one lingerie shop in the Realm, and it didn't have half as many things as the shops here.

"Let's d—"

"Nikki, we don't have time," Jacob complained, but Ax was already turning his back to me.

"I'll have us back in fifteen minutes," he repeated, then looked at me. "Hop on, Damsel."

"You're joking." I was grinning ear-to-ear. "You're gonna *carry* me?" Was he serious?

"Just to make sure we make it back on time," he said with a wink.

No need to convince me more. I hopped on his back, locked my arms and legs around him tightly, and...

"Hey, wait!" Jacob called, but Ax took us forward, too fast for the human eye to see.

He carried me on his back all the way to the mall and inside.

THE WIND on my face felt mighty fine. Who knew riding on someone's back would be so much fun? I couldn't stop laughing when we finally stopped in front of Jacob's truck. He was sitting in the driver's seat, feet up on the dashboard, heartbeat accelerated.

Yeah, he was still pissed.

"Fourteen minutes," Ax said proudly, opening his car door and throwing the four paper bags inside. So many things—and there'd been no time to try anything on, so we'd just gotten every pair *he'd* liked and every pair *I'd* like, too. I'd never paid more in a shop before, especially not for underwear, but fuck, I couldn't wait to try them all on. And

I would need to figure out a way to make sure Ax wouldn't tear them off me, too. Way too pretty to end up in pieces.

"Wasted time," Jacob said, getting out of his truck, looking at me like he was *disappointed*.

"C'mon, it was just a quick stop." Fourteen minutes weren't gonna make a huge difference.

To us, though, they would. Because once we made it to the Realm, Ax said he'd lock me up in his bedroom and I could forget about going outside for at least a few days. I had no complaints whatsoever, and it wouldn't hurt to be a bit *prepared* for it, too.

"I'm gonna go get us blood," Ax said, closing the door again, before he threw the keys to me. "Be right back." He kissed my cheek and disappeared so fast I only felt his lips on my skin.

I felt Jacob's eyes on me, too.

I put my hands on my hips. "What?" It was just fourteen minutes, for fuck's sake.

"Nothing," he mumbled, shaking his head.

"We'll be there in no time, Jacob. Just…relax." We said we'd take him to the Realm, and we would.

"It's not that," he said.

"Really?" Because he'd looked pretty pissed. "So, what is it?"

He shrugged. "You look happy," he said, scratching his chin. "I've never heard you laughing before."

I flinched. *Ugh*. Out of all the things that had ever made me cringe, that definitely took the cake.

"It's Ax's fault," I spit. "He just gets in my head." And while he was there, it felt perfectly natural to want to *laugh* and be stupid.

Jacob laughed. "You realize that's not a *bad* thing, right?"

"It's—" *much worse than bad,* I was going to say, but a sound reached my ears, and both our hearts skipped a long beat as we turned to look around us.

A wolf's gut-wrenching howl in the middle of a damn city.

"Is that—"

"Ethan," Jacob said, reaching under his jacket. "That's a warning, Nikki."

"Ethan's *here*?" Was he kidding?

"I had him stay close so he could warn us in time in case he heard or smelled something," Jacob said, moving farther away from his truck, deeper down the sidewalk, searching every face around us, same as me.

And... "Ax," I whispered, when I remembered that Ax wasn't with me.

I took off running to the other side of the street where he'd disappeared, everything else forgotten. Jacob called my name, but I didn't answer. And the moment I turned the street corner, I saw Ax with a bottle full of blood in his hand as he looked at the people around him.

I stopped running, so fucking relieved I could cry.

"Did you hear it?" I asked, though it was pretty clear he'd heard the howl, too.

But when Ax looked at me, he didn't look relieved.

"Damsel, *move!*" he shouted, fangs extending down his upper lip lightning fast before he jumped.

I jumped, too, but it was too late. The bullet buried straight in my chest from gods knew how far away. It pierced my heart and threw me against the asphalt before I could even realize what the hell was happening. I could hear a bullet coming. I could hear a gunshot...but that had been no gun. Whoever pulled the trigger, they were too far away from me to have heard it. And the whoosh of the bullet had been lost to my own distraction and the many hearts beating in my fucking ears around me.

People screamed. The spicy scent of magic filled my nostrils so fast, I knew it was coming even before it slipped under my skin, pushing me down under even more. My heart still beat—it would take more than a bullet to stop it completely, but it would also need time to heal. That magic was already poisoning my blood and my mind wasn't going to let it.

Just a minute—that's all I'd need. The screams in my head would keep me distracted. The magic in me would fade, and then I'd be able to stand up, to see better, to run. And I did manage to make it on all fours. The magic was fading, and my arms kept shaking, my heart pumping slower than usual…

Something hit me in the back of my head so hard, it slammed me on the sidewalk again. My skull cracked. Asphalt broke.

"There you are, bloodsucker," Ray's voice reached my ears. I pushed myself up again, already knowing what was happening, and the spirit in me went mad.

If Ray was here, so were the others.

And if the others were here, so was Will.

But before I could move away from his grip, Ray grabbed me by the arms, pulled me back, and he'd had his leg up, too. I slammed onto his foot with my back. Bones cracked again. I called the spirit forward with all my strength.

The transformation began immediately, shifting my bones, my skin, my mind…until something sharp and ice cold went right between my shoulder blades.

My legs gave up and I hit the ground on my knees. Black dots in front of my vision, and I was losing my mind, even though the spirit kept on shifting my body. I wanted to think that it would stay awake, that it would win against whoever was stabbing me, shooting me, breaking my bones.

I wanted to think it would *win* against all odds, but the truth was, I didn't know. And I had no choice but to let go when my mind shut down.

When I woke up again, I was no longer in South Dakota.

CHAPTER
EIGHTEEN

Everything hurt. It hadn't been that long since I'd been used to waking up to my entire body throbbing with pain, but when I came to, even my heart felt like it was *hurting* every time it beat. A bullet had gone through it—it wasn't there anymore. A knife had grazed it, too—not to mention the magic I'd been hit with.

But my heart had healed. The taste of *metal* coated my tongue, though, and I had no idea where it came from. My body had healed—it was my mind that was screaming still. The monster demanding control even before I saw what was around me...

Ax, wrapped up in a glossy magic shield not twenty feet away from where I was lying.

A loud growl escaped me, and I jumped to my feet, ready to run and shift and claw that fucking magic to pieces. It didn't occur to me to try and see what the hell was around me—*who* was around me. All I cared about was that Ax was sitting in there, eyes bloodshot, fangs in full display as he watched me...and I was free.

I wasn't locked under magic. I didn't even have a

fucking rope around my hands, so that when I jumped, I landed on the grass, almost at the magic shield.

"That's far enough."

Every hair on my body stood at attention. Will Thorne was standing right to the side of the magic shield, hiding behind Fallon, Ray and Dylan, his arms outstretched toward Ax.

And behind me was Jacob, too, with a thick chain wrapped around his wrists and around a tree trunk by his side.

Because we were in a woods somewhere.

No—not *somewhere*.

We were in Arizona...and the den of spirits was just down the slope between the mountains.

For fuck's sake, how long had they driven to get us here? How long had I been unconscious?

"Your choices are simple," Will Thorne continued. "Get in there, seal that Vein, and he walks away. Refuse, and I will be cutting him to pieces until you do as I say."

I took a step forward, a smile curling my lips. Because the fucker had no idea what the hell he was talking about.

"Look close, Nicole," Thorne said. "Look really close because I've come prepared."

"You—" Before the next word left my lips, Ax moved, raising his hand toward his neck.

Toward the metal band wrapped around it, and the small red dot that blinked in and out of existence to the side.

My limbs locked instantly.

"That's right. He's got a bomb around his neck. Military issued. Fancy stuff," Will said, and by the sound of his voice, he was damn proud of it. "If he tries to take it off, it will activate within two seconds. If you don't do as I say or try to come at me, I can activate it within *one* second. Do you understand me, Nicole?"

I looked at Ax, looked at Thorne's hands and the small square remote in his hand, the way his thumb had turned white by how hard he was pressing on the round button. My body let go slowly and I hit the grass on my knees, shaking my head at myself. At Ax.

This wasn't happening. It was fucking stupid—this *wasn't* happening. We were on the road, almost to North Dakota. And we were gonna make it to the hidden Realm, home, where we were safe from sorcerers and snipers and fucking bombs. There's no way this was even real. It couldn't be.

"Damsel, do not go in there," Ax said, his voice rough, full of sharp edges.

"No," I said. Just *no*. This wasn't happening, damn it!

We were gonna make it home. We were gonna be safe. We were gonna be together!

"Look at me, baby. It's fine. Don't go in there, no matter what," Ax told me. "Just run, okay? *Run.*"

I would have laughed any other day.

As it was, I looked at Will Thorne, at his wicked smile, those ice-cold ice. What the fuck had I done to him? Why couldn't he just leave me alone?

"You think *I'm* a monster?" I asked him despite my better judgment. "Look in the fucking mirror, you goddamn prick."

But he didn't give a shit. And Ax was moving, coming closer to the magic. "Damsel, look at me." But I couldn't look away from Will. How was I going to stop him? How was I going to get him to leave me alone? Leave Ax alone?

"For fuck's sake, look at me!" And Ax slammed the backs of his fists on the shield hard.

I screamed just as the magic threw him back and slammed him against the ground. I knew exactly what that felt like. Even my spirit hadn't been able to break through Will's magic without Jacob's help. Ax had no chance, and I knew exactly how much it would hurt him if he kept trying.

"Stop it," I hissed when he raised his head, a bit of blood slipping from his nostrils.

"The sun will be up in about twenty minutes," Will warned.

"Let him go first," I said. "Let him go, right now, and I'll do whatever you want." And I meant it.

"No," Ax growled, but I didn't even look at him.

"Do it. Let him go. Take that thing off him, and I'll go. I'll do whatever you want." I'd go back into the den of spirits. Fuck it, so long as Ax was okay, I didn't care.

It didn't even matter that I could hear the haunting cries of the spirits. It didn't matter that my own spirit was going to make me fucking collapse soon—if he let Ax go, I would go in there.

"She can't do it on her own!" Jacob called from where he was chained to the fucking tree trunk. "She can't break it! She's already been in there—it will suck her—"

"Don't you worry your empty little head about it, boy," Will spit. "You're a fucking disgrace. A stain on the family name! Don't you dare tell me what to do."

"She *can't* do it alone!" Jacob shouted anyway, but Will wasn't even looking at him anymore. His eyes were on me.

"You're gonna grab that bag over there. You're gonna light up all that dynamite inside that cave. Once it goes off, I'll do the rest," he told me, pointing at a green army bag resting against the tree at his side.

"Damsel, don't fucking touch it," Ax said and again he

slammed his fists on the shield. Again, the magic threw him back.

"Stop it!" I said, and my voice shook. He didn't need to go through all that pain. He didn't need to *try*—it was over. He couldn't get out of that magic. He couldn't fucking get that bomb off his neck fast enough, either.

It was *done*. We were here now.

"Damsel," he warned, his arms shaking as he pulled himself up.

"I'm sorry," I told him, feeling like the entire world was on my shoulders. "I'm sorry I didn't listen to you. You were right. You were always right." Since day one, he'd been right.

I wished I'd hopped on a plane with him to go to Paris or Rome or anywhere in the world. Maybe I'd have had a few more days. Will Thorne would have still found me, but maybe, if I'd listened to Ax, I'd have had him for just a little while longer.

"Keep moving," Will said.

"Damsel, stop," said Ax.

"It won't work!" Jacob shouted.

"Grab the bag. Go in. Light up the dynamite," Will ordered.

My gods, it felt like there wasn't enough air left in the world to breathe properly, but I somehow managed to ignore Ax's pleadings and stand up. I somehow managed to step to the side, closer to Fallon and Ray and Dylan, whose faces I couldn't even make out properly. Not when my whole attention was on Will hiding behind them, that remote in his hand, thumb still pressed to the button.

What would happen if he accidentally let go?

He would fucking blow Ax's head up.

Every monster inside me roared in unison.

"Let him go first," I said, and my voice came out robotic, almost as if I had shifted into the spirit.

"No. I will let him go only when you get in there. Only when the Vein is closed," Will said, nodding at his laptop on the ground next to his feet, the screen showing a map of colors. It was the same map he'd showed me on his phone the day he ambushed me and locked me up in Minnesota. "I'll see it the moment you do it. I'll let him go that same second. You have my word."

A sick smile stretched my lips. "I don't trust you, Will Thorne."

"I don't trust you, either, hence why we're in this position. You don't understand what this thing is, how much magic it has." He nodded at the screen of his laptop. "You don't understand what it will do to the world if we don't stop it, and that's okay. You don't have to understand—or trust me. Just trust that I will do whatever it takes to get rid of it."

And just like that, all my choices were taken from me.

I don't know how I managed to turn around. How I kept my eyes focused ahead and didn't look at Ax when he called my name, demanded I run away and leave him here to die all by himself...*because of me.*

If he really believed that I would even consider that for a second, he didn't know me at all. I'd take that fucking bomb around my own neck if I could. Of course, I was going to grab that army bag from the ground while they watched me. Of course, I was going to put it over my shoulder and move toward the mountains, toward the cries of the spirits and the glowing yellow light coming from them.

I felt Ax's pain in my soul every time he called for me, every time he slammed his fists on the magic. I felt all of it as if it were mine, but I didn't dare turn to even look at him for fear I'd cave. And I couldn't afford to do that. Not anymore.

My spirit was making me see double, but I pushed it down with all my strength. Not yet. Not until we were in there. Not until I did what Thorne wanted me to do.

And not until I knew for a fact that Ax was safe.

Then, I could give up. I wouldn't need control anyway. I would be dead.

"It's okay," I whispered to myself as I went. I'd had eight days. I'd had the most beautiful time of my life. I was with him. I *lived* for once in my miserable existence, and it was absolutely worth it.

I would always have the memories, no matter where I went from here. No matter what hell awaited me, I'd get through it because I knew what he felt like. What he sounded like. What he tasted like.

When I reached the slope between the mountains, I finally saw the howling spirits again. There were so many more of them than the first time, my knees shook. My body threatened to give. Even the spirit in me wanted me to turn around and run because I remembered what it had been like last time. I remembered the magic. The scent. The pull.

I remembered the spirits that had floated out of the cave, the warmth that had come at me in waves every time those large bubbles exploded on the surface of the lake contaminated with magic. But it was all so much more terrifying now. And I felt it all...felt Will Thorne and his minions coming after me, slowly. They could see me, could see the spirits, and they would make sure that I would go in there one way or the other

Ax still screamed my name from fifty feet away. I still heard the way his his skin burned every time he tried to break the magic.

But it was okay. This didn't have to last long—it would be over in no time.

Raising my chin, I looked at the sky for a moment, at the darkness that was lighting up by the second as the sun came out. I wasn't afraid of unconsciousness. I wouldn't be able to shut my mind down if I tried.

And the spirits watched me, their lifeless eyes made out of greenish yellow light, their mouths opened as they cried out, their shapeless bodies changing every second as they floated on air.

The lake. The cave. The larger monsters waiting.

"Go on," Will Thorne said from behind me. My hands shook as I took the bag in my hands. I opened it, saw the dynamite sticks inside, too many to count. All I had to do was put them in that cave and light them up. There was a small pocket to the side, and I found a Zippo lighter there, too. I held it in my fist and put the bag over my shoulder again.

My gods, the spirits were waiting for me. They knew I was going to go to them now, and they were eager. They couldn't wait to fucking devour me whole.

"Move!" Will said, and my legs shook harder when I took a step forward. The magic of the ward that kept the world safe from these spirits was right there, the warmth of it coating my skin. Last time, it had barely let me through. This time, it would probably be no different.

"*Damsel!*" Ax called with all his strength, but I didn't stop. And when I was right in front of the ward, I prepared to jump, just like last time.

But...the ground shook before I could blink.

"What the—"

Before Will could finish speaking, the mountains roared. The ground shook harder—just like it had that first time I'd been in the den. Just like it had when the cave had been trying to suck me in.

Fear crawled all over my skin as I watched the spirits screaming in unison now, and I waited for the pull…

And I waited…

"Oh, my gods," I whispered to myself when the spirits began to be sucked back.

The spirits—*not me*.

I watched in awe, unable to even blink, as the cave or whatever was inside it, pulled back the hundreds of spirits made out of glowing light around them. I watched as the light of them disappeared in the depths of the dark cave that looked like a monster's mouth about to eat me raw.

I watched as the yellow glow of the lake around it began to lose strength, grow dimmer, and the bubbles exploding on its surface become smaller…

I watched until the very last screaming spirit was sucked into the cave.

The silence that fell in the woods was sudden and absolute.

"What did you do?" someone asked—probably Will, but I couldn't answer.

My legs gave out, and I fell on my knees, barely any strength to raise my hand. But I needed to feel the magic. The slope was right in front of my knees, and the ward should have been there, too, but…

There was nothing but air going through my fingers. No ward. No spirit. No bubbly lake.

No magic.

"What the hell did you do, bloodsucker?!" Ray growled.

I shook my head, but no word left me. Was that *me*? Had I actually spooked all those spirits back to wherever they had come from?

Had I really taken all that magic away from the water, too? Because the water was dark and it looked filthy, but it wasn't glowing anymore. And no bubbles were popping on its surface.

"Doesn't matter," Will said from behind me. "There's no more magic here. Get the bag, Ray. Let's bring that cave down."

My eyes refused to blink. My body refused to move. I just felt it when someone pulled the bag from my shoulder. I saw the silhouettes as they rushed forward, jumped, and weren't met by magic. Weren't met by spirits, or any kind of resistance.

And a voice in my ear whispered, *something is not right.*

I'd be damned if I didn't believe it.

CHAPTER

NINETEEN

THE WHISPERS WERE GROWING LOUDER. I DUG MY FINGERNAILS into the soil and waited. Just a little longer.

Just one short minute, that's all.

"Damsel," Ax said from the inside of the magic shield. The sun was already up, but I'd never been more awake. That thing was still around his neck. That magic was still keeping him prisoner.

"It's all right," he told me. "This is the perfect time to run."

"Does it hurt?" I asked instead. Because he knew that he was wasting breath with those words, and I really didn't have the patience to do the same.

"I don't feel it," he said, and it wasn't a lie. "Damsel."

"Stop." He kept saying my name like that, like he wanted to remind me of what mattered. Like he thought that I had forgotten.

I hadn't—all he cared about was that I got away from here with my life. But all *I* cared about is that *he* got away with his.

"It's accurate," Jacob was saying as he and his uncle came closer. Yeah—Will had removed the chains from Jacob because he needed him to confirm what we all already knew. The fucking Vein was gone. Disappeared. Not here anymore.

"There has to be an explanation for this," Will insisted when they stopped and squatted down barely five feet away. All of them were looking down at the screen of his laptop, too. "A Vein doesn't just stop existing."

"It's useless to try to blow up the cave. What would we accomplish? There's no magic here anymore," Jacob said, and he sounded really curious, too.

I just wished I gave a shit.

"I did what you asked. Let him go."

My own voice sounded strange to my ears. I didn't move from where I was kneeling on the ground, right in front of Ax. I didn't even breathe while I waited for an answer because I already knew what the answer was going to be.

"I've got much more important things to deal with," Will Thorne spit, then went back to his laptop.

I smiled, raising my finger to touch the magic keeping Ax locked in there.

"It's okay," Ax said, the corner of his lips curling up a bit. "It's fine."

I smiled wider. "It's perfectly fine."

"What possibilities are there? We know what causes an outburst of magic, and—" Jacob was saying to his uncle, when I cut him off.

"I did what you asked. Let him go."

Second try. I promised myself I'd give them three.

"For fuck's sake," Will muttered. "This was *not* an

outburst—this is a Vein! It's different..." and he continued to speak to Jacob.

The magic of the shield burned my fingertip when I went too close. The whispers in my head halted for a moment, as if waiting to see what decision I was going to make.

But I'd already made it—they just didn't know it yet.

I barely breathed. My skin burned from standing so close to the magic and from the sunlight. There was no heat yet to the rays falling on my side, though, so at least I had that.

"Damsel?" Ax whispered, barely blinking his eyes as he watched me.

"One more left." Three tries—that's what they would get. Then my conscience would be squeaky clean.

"You can run. I'll find you. Go find a place to sleep," he said, leaning closer to the shield, a wicked grin on his beautiful face because he knew perfectly well that he was wasting breath. "I'll be there when you wake up."

His wide eyes shone like gems, and I saw them clearly, even though it was daylight. Maybe my imagination filled in the gaps where my eyesight failed and wasn't it beautiful how well I knew him?

Suddenly, it occurred to me that this might not end all that well for me.

And though I knew him, did he know *me* well enough?

Probably, but I got the urge to tell him anyway. So, I did.

"Did you know that I'd given up before you?" And to think about that right now was almost ridiculous. *Impossible* that there'd been a time when I hadn't felt so motivated, so full of will to be alive. "I always went to bed feeling worthless, *half,* and I woke up worse." It had been a vicious cycle.

"Damsel," Ax warned, but I just needed to let it out.

"You complete me, Savage." I pressed my finger to the magic and fucking loved the way it shocked my entire system awake. I loved how it opened my eyes wider and made my senses sharper, even if only for a moment. My fangs extended, too, and when Ray and Fallon came closer, I didn't even look at them. What was the point?

"You—"

"No," Ax cut me off. "This is not goodbye." And he was dead serious.

"It isn't." I wasn't saying goodbye. "But I—"

"So, you will tell me those things when I'm not in here anymore. I'll want to hear them then," he insisted.

And you know what? He was right. Because if I were touching him, kissing him, I'd be able to share everything I'd ever thought about in my life, every small thing that had ever crossed my mind.

So...

"I did what you asked. Let him go."

Third time.

Will stopped talking. Ray and Fallon moved even closer to my side, slowly, cautiously.

"What the fuck is the matter with you?!" Will Thorne spit.

Well, I tried.

Now, I let go.

I held Ax's eyes as the spirit took over me. It was okay. I could take the pain. I didn't have to close my eyes and writhe in it until it was over. I would just let it run its course.

"I think it's time you kept your word, Uncle," Jacob said, and I heard him standing up, though my head was a mess of whispers and screams, and my eyes were locked on Ax's.

"Let Ax go."

I heard it perfectly when Will's heart skipped a beat. His blood began to rush in anger, too.

"You little—"

I jumped.

I wasn't shifted all the way yet, and the pain was still there as my bones rearranged themselves, but the strength in me had already doubled. That's why I had no trouble reaching the branch of a large tree right next to where Ax was trapped. I grabbed it and spun myself around until I jumped over it, preserving my balance perfectly. And by then, the shift was complete. I was no longer a vampire... and I'd barely felt the pain.

My lips stretched into a smile as I looked down at the others—Jacob with his arms raised toward me, telling me to calm down, Will Thorne with one hand covered in his red smoke, the others all ready to throw their magic at me, while Ax sat on the ground cross-legged and watched me through the magic, a wide grin on his gorgeous face. The way he pulled at my heart just by looking at me was ridiculous.

But there was no time to stare at him now. No time to go after that shield, like the spirit in me wanted. It could break it with my brand-new claws, but that would give Will Thorne time to throw his magic at me, and we couldn't have that.

The spirit agreed. I don't know whether it did it willingly, but what mattered was that I had a say in how it acted. So, I made a plan and I saw it through with such ease, you'd think it was all a dream, not reality.

I jumped from one tree to the other too fast for their eyes to see me, until I landed right behind Will's back, one hand wrapped around his, where his thumb was pressed to that remote, and the other on his face, fingers between his teeth, my claws pressing onto the roof of his mouth.

His magic vibrated in his hand and he raised it, trying to slam it to my face, but I hid behind him, then pressed my claws into the roof of his mouth harder.

"Step back!" Jacob called, pushing the others away, and Will bit hard onto three of my fingers until he drew blood.

I welcomed the pain, same as my spirit, and continued to make bigger holes in his mouth until he stopped biting and grunted like a wounded animal.

"Nikki, calm down," Jacob was saying, but I was calm. I was perfectly calm. Will's hand was in mine, my thumb pressing onto his, on the button of the remote. My claws were on him, and it would take but a little tug to break his skull in half. He knew it. I'd be faster than this magic—or if I wasn't, the spirit in me would continue to pull him apart even if *I* was knocked out by that magic.

I'd underestimated him that day when he ambushed me in Jacob's house. I hadn't known what to expect from him, and...

Wait, that's not right.

It wasn't *him* that I'd underestimated. It was just that I'd only had *my* life to lose against him, and that had never really been much of a motivator for me.

Ax's life, on the other hand...

"You've got three seconds," I whispered behind his back, pushing my claws deeper by the second. My voice sounded worse than I remembered, but he heard the words. I felt his magic, smelled the scent of it, but also knew that it would not stop me.

"Do it!" Jacob shouted. "Fucking let him go!"

"*One*," I whispered, running one claw down the roof of

his mouth and to his throat. He grunted and tried to push away from me, his magic warm and vibrant, ready to consume every inch of me if it could reach me. If Will didn't know for sure that he'd be dead by the time his magic actually managed to stop me.

"*Two...*" A second finger joined the first.

"Do it!" Jacob shouted.

Ax was laughing. The sound of it vibrated through me. It would have made my toes curl if they weren't tipped with claws right now.

"*Three...*" I whispered, but before I could drag my third claw down to his throat, magic released into the air with a hiss.

Thorne growled as the magic filled the air with tension and that spicy scent I both loved and hated. I pulled my fingers out of his mouth, bloody, skin broken where he'd bitten me, but I hardly felt the pain. I pushed myself to the side for just a second to confirm that the magic shield around Ax had disappeared.

It had. He was standing now as he smiled, shoulders wide, chin up. I fucking loved that man so much, it made my insides twist.

But that band was still around his neck.

I still held Will by the neck when I pulled up his hand with the remote stuck in it. He tried to resist it, but he wasn't stronger than me even when I was merely a vampire. The spirit could crash his knuckles without effort.

"The...the computer..." he said, his voice strange as I held him by the neck.

And Jacob didn't hesitate. He kneeled in front of Will's laptop and started pressing on the keyboard frantically.

Ax slowly came closer—I could barely see him over

Will's shoulder even though I was on my tiptoes. He was a tall guy.

But the others were already moving for Ax, too, and Jacob was too busy with the computer to tell them to move back, so Ax had no choice but to stop.

To my surprise, he was ignoring Will and the others completely as he watched me.

"It's fine, baby. Let him go. I'm out," he told me.

I growled—this was *not* the part where we trusted Will. Or even Jacob. Anybody in the fucking world—not when he had a thing around his neck that could blow his brains out. On that, I wouldn't compromise.

"C'mon, Damsel. Step away from him," Ax said, a bit more impatient now. "Don't kill him."

Oh, I knew exactly what he was doing here. *Don't kill him*...because *he* wanted to be the one to do it.

And if he did that, there would be no stopping the others.

My spirit thought it was a fine idea, obviously. But my spirit—and Ax, apparently—didn't think farther ahead than two minutes into the future nor did they think with a sound mind. They thought with their egos.

So, when the light around Ax's neck turned green and the band released with a hiss, falling on the ground in front of his feet, I moved, too.

I let go of Will, pushed him back, and I moved in front of Ax. I kicked the stupid bomb away, just in case it could still explode.

His eyes were locked on Will, who was resting against a tree trunk, breathing heavily as he spit out blood. The others were already at his side, watching, waiting, knowing that all hell was about to break loose.

"Easy," Jacob said, stepping between us and Will. "Easy now. It's all good."

I looked up at Ax, and when he refused to meet my eyes, I grabbed his chin in my hand and lowered his head violently.

He was surprised for a second, but he recovered quickly. And I growled, because for some reason, my spirit really liked to avoid speaking. It made it feel like *less* of a spirit or something, and Ax understood the sounds of me perfectly.

He grabbed my face in his hands and came closer, looking into my eyes like I was the most fascinating thing he'd ever seen. Did he see *me* in there? Or just the spirit?

I got my answer when he grinned widely. He could see me just fine.

But there was only so long I could keep my spirit under control. And my instincts were sharper now, even though the sun was still shining.

"Nikki, go," Jacob whispered. "Just run."

I turned to him, to Will and the others who'd already recovered themselves and were waiting for me to make a move before they released their magic at me. And Will looked so pissed, he might have killed me on the spot with his eyes alone.

But he didn't say anything, didn't tell Jacob to shut up. Didn't attack.

And for now, that was the best I was going to get. The spirit had taken over. I could make myself run if Ax followed me. I could make myself get to safety, then force myself to shift back to vampire again. But if I stayed, and if Will Thorne provoked me, the spirit would lose it and I wouldn't be able to stop it. I wouldn't even want to.

So, I turned to Ax again and grabbed his jacket in my

fists, making holes in it with my claws in the process. Would he make this easier for me and just run?

Or would he make this easier for my spirit? I waited, and my spirit waited, too, and...

He leaned closer, and my head moved to the side—the spirit, *not* me. "Meet you by the road."

And he took off running without warning.

CHAPTER TWENTY

I *NEVER* WANTED TO GO THROUGH THAT AGAIN. NOT EVER.

I lay in Ax's arms, shifted back into my original self—for the second time now, without losing consciousness—feeling like I had a million needles prickling my skin from everywhere at once. The sun was up in the sky. We'd made it all the way to Albuquerque. It was almost noon, and though I couldn't keep my eyes closed, my mind was in chaos. It just wouldn't shut up.

We were safe. Ax had taken us away, and he'd broken into the basement of an empty house two hours away from the Tonto Forest. He held me in his arms as we lay down on the dirty mattress, surrounded by bugs and mice and dust. He wasn't asleep. He was wide awake, alert—I knew that just by hearing his slightly accelerated heartbeat. I trusted him to know if Will or anybody else came even close to us, but my mind still wouldn't shut down.

The fear wouldn't let it.

Seeing Ax trapped under that magic, with that thing around his neck...it fucking terrified me. Had I been anything less than what I am...had I been *alone* in my body, merely a vampire, not the monster that I was...

What exactly would have happened? Would Ax be here right now? Would his head still be attached to the rest of him? Would this heart that was beating right under my cheek still beat?

"Stop it, Damsel," he whispered. I'd gripped his shirt tightly even without realizing it. He put his hand over mine and caressed my knuckles until my grip loosened. "Sleep, baby. We're okay."

And I trusted him—we were okay now.

But would we be when Will, or anybody else, found us again?

Would we be fine when the next time he ended up in that position, I was free of this spirit inside me that I'd spent a lifetime hating with all my being?

I was never a fan of sugarcoating things for myself, and I wasn't about to start now. The ugly truth was that *no*, we wouldn't. We wouldn't be fine if I couldn't protect him against everything and anything out there. Against magic and monsters and fucking bombs, too. We would *not* be fine.

I wanted to hug him to me tighter, but my energy was minimal. My body too heavy. But I'd already accepted that he'd been right all along, the asshole. Those words he'd said to me on that rooftop lulled my mind to unconsciousness faster than magic...because my decision was already made. That's all it took—a lifetime of wanting to do everything in my power to be free, and then Will Thorne goes and threatens the only thing I cared about in the world more than myself.

You don't have to change a hair on your head because you're perfect, vampire, Vein spirit and all. That's what Ax told me that night. I didn't believe him then.

I still didn't believe him now—I was far, *far* from perfect. But I was *his* perfect, same as he was mine.

And I could believe *that* with all my heart.

Damsel.

My eyes opened, but I didn't see anything until I blinked at least ten times. Darkness around me, but I could still feel the sun shining up in the sky.

Strong hands around my shoulders pulled me to sit, and I could finally make out Ax's face in front of me. He touched my cheeks, kissed my lips, just little pecks, until I was fully aware of our surroundings again.

I'd slept, apparently, and we were still in that dirty basement, on that dirty mattress, with the mice and the bugs all around. It wasn't nighttime yet, but the sun was setting.

And Ax looked a bit alarmed.

"There you are," he said, trying to force a smile. He shouldn't have bothered—I could tell.

"What is it?" I said, and my voice came out dry, hoarse. Fuck, I needed water.

"They're coming our way," he said. "It's daylight, baby, but we need to move."

"All of them?" I asked, pushing myself up to my knees. He stood up and pulled me up by my hands.

"Just the Thornes," he said, holding me by the waist. "You good?" He searched every inch of my face so carefully, it would have made me blush under different circumstances.

"I'm fine," I promised him. "What the hell do they want now?" I moved to the side, and my legs still shook, but I managed to keep my balance. The memories from last morning came back to me with a vengeance...the spirits, the way they'd howled and screamed, and then—

"They disappeared. They just...disappeared." Just like that. They were sucked into the cave right in front of my eyes.

"Good riddance," Ax mumbled, nodding at the stairs.

"You think that was me?" Had *I* somehow chased those spirits away?

"If you could do that, you'd have done it the first time around," Ax said, reminding me that I'd actually been inside those wards before, when the spirits were still there.

Chills rushed down my spine as I followed him up the stairs, into the dust-covered house, and outside. The orange hue that the setting sun cast on the houses around me would have probably looked beautiful to me had I not been in such a foul mood.

"What do they want from me now?" I wondered again. Will had wanted that Vein gone—it *was* gone already. Why come after us again? Did he *want* to fucking die? Because I'd kill him, pull his head off his shoulders with my bare hands before I allowed him to hurt Ax again. I would not hesitate, not after what I witnessed him doing. What I knew he *could* do with fucking bombs.

"Does it matter?" Ax asked, stopping in the middle of the wide street, sniffing the air hard. He seemed like he couldn't care less that the sun hadn't retreated completely yet. He wasn't even sweating; meanwhile my shirt was sticking to my back uncomfortably already.

"Wet dog hair," he mumbled with a flinch.

I turned around, searching the humans walking by, the

ones sitting on their porches, inside their houses. Some watched us, some ignored us just fine.

"Werewolf," I said, the image of Ethan's grey wolf coming before my eyes. Hadn't Jacob said that out of all five of them, Ethan was the only one who hadn't gone behind his back to Will?

"I'd actually love to see that," Ax said, eyes suddenly sparkling with curiosity.

But I grabbed his hand. "Let's just get the fuck out of here first."

He looked at me. "Want me to carry you?"

"I'm good. The sun will be gone in two minutes." I just didn't want to wait around for Will to show his face, provoke me, and make me murder him in front of all these humans.

We ran down the street together, not really caring if anybody could see. I was way too tired, way too irritated to bother right now. I just wanted to get away.

And we would have...had I failed to hear Jacob's voice.

He wasn't close by any means—he was at least a few hundred feet away from me, but he was *shouting*. I didn't hear him at first, too focused on trying to save energy while I ran, afraid I might collapse soon. But Ax heard him, and when he stopped, so did I, thinking he saw something ahead.

It was just Jacob, calling my name.

Ax growled, hands fisted tightly by his side as he looked behind. I wanted to tell him to move. I wanted to beg him to just keep running, don't stop, don't look back, but...

"*Nikki, please. Don't run. I need to talk to you!*" Jacob called from the gods knew how far. I couldn't even smell him, or hear his heartbeat, just his shout. "*One second! Please, wait one second!*"

Cursing under my breath, I closed my eyes and forced my mind to calm down. The growing darkness felt mighty fine, and when the sun disappeared behind the horizon completely, that's when my mind woke up fully. My senses came back to me, and my heart slowed down the beating.

Ax didn't ask me what I wanted to do. He didn't tell me to wait or to run—he was curious, too.

Or...he just wanted a chance to murder Will Thorne. Jacob would know that, and if he was bringing his uncle to us again...well, I was just going to assume that he did it on purpose.

"Don't attack yet, okay?" I whispered to Ax two minutes later, when I began to hear Jacob's heartbeat and smell the spicy scent of his magic.

"Well, it depends," Ax said.

"On what?"

"On whether he shows his face."

"Ax..."

Will Thorne showed his face.

He and Jacob turned the corner walking side by side, each with a bag around their shoulder. When they saw us, they both stopped, and Jacob raised his hands in surrender, as if to show me that he wasn't going to attack. There were still humans around us, and now that night had fallen, I could hear their heartbeats clearer, and the craving for blood was growing stronger, too. Maybe we should have kept going until we found a butcher's shop.

"I don't suppose you'll let me go to them alone?" I asked Ax, even though I already knew the answer.

"Not a chance," he said, and I heard the grin in his voice. I had yet to know a man who was more excited at the idea of fighting and killing as he was.

"Okay, then. Let's hear what Jacob has to say first. We owe him that."

"We don't owe him shit anymore," he spit, but he walked with me. "He set us up."

"He wouldn't." Of that, at least, I was sure.

"He's equally guilty for not assuming that his uncle would follow him and for not doing what he needed to do to prevent that from happening," Ax said, eyes on Will as he stayed in place, and Jacob came close to us slowly. "Stupidity should be punishable by death."

I would have laughed. "Let's hear him out first." Because I was curious, too. I wanted to know what the hell had happened with that Vein. I wanted to know where those spirits had gone to, what had caused them to run, or what had sucked them back. *If* they were ever coming back up here again, too.

"I know you're pissed," Jacob said as he approached, skin slick with sweat, blue bags under his eyes. He looked almost as bad as the night we first met.

"No, no," Ax said, shaking his head with a wicked smile. "*Pissed* isn't really the word for it."

Jacob swallowed hard, then looked at me. "I'm sorry, Nikki. I had no idea."

There were things I wanted to say to him, but I stopped myself. What was the point, anyway? I knew he was sorry. He knew I was sorry, too. But we had much bigger things to deal with here.

"Are they back?" I asked, which was the only reason why I'd stopped to wait for him in the first place.

Jacob flinched before he looked down at the ground for a moment. That alone told me that whatever he was about to say, I wouldn't like it.

DEADLY MATCH

"No, they're not back," Jacob said, shaking his head. "There's...something else."

I raised a brow and looked at Ax, to see if he was just as curious, but he was looking at Will Thorne instead. And the asshole sorcerer looked back at him, arms crossed, a small smile curling his lips. He was *challenging* him even now, and for how much longer could I realistically expect Ax not to lose his shit on him?

"You might want to get to it faster," I told Jacob, and his eyes moved to Ax immediately. When he saw him grinning like a fucking psycho, he turned back to Will Thorne as his heart skipped a beat.

Jacob was afraid. He was scared shitless—even more so than any other time I'd spoken to him.

And that was the second indicator that I wasn't going to like what he was going to say next.

"He won't attack," Jacob told me, then reached for the green army bag around his shoulder. Come to think of it, it was the same one that had been full of dynamite back in the Forest. Now, it only carried Will's.

"I'm not worried about your uncle, Jacob," I told him as he dropped the bag to the ground and pulled the lid of the laptop open.

"Axel," he said, drawing Ax's eyes to him for a moment. "Just...just take a look at this first." And when Ax raised a skeptical brow, he said, "*please.*"

That surprised Ax more than anything. He turned to me, almost *shocked* because...what in the world could make Jacob Thorne, the same man who'd almost killed him twice—and called him a monster—*plead* with him now?

We both found out when Jacob turned his laptop around to show us the screen. It was a map, a nameless map, and the thousands of different shapes were all colored, just like always. The greens, the yellows, the oranges…and the red, too.

I'd seen the color red on Will's phone the day we met. I'd seen the red on the laptop back at the Forest, too. It had been showing *me* and the Vein location, but now…the red was showing something else. Something much *bigger*.

"Why the fuck would you make a program with a map without *names*?" It really defeated the purpose here. I couldn't tell where the hell the red was.

"That's North Dakota," Jacob said, swallowing hard. "It's the Hidden Realm."

At least I was right. I definitely did not like the sound of that at all.

Ax wouldn't stop looking at Will. It didn't help that he was closer now, standing right next to Jacob, and that the three other touched sorcerers had showed their faces, too. They kept their distance for now, but it was enough to know that they were there. Watching. That one of them had shot me through the heart two nights ago. That they'd helped in locking up Ax like that.

And my spirit didn't like that.

The sky was pitch-black and my strength had returned to me completely. The anger, too. The more I thought about it, the more I wanted Will's head. *All* of their heads, except maybe Jacob's. And Ethan's. Though I didn't see him, I smelled his fur, too, now that night had fallen. If it came to it, would he come out from wherever he was hiding?

"It appeared about five minutes after you left," Jacob was saying, showing us the red screen and the nameless map of the United States. "It's almost like the spirits were sucked out of Arizona and somehow brought up to North Dakota."

"The Hidden Realm *is* magic," I reminded him. "A shitload of magic." Which could be the reason why it was showing *red* on that map, too.

"No, it never showed like this before," Jacob said, shaking his head. "Only you, and that site at the Forest ever registered as red in the program, Nikki. Nothing else. Only Vein spirits would have that much power, that much magic gathered into one place."

I raised my brows. "Are you insinuating that there's Vein spirits in the Hidden Realm?" Because that sounded ridiculous. Vein spirits couldn't even get through the gates or the walls that surrounded the Realm. They couldn't get to vampires at all, which was one of the main benefits vampires had when they signed that treaty with the sorcerers. To assume that there would be spirits in there was just absurd.

But...my eyes closed for a moment because, the truth was, we didn't know. We didn't know for sure that spirits couldn't get through the gates.

A spirit had lived inside those walls since they were first created—inside *me*. And Marie had walked through the gates with Ax, too. Nothing had stopped her.

Nothing had ever stopped me, either.

"I don't know, to be honest. I don't know what the hell it means, but we have to check it out. We have to get to the Realm and see for ourselves." Jacob closed the laptop and took half a step closer to me. "We *have* to see what's going on, Nikki. This is too big. You know what all that magic means. You experienced it firsthand."

And I had. When I was inside that ward in the Forest in

Arizona, I'd experienced all the magic, all those spirits, the incredible pull toward the cave...

"If you could just take us to the Realm, and if we saw what was happening in there—"

"We already know what is happening in there," Will Thorne cut him off, his eyes never leaving Ax's. "An incredible amount of magic is being used. It doesn't matter what it's coming from—it's equally dangerous. If we don't stop it, it could destroy the Hidden Realm, which I have no complaints about, to be honest, but magic keeps growing. It keeps consuming. If it consumes your Realm, it won't stop there."

No—it would spread to the rest of the world, too. Especially if there was an actual Vein in the Realm somehow. If there were *spirits* roaming around there, free to kill every vampire they found. *All* of them.

My heart skipped a long beat. Anya. Ivan. Jones...even Marie and Marcus. They were in the Realm.

The whispers in my head turned up instantly.

"We have to go," Jacob said to me. "Nikki, we need to see what's happening."

I licked my dry lips. "How do we know he didn't just make this shit up? I'm not gonna fucking trust him, Jacob."

"You fancy yourself too important," Will spit. "I wouldn't have wasted my time."

"Oh, yeah? Just like you didn't waste time keeping me under magic for two weeks, then tracking me down and taking me to Arizona, too?" I didn't even want to talk to him. I didn't want to fucking look at his face at all.

"Nikki, this isn't made up," Jacob said. "And you don't have to trust him. But you can trust me."

"Are you insinuating that you can keep him on a leash?" Ax asked, his voice low, full of sharp edges.

We both heard it when Will Thorne's heart tripped all over itself. "I'm not a fucking dog!"

"I can't, but he knows this is bigger than all of us together. Bigger than anything. He will be no threat," Jacob said, looking at his uncle like he wanted him dead on the spot, too. "Right, Will?"

And he grinned. "I'll give my word, if you give yours."

Despite everything, I smiled.

"Of course. I give my word that I will not touch you. I wouldn't—not if something's going on in my home," Ax suddenly said, and I did a double take. Was he serious?

Because he sounded serious. He sounded *honest,* too. Which just...what the fuck?

"Really?" I whispered to him, still unsure, even though I always knew when he was lying. His body gave him away, same as mine gave me away.

"Of course," Ax told me, and when he met my eyes, there was no hint of amusement in them. He wasn't lying.

He fucking meant it.

Well, damn. The Hidden Realm meant more to him than I realized.

"And I give my word I won't touch you, either—only until this is over, Savage Ax," Will Thorne said without missing a beat. "But when it is, I'm coming for you. Best to remember that."

And Ax smiled. "If you get there, it will only be fair."

Jacob was relieved. I was still very, *very* suspicious. I mean, it was Ax. Who even knew what went on in his head?

"Right," Jacob said, putting the laptop away as he nodded at himself. "We're gonna need about seventeen hours to drive to the Realm. You can join us, or—"

"Thanks, we'd rather run," I cut him off. No way was I

going to be in Will Thorne's presence for longer than I absolutely had to. Ax gave his word, true—but *I* hadn't.

"Fair enough," Jacob said. "Your way will be clear. We'll meet you in Lowin in North Dakota."

The very town where we first met. Where this whole madness even started.

"Try not to take too long," I said, sliding my hand into Ax's. He squeezed my fingers tightly.

"Thank you, Nikki, Ax," Jacob said, and though he meant that *thank you* to me, he forced himself to say it to Ax, too. But Ax didn't give a shit, and neither did I, really. We didn't need a *thank you*. We just needed to get this over with.

"Gentlemen," Ax said with a curt nod, then looked at me.

We could read each other's expressions perfectly by now so when we took off running, we did it at the same time.

CHAPTER
TWENTY-ONE

Ax Creed

I booked a suite on the top floor of the hotel because I wanted to be as far away from other people as I could. Lately, they were getting to me more and more.

Or maybe it was just the sorcerer Thorne. I could barely sit still every time I thought of him.

Not yet.

But...soon.

Damsel came out of the bathroom, wearing a new purple skirt and a black top we'd gotten at a store before we stopped for the day. We'd had no choice—both our clothes were torn, and our car with all the clothes we bought at the mall two nights ago was way too far still.

The Thornes and their minions would need to rest before they hit the road again, anyway. And we'd get to the Realm long before they did. That's why we decided to spend the day here in Albuquerque.

I sat on the large brown sofa, sipping whiskey from

the small bottle, watching her. She came to me slowly, sat on my lap, taking the bottle from my hand and putting it on the coffee table. Then she grabbed my face in her hands and kissed the breath out of me, wiping my mind clean for a second. I loved how much power she had over me.

And I also loved that she wasn't wearing any panties. I wanted to be the one to put some on her, so that I could tear them off her body.

At first, I'd just loved the sound of the fabric coming to pieces. I'd loved both our hunger. But then I felt how much *she* loved it, too, when I did it. Despite her protests, she loved that I couldn't wait long enough to take her clothes off properly.

"What are you thinking, Savage?" she whispered against my lips. "Tell me what's on your mind."

I ran my hands up her naked thighs, under her skirt, and gripped her hips tightly, making her moan. "I'm thinking I want to put some panties on you."

She smiled lazily and started grinding against me. The way her hips moved in my hands, the rhythm of them, the slow, sensual movement made my cock stand at attention immediately.

"No—I mean about the...situation," she whispered, grazing my lips with her teeth.

"There's nothing to think about. We'll take them to the Realm. We'll find out what's happening there, then deal with it." I moved my hands down her perky ass and dug my fingers in her flesh the way she liked. Fuck, the feel of her was better than anything in the world. My hands slid on her smooth skin, and our bodies had already fallen into a slow rhythm, moving together in perfect sync. Even without the mating instinct, it had been obvious to me that we were made for each other the first time I was inside her. The first time I tasted her.

"Aren't you afraid, though?" she asked, eyes squeezed shut while I kissed down the side of her neck and guided her hips against my hard cock, a bit faster by the second.

"There's no reason to be afraid, baby," I told her. "Whatever is happening in the Realm, we can handle it." I knew my strength—and I also knew hers, too. I knew what she became. The memory of her while I'd been trapped in that fucking magic shield was right in front of my eyes.

Will Thorne had held a gun at Damsel, had put the barrel inside her mouth, and threatened to blow her brains out while she was unconscious if I didn't stand still long enough for his minions to put that collar on me. Then, he'd made me stand still another five seconds, until he wrapped me up in that magic.

And I'd been completely powerless when there was a fucking gun inside Damsel's mouth, and she wasn't waking up. I'd had no choice but to obey, but I'd known. I really believed the two of us could make it out of *anything*, but I still hadn't forgotten, the helplessness I'd felt. The way I'd lowered my head and folded like I hadn't done since I was sold as property when I was a kid.

"I know," she said, suddenly wrapping her arms around my neck, holding me to her chest tightly. I wrapped mine around her waist, too. "I'm not gonna do it." Her voice came out muffled, but I understood every word. "I'm not gonna take the spirit out."

I kissed her shoulder. "I know."

She pushed herself back for a moment. "You do?"

"Yeah, I do." She'd seen me locked in that magic, with that bomb around my neck. She would have done anything in the world to get me out...*anything*.

Just like I did *everything* I had to do when there was a gun barrel inside her mouth. And now that she knew I *could* end up like that again, she was going to make sure she could get me out of it no mater what. Just like I knew that I wasn't going to rest until I found a way to keep her out of reach of everyone and everything. Whether it was magic or weapons didn't matter—anything would do. I'd figure it out.

"How?" Damsel asked, pressing her lips on my forehead gently. She always felt better to share with me what was on her mind when I was kissing her. Right now, it was really easy for me, too.

"How else are you gonna get me out the next time someone traps me like that?"

I felt her muscles clenching for a second, and she slammed onto my chest again, squeezing me so tightly I could hardly breathe. I didn't stop her. I didn't fucking need air right now.

"I've never felt more helpless in my life," she whispered.

"I know, Damsel." I never felt more helpless than when people threatened *her,* either.

But it was okay because we could make sure it would never happen again. I was a vampire. I was fast. I was strong. I never slept. Somehow, even all of that wasn't enough, but it was still okay. I'd improve. I'd become better. *Whatever it takes.*

"Will Thorne is gonna play dirty again," she said, making my heart skip a beat. Didn't I know that already.

That man was one of the few true threats I'd ever encountered in my life—and not because of his magic. But because he was driven by the same instincts as me. He had his own *whatever it takes,* and as long as he was alive, we weren't safe. Damsel wasn't safe.

But right now, she needed some peace of mind. Right now, she needed me in a different way—not to save her life, just her sanity. Not to protect her, just to fill her up, heart and soul and body.

So, I pushed her back until I saw her wide, pale eyes. Her wild hair was all over the place, handing around her like an aura. My little piece of perfection. She was even more beautiful than a piece of art.

"I need you to do something for me," I said, and she squeezed my wrists, holding my hands on her face.

"Anything," she whispered.

"I need you to clear your mind and focus only on me, baby. On my hands. On my lips. On my cock. Can you do that?"

She nodded, closing her eyes as I touched my lips to hers. "I need your mind empty right now. I need you to be completely mine. All of you—including your attention."

And Damsel didn't hesitate. "Yes," she whispered, making me smile.

The more she gave to me, the more I wanted. I already knew this was a game I was *never* going to win. Nor did I want to.

"Good girl," I said and enjoyed it when her skin broke in goose bumps. She loved to be a good girl for me, just as much as she loved to be my little slut. She gave me everything, in all levels, in all angles. I couldn't fucking believe she was mine.

I held her in my arms when I stood up and took her to the bed in the master bedroom. My ears were sharp, my attention not completely on her, because it couldn't be. Not yet. I lay her on the bed, then grabbed the paper bag from the ground, and put everything we'd gotten at that store on the bed. It wasn't much, only two sets of lingerie. I chose the red one, the color like blood, half of it smooth satin, half lacy roses.

"Feet up," I said, kneeling in front of her, so I could put the G-string on. Her eyes were already more vibrant, brimming with life. The more she trusted me, the more she obeyed me, the more relaxed she looked. I loved her when she was completely submissive, just as much as when she fought me.

Her body must have been drawn because every inch of her was perfect. I put the panties on her, and though I wanted to keep that skirt on her, too, I couldn't. I need to see, so I took it off. And I took off her shirt, too, then put on the bra. It was padded, so it made her tits push up so fucking deliciously, I wanted to devour them. Good thing I would in a second.

"Are you gonna tear them off?" she asked, running her hands up and down her body as I watched her. The sight of her touching herself could bring me to come all on its own. If I'd had patience, I'd have ordered her to get on the bed, spread her legs, and make herself come.

"Maybe," I teased, taking my own shirt off. Her hands were on my jeans immediately when I approached her, and she was impatient, too. Because as soon as the button was undone, she stuck her hand under them and grabbed my cock, squeezing tightly.

Fuck, the feel of her.

"How do you want me?" she whispered, running her hand up and down me while her hips moved with the same rhythm.

I pushed off my jeans myself as she played with me and thought about what she asked. How the fuck was I going to choose?

But I knew how. This was about her. Tonight—and

every night, but tonight especially—it was all about her. "I want you to sit on my face first, baby," I said, and when her heart skipped a beat, and she tightened her fists around my cock, I knew it was the right thing to do. I grabbed her ass and slammed her to me, just to hear her moan. "Then, I want you to ride me whichever way you want." I moved my hand lower, between her ass cheeks and down to her wet pussy, growling. Those panties were in my way, but I didn't want to tear them yet. I wanted to eat her pussy with them on first because she'd like that. "And then I'm going to lay you down here, fuck your tits, and your mouth, then flip you over so I can fuck your ass, too. Would you like that?"

"Yes," she breathed without hesitation, pushing her ass back so that my fingers reached all the way to her clit. Fuck, she was so wet, and she was jerking me off so well my knees were shaking a bit.

The moment I lay on the bed, she sat on me, running her hands on my chest. I grabbed her ass and pulled her up, watching her eyes light up the closer her pussy was to my mouth. Fuck, she looked good enough to eat for real in red. In lace. In satin. In *everything,* and especially in *nothing.*

"How do you want it, baby?" I asked when her knees were on either side of my neck. I pressed my thumb over her clit and watched her back arch as she cried out. "Do you want your pussy devoured or worshipped slowly?" Pushing the panties to the side, I ran my tongue over her wet folds. The taste of her was fucking intoxicating, and the swollen bud of her clit felt mighty fine on my tongue. She cried out, already lost to the sensation, and brought her pussy to my mouth.

It was all I could do not to dive in already, but she still hadn't given me an answer, so I held her thighs back for a moment.

"Tell me, Damsel. Do you want to be fucked like a good girl or like a little slut?" I begged, and she didn't hesitate.

"Both," she said, holding onto the bedpost. "I need both."

"Better hold on tight."

I grabbed her hips and brought her pussy down on my mouth. I wanted both, too, but right now, I just needed her to come really fast first. I'd make the second time slower. So, I thrust my tongue inside her as she writhed over me, moving her hips, fucking my mouth while she cried out my name. I'd never felt more powerful than when she screamed out my name like that. I sucked her folds inside my mouth, then her clit, and the taste of her made it really hard to keep half my focus on our surroundings the way I needed.

But I made do. I kept going, desperate to feel her coming, to smell the orgasm on her skin, to feel her shaking between my hands.

I didn't make her wait at all, didn't hold her back as she moved, so it only took her thirty seconds to explode. She cried out my name over and over again, her shaking arms barely holding her up while I kept licking her so that the orgasm would last a long time.

And when she came down to earth again, there would be no time to rest. She'd ride my cock, then I'd fuck those tits that were bouncing fucking magically every time I thrust my tongue inside her.

Then, we would really begin.

CHAPTER
TWENTY-TWO

It had been a while since I picked up a cigarette. I'd honestly forgotten all about it until the guy who sold me the cylinder offered me one. I took it because why the fuck not? I didn't have shit else to do while I waited, anyway.

The sun was at my back, and I hid in the shade of the large chimney of the building in vain. The heat still reached me, but it was okay. I liked the discomfort. The hard part of the day was done. Now, all I had to do was wait. Wait and strain my ears, listen to that heart beating…until it stopped.

Sweat on my forehead. It had been a while since I'd been actually nervous about something like this. Finding Will Thorne and his entourage wasn't hard. We'd driven our car here, too, same as them, so I found them barely two towns away from where we were staying. Picking up Jacob's scent had been easy. I already knew it well enough to recognize it even a day after he'd been at one place. And I knew they'd need to rest, that they'd stop by an inn or a hotel for at least a few hours eventually.

A few hours was all I really needed.

Finding a carbon monoxide cylinder hadn't been difficult, either—all it had taken was a Google search to find a Craig's List entry, a phone number, and the right guy who smoked cigarettes like they were oxygen, not actual poison to his human body.

But the difficult part had been to put it inside Will Thorne's room.

He'd be a light sleeper, I had no doubt about that. And he wasn't alone—another four people slept in the rooms and floors around him. I'd had to climb up to Thorne's balcony, get the half open window to pull up all the way without him hearing me, before I could even put the cylinder inside.

He was a sorcerer, and they had spells to even enhance scents, not to mention the touched sorcerer minions they kept about them at all times. Who knew which one of them had enhanced hearing because of their spirits?

That's why I'd chosen carbon monoxide. It was gonna take a while to kill Thorne—probably about four hours, but it was odorless and invisible, and since the sorcerer was asleep, it would kill him before he had the chance to realize he was being poisoned. Clean. Slow, but effective.

And my promise was perfectly kept. I hadn't laid a hand on him at all.

I lit up the cigarette on the rooftop of the building across the street and looked at the windows of Thorne's room on the fourth floor. I'll admit it wasn't ideal to leave Damsel all alone right now, but her biggest threat was right here. I'd be back in time before she woke up, anyway. By then, the heart that was beating steadily in Thorne's chest —and in my ears—would stop.

And the world would realize, once again, that they shouldn't mess with what is mine. Because I'd find a way. No matter the limits set before me, I'd always find a way.

The consequences didn't really matter. Will Thorne had hurt me and mine. I'd killed men for much less. I'd deal with the outcome of this one way or the other.

Right now, I just enjoyed the cigarette, the discomfort of the heat of the sun at my back, and the gradual slowing of Will Thorne's heartbeat.

Minutes blurred together, and so did hours. My mind was lost out there in the world. In everything that it meant now that I had a purpose. So much to see. So much to do, and I couldn't fucking wait to get started yet.

It was almost two in the afternoon when Will Thorne's heart stopped beating. The cylinder should have been empty by then, too. I couldn't hear it from so far away. And the others were waking up. Jacob Thorne left his room a floor below, and soon he'd climb those stairs, knock on Thorne's door, and when he got no answer, he'd break it. When he broke it, he'd find the lifeless body of the monster disguised as a man on that bed.

It's what I fucking hated the most about people. You're a monster? Fine, fucking be one. Don't pretend. Don't hide. Own it. Don't cower behind big words and masks. Don't fool yourself into thinking you're *good*. Nobody's fucking good.

But my job was finished, so I didn't stick around to see the outcome. I just jumped onto the rooftop of the next building and made my way back to Damsel.

CHAPTER
TWENTY-THREE

NIKKI ARELLA

NORTH DAKOTA.

To be honest, I didn't think I'd get here again under these circumstances. Right now, I was nervous as hell, though. Still another four hours until sunrise, and that meant that we would get to the gates just in time for *everyone* to see us.

Anya would be awake, which I was counting on, but...so would Jones. I had no doubt in my mind that once he found out I was in the Realm, he'd come see me. I'd have to look him in the eyes, and...*what* exactly? What the hell was I going to say? Was I going to accuse him of keeping me isolated from the rest of the world my whole life, for letting me think I was the only one of my kind out there, for letting me feel like a freak with no place to belong...for not telling me that there was actually a chance for me to be *free* of my spirit?

What would be the point, anyway? What happened had

already happened. No amount of talking about it was going to change anything.

"Come here," Ax said, sitting down on the ground, his back to a tree trunk. My body moved without my even having to think about it.

I went and sat on his lap, resting my back to his chest. He wrapped me up tightly in his arms, pressing his cheek to mine, filling me with his warmth. Calming me down better than a magic spell.

It no longer even freaked me out. I no longer felt *guilty* for being relaxed. At least not when I was with Ax. And the voices in my head just kept getting lower and lower when he held me like that.

"It's still exactly as you left it," he said, knowing what I was thinking. He always knew.

"I know, but *I'm* not the same person I was when I left."

"You're not?"

I smiled. "I haven't had a drink in almost three months, for starters."

"Oh, yeah. I noticed that," he teased, kissing the side of my head. I leaned to the side so he could kiss my cheek, too.

"Also, I'm able to control my spirit now." I flinched. "More often than not."

"Mhmm," he said, biting my jaw slowly. "What else?" And I knew exactly what he wanted me to say.

"I don't know..." I teased. "I mean, my hair's longer."

"And?" he pushed, sticking his tongue in my ear, making me laugh.

"I'm more...*mature* now. A proper adult," I continued, and he squeezed me tightly, emptying my lungs. "Stop it!" I said, laughing.

"What else is different about you, Damsel?" he insisted,

biting my neck next, and no matter how hard I thrashed, he didn't let go.

"I know more about magic now. I know—*stop it!*" Fuck, that tingled like hell.

"What more?" he demanded. "I'm not gonna stop until you tell me."

"*You!*" I shouted, body shaking with laughter. And he finally stopped biting that spot under my ear that made me ticklish as fuck. I could hardly breathe. "You, asshole."

"What about me?" And he still didn't loosen his arms from around me.

"*You*'re different. I'm with you."

"*With* me? You're not just *with* me, are you?"

Even though I knew what he wanted to hear, I didn't say it right away. "I am. I'm your girlfriend."

The next second, he pulled me up and spun me around like I weighed less than a feather. I was straddling him, and his arms were around me again.

"You're not my girlfriend," he growled, eyes a bit bloodshot. I loved that I could get to him so easily.

"I'd need a ring on my finger to say *wife*, and we're not exactly mated, so..." I shrugged, running my tongue over his bottom lip. The most delicious thing I'd ever tasted in my life.

"You're not my wife, either. You know what you are," he said, squeezing me tightly. "Say it, Damsel."

"Why would I? You already know," I teased, and he was going to fucking break my ribs.

"Because I want to hear you say it," he insisted.

"You're so insecure, Savage," I said, and he pulled both my lips into his mouth and sucked hard. My hips moved against him on instinct, and I found him half hard already. Damn, the way he played my strings.

"*Yours!*" I said, desperate for some air—and for more room to move against him. His arms loosened a bit instantly. I smiled, taking his face in my hands. "I'm yours, Ax Creed. That's the *biggest* change of all about me," I said, knowing that was exactly what he wanted to hear. It wasn't hard to say it because it was undeniably true, but it was fun to watch him squirm, especially when I knew I could get him there about the exact same thing tomorrow, too. And the day after.

Oh, I was going to have my fun with this guy for the rest of my life.

Grabbing my hips, he pulled them to his, his hard cock pressing against my center, and he devoured my mouth in a burning hot kiss, swallowing my moans as they came. His touch could break me if he willed it, and it showed me how desperate he was for me so well that I'd take all the pain in the world just to have him hold me the way he did every single day. He couldn't live without me. He couldn't breathe without me. His need for me was all consuming, just like mine was for him.

But the heartbeats that were getting closer by the second squashed any hopes I'd had at fucking him against this tree right now. It was okay, though. We were two hours away from home.

And once we got there, and I got everything out of the way, it would be just us, just like at the cabin, for as long as we wanted.

I COUNTED FOUR HEARTBEATS.

By the time Jacob came into the woods, there were only

three men behind him—Ethan in his human form, Ray, and Dylan.

Jacob looked like shit—dark circles under his eyes, a layer of sweat covering his skin, a murderous look in his dark eyes. We waited for them to approach, and Jacob turned a flashlight on, too, because there were no lights around us.

"Where's your uncle?" I asked Jacob, holding a hand in front of my face when he shone his flashlight at me.

He didn't say anything, but his heart did skip a beat, and when he finally stopped in front of me, he squinted his eyes like he was *waiting* for something.

I raised a brow. "What?" Why was he looking at me like that?

And Jacob smiled, shaking his head before he looked at Ax, standing by my side with his arms crossed in front of his chest.

"You're a piece of work, you know that?" Jacob said bitterly.

I looked at Ax, too, and...he refused to meet my eyes.

What the... "Ax?"

"Yes, Damsel?"

"Where's Will?"

At that, he looked at me, pulling his lips inside his mouth like he was trying to keep from *smiling.*

Oh, my gods. My jaw hit the floor. Was he serious right now?

"You *promised!*" I hissed, not even believing the look on his face. "You fucking prick, you promised!"

"I didn't touch him," he said, shaking his head. "I promised that I wouldn't, and I didn't. I swear, I didn't lay a hand on him."

"No, he just poisoned him with carbon monoxide while

he slept," Jacob said, his voice as bitter as the look in his eyes.

For fuck's sake... "Ax, you—"

"He was never gonna live, Damsel," he cut me off, and he did look sorry, but not because he'd done it. He was just sorry because I had to find out about it. "He hurt you. He was *never* going to live."

Fuck. It pissed me off so much I saw red, and when he made to grab my hand, I slapped it away. He'd promised me that he wouldn't touch him—and he knew exactly what that meant. He fucking knew. And he'd gone behind my back to do it?

"We *needed* him," Jacob spit. "We needed him for whatever is in the Hidden Realm."

"We'll make do just fine," Ax said without even looking at him. "We'll be fine, Damsel."

"That's not the fucking point! You promised," I hissed, and I hated that I had to do this in front of Jacob. In front of the others.

"I kept my promise. I also kept the one I made to myself," Ax said instead, raising his chin. "We can waste time talking about it, or we can just get home and get this over with."

There was so much I still wanted to say to him, but I resisted. It was nobody's business what went on between us, but he'd hear all about it as soon as we were alone. Anger coursed through my veins the longer I looked at his face, so I looked away. There was time. I'd make him regret ever going behind my back again. Whatever it took.

"I'm sorry, Jacob," I said, and Ax growled. Actually growled like a fucking animal, but I could pretend he wasn't even there. "That was not part of the deal."

"Not your fault," Jacob said. "We still need to make it to the Realm."

Ax's presence, his stare was like flames licking my skin, but I didn't turn. Didn't even acknowledge he was there. I just looked at the others.

"They're all coming?"

"Yes," Jacob said while the others flinched at the sound of my voice. Not like I gave a shit. "Fallon decided to stay behind after we found Will's body. It's just us." And he wasn't happy about it.

I nodded. "Let's get going."

CHAPTER
TWENTY-FOUR

I didn't talk to him the whole way there. I didn't even look his way at all as we went through the woods. He didn't try to talk to me, either, for which I was thankful. If he did, we'd have an argument right there. He knew it, too. That's why he stayed ten feet behind us the entire way.

The air changed so abruptly, it caught me off guard. I'd forgotten just how much magic surrounded the Hidden Realm, and I jumped back, half expecting a ball of magic to come my way.

Nothing did.

"Home," I whispered to myself when I could make out the dark wooden gates about five feet away, and the walls that surrounded the Realm, covered in green. Jacob and Ray shone their flashlights at it, too. Still another hour to go until sunrise. Plenty of time to talk to everyone, especially that sorceress.

And then we could go...*where*? I turned around to look at Ax standing there with his arms at his sides, watching the edges of the wall of the Realm curiously. Were we going back to his place?

But the look in his eyes...

"What is it?" I asked, recognizing his caution as he slowly came closer.

"They're not here," he said, stepping closer to the gates. He then took his phone out of his pocket. "I texted Robert to send someone for the gates."

"They're probably on their way," I said, not really worried yet, until...

"I texted him an hour ago."

Shit. I watched him put the phone to his ear. "What does that mean exactly? Maybe he was busy and missed the text?"

"Not for this," Ax said, shaking his head as he put his phone down. "His phone is off." Then he proceeded to press something on the screen. I moved closer, the anger halfway forgotten. Something inside me insisted that something wasn't right. Maybe it was the voices, recognizing the magic of the Realm. Maybe it was just my instincts. Either way, it had my jaw itching as my fangs tried to come out. I pushed them back for now.

And then Ax's heart skipped a long beat.

"Off. All their phones are off," he said, putting his phone back in his pocket.

"Can we get in there?" Jacob said, coming closer. "Can you get through the wards?"

"There are ways," Ax said. "There are weak points. All of which takes time." He looked at Jacob. "Unless you break the ward."

Jacob raised his brows, shocked. "Are you joking? It's the Hidden Realm. Of course, I can't break the ward. That would mean every vampire in there would be free to come out."

The next second, I was in front of him because it

seemed to me that he wasn't quite understanding the situation there.

"Jacob, vampires are always up at nighttime. They never turn off their phones."

"You don't know that," he said, shaking his head.

"You've got Abraham Jones's number, don't you?" Ax told him. "Give him a call."

Jacob opened and closed his mouth a couple of times, unsure of what to say. The fear in him grew, I could see it in his tired eyes.

"Do it, Jay," Ethan said from behind him. "Because something feels off here."

Jacob finally took his phone out of his pocket. I turned my back to him and looked at Ax, who seemed almost as worried as he had been when he had that bomb around his neck.

"What is it?" I wondered, not really expecting an answer. He gave me one anyway.

"Alida," he whispered, and chills washed down my back. That sorceress...

"Off," Jacob said from behind me. My fangs came out all at once, and I didn't even try to hold them back.

Ax grabbed my hand and pulled me to the side, his eyes on Jacob. "Do it."

"If there's something in there—" he started, shaking his head, but I didn't let him finish.

"If there's something in there, we won't get to it until it's too late."

Ethan growled behind him, pulling his white shirt off. The next second, he began to shift without warning. Grey fur sprouted from his skin all at once, and his bones broke —I *heard* them. He whined a couple of times as he fell to the ground, half covered by the overgrown grass. The process was almost the same as *my* shifting, except when it was over, Ethan became a wolf. A large wolf howling at the dark sky.

"Goddamn it," Jacob spit, throwing his bag to the ground. "Stand back."

He stepped closer to the gates, and Ray and Dylan followed, while Ethan's wolf slowly moved to the other side, sniffing the wall, his footsteps barely there.

"What do you see when you look at him?" Ax whispered to me, nodding at the wolf as he moved farther away.

"A werewolf." Literally—that was it.

"Do you see a monster?"

"No. I mean, technically, he is, but it's not bad. He's just...*touched*." Fallon had green hair and scales on her skin, but even she didn't really look like a monster. Just touched by something foreign.

Ax squeezed my fingers tightly. "You don't look half as bad as that."

I rolled my eyes. "That's not like me."

"It's *exactly* like you."

"My spirit is different."

"Your spirit is a spirit," he insisted. "And you keep referring to it as *the monster*. You shouldn't."

"Are you seriously gonna pull that psychology bullshit on me right now?" Because Jacob and Dylan had already begun chanting while Ray shone the flashlight on the symbols they'd drawn on the wood of the gates with chalk. The magic in the air was intensifying, too.

"It's not bullshit—it's the truth. He actually looks kinda cool, and you look even better," Ax said, eyes on Ethan who was making his way back to the gates slowly.

I looked, too, and he took advantage of my distraction, then snaked his arm around my waist, pulling me to him.

"Hey—I'm still mad at you," I said, but it was useless. He kissed me anyway.

"That's okay," he mumbled. "Be mad. I don't mind."

"You killed him behind my back."

"I didn't. Technically, you were sleeping," the asshole said.

"Technically, you're a fucking prick," I hissed, and all I managed to do was make him pull me closer.

But before our lips touched again, the magic in the air whistled, making us break apart. Heat waves crashed onto us, and they were coming straight from the wall—from where Jacob and Dylan had been chanting at the symbols on the gates.

"It's not gonna hold," Jacob said, breathing so hard I was afraid he might pass out. "We need to get in there, now!"

"Get the skinny one," Ax said. Before I could blink, he had Jacob over his shoulder and jumped right on top of the Realm's wall.

Ethan's heart-stopping howl made chills run down my back as he jumped, too.

Cursing under my breath, I materialized behind Dylan before he could turn to me. I grabbed him by the arm and jumped.

Quiet.

Way too quiet for this time of night. We were in the Hidden Realm and the magic still infused the air, but there was no soul in sight around us. No heartbeat in our proximity.

"It's cool," I said, more to myself than to anyone. "We're

at the very edge of the city. It's a five-minute walk to the main road." And then we could see better, probably every vampire here, hiding from us because…*why*? Because somehow, I really didn't believe that they'd planned a surprise party for us.

My heart was skipping too many beats to count.

"Let's run," Ax said, preparing to move forward, but I grabbed his hand. We weren't alone. If we left Jacob and the others to fend for themselves here, that would be plain cruel. Yes, they could absolutely handle themselves, but in a place with over ten thousand vampires?

"We can't. We have to walk, stay close to them," I reminded Ax, and he flinched at the sight of the sorcerers—and the werewolf—as if he'd suddenly forgotten they were even there.

But he knew just as well as I did that it was way too dangerous for them, at least until we knew what was going on here, so he forced himself to nod.

"Let's see how fast you can walk," he told them, and we all rushed deeper into the woods, toward the main street, secretly praying that what we found in there wouldn't be as bad as we all feared.

CHAPTER
TWENTY-FIVE

It was worse than any of us feared. Not a single soul around us when we reached the road, or when we hurried along it to get to the heart of the Realm. The closer we got to the first row of buildings, the clearer it became that there was something very wrong here. Vampires were in their beds, all of them breathing, their hearts beating...all of them unconscious, but not naturally. Magic hung onto their bodies like it did on the gates of the Realm. All these people had been spelled to remain unconscious even at nightfall. For how long had they been like that? Jacob couldn't tell, and I really didn't want to know. Not when Anya was here. And Marie and Marcus, too.

Had it gotten to Jones, too? Because the idea terrified me.

We went deeper into the city, barely whispering any words to one another, and I thought we'd have a hard time finding whoever was responsible for this, but we didn't. We didn't even have to try—we found out when we reached the main square right in the middle of the city.

The square was set with cobblestones, with benches

and lampposts to the sides, patches of grass and flowers growing here and there. A large square piece of stone was in the very middle of it, with the name of the Hidden Realm engraved on it, and the date on which it was created. Nothing special about the looks of it, but when vampires were awake, they made it so. There were people who played instruments, others who played cards, and hung out with friends after work until dawn. It was always loud and crowded in the square.

Except tonight.

Tonight, only three people were here.

Marie sat cross-legged on the ground, eyes closed, arms raised by her sides as she whispered words I didn't understand. Her dark hair floated around her as if she were underwater.

And across from her stood a woman I'd never seen before. Her grey hair was tied up in a bun behind her head, her grey dress covering her all the way down to her ankles, and her wrinkled hands didn't shake as the dark green magic came out of her palms, spinning around her feet before it disappeared into the asphalt underneath her.

To their side sat Marcus, arms around his knees, his wide eyes on me. He wasn't afraid—on the contrary. He just looked surprised to see me.

I stepped closer, unsure what to even think yet as the voices in my head became louder. The spirit wanted control, but I pushed it back. It wasn't time yet—I needed to know more. I needed to understand.

The others were right behind me, but before I took another step closer, Jacob grabbed me by the arm and stopped me.

"Don't," he whispered.

"I just need to—"

"It will burn you," he cut me off. "That magic...it will burn you. It's way too strong." And he sounded in fucking awe.

But I'd witnessed worse. The magic close to that cave, to that contaminated lake in Arizona...*that* had been so much more than this. The same spicy feel, the same *flavor* to it, but this had a bit less intensity. And my spirit could feel it much more clearly than me.

"Can you break through?" Ax asked, eyes stuck on Alida. On Marie.

"No," Jacob spit, looking at him with all the hatred in the world. "My uncle could have."

"Your uncle isn't here," Ax said calmly. "Stand back, Damsel."

But I wasn't going to. "Just hold on a second," I said, eyes on Marie's face, hoping she'd look at me. "Marie!" I called, not even sure she could hear me through all that magic. "Marie, it's me, Nikki!"

Her eyes finally opened. She saw me, barely fifteen feet away from her, and she looked positively shocked.

The other woman opened her eyes, too.

I could have sworn that time stood perfectly still while they analyzed every inch of me, as if they were trying to make sure that I was really here. That we all were.

"What are you doing?!" I called at the top of my lungs.

None of them answered me, only kept staring at us.

I pushed forward, jerking my arm away from Jacob. The magic pushed me back, but I resisted. It burned my skin but not enough to make me back off.

"Marie! What the hell are you doing?!" I tried again.

She finally stood up, slowly turning to me.

"You're alive," she whispered.

"Of course, I'm alive," I spit. "What are you doing? What have you done to everyone?"

And Marie smiled at me, leaning her head to the side like she was suddenly looking at a *child*.

"We're doing what should have been done a long time ago, Nikki," she said, her sweet voice, light as a breeze. "I'm sorry—you weren't supposed to see this at all. You were supposed to be dead." Then her eyes moved to the side, to where Ax was standing. "And so were you."

I shook my head, disbelief still clouding my mind. "We saved you."

But at that, she chuckled. "You didn't *save* me, Nikki. You simply played your part."

My *part*? What the hell was my part?

"What—" but I was cut off.

"That's enough."

The sorceress had stopped producing that green smoke from her hands, too. I assumed that was Alida Morgans. "You are interrupting something very important. I would ask you to leave, but I'm afraid I can't let you do that anymore."

Suddenly, she raised both her hands our way.

Jacob stepped in front of us before we could blink.

"Alida Morgans, huh," he said, raising his own hands. "I would suggest you save your energy. I wear the Magma."

The old woman's grey brows shot up. "A Thorne," she said, as if that made perfect sense to her and she was delighted. Maybe that's what Jacob's family heirloom spell was called—a Magma.

"What is the point of this? What exactly are you trying to do with all this magic? And how..." Jacob looked around the empty streets, the lampposts burning orange every few feet. "How are you doing that? This is the Hidden Realm."

And it was a damn good question to ask. I looked at Ax, hoping he'd somehow have an answer, but he didn't. He just growled, intertwining his fingers with mine, squeezing so hard I thought he might break my bones.

But I knew what that touch meant. He was preparing. He was telling me to prepare, too.

A fight was going to break out here any second now. That was inevitable. But how were we going to fight this woman when she had all that magic wrapped around her?

"This is the point of the Hidden Realm," the sorceress said, raising her chin as a small smile played on her lips.

"I don't understand," Jacob said. "Why would you fake your own death? Why come here? Just...*why*?" But did it matter?

Not to me, not anymore. They'd made their choices. Whatever they'd done to the vampires here, they could *undo* it, too. And if they couldn't, then when they died, Jacob would do it. I knew he would—he was a *good* guy like that.

"I *really* wish you hadn't killed Thorne right now," I hissed, and Ax flinched.

"Me, too," he admitted reluctantly.

As much of a prick that he was, Will Thorne was the most powerful sorcerer I'd ever met. And *my* prick had fucking killed him with carbon monoxide. Go figure.

"Any way around it?" I wondered, though I could see that there wasn't.

"Nothing. The magic goes all around," Ax whispered, just as the sorceress began speaking again.

"Because the world is suffering from these parasites, Thorne," she said in a honey-sweet voice. "And there is no way all sorcerers can unite to get rid of them. I saw it all when I was barely a girl." And she closed her eyes, bringing her hands to her chest. "I saw a world free of vampires. I saw a world as it was always meant to be." She sighed. "Did you know that vampires are a product of sorcerers? An *experiment* with the wrong spirits, with the wrong spells. *We* made them with our own hands. It is up to us to get rid of them, don't you think?"

That's how I knew she was fucking crazy.

"No worries, though. I have a plan. I'm going to see it through." And she opened her palms to the ground again.

"Fuck you," I told her, shaking my head. "You're not gonna see anything through."

And the woman…burst out laughing.

"Nicole," she said in that sweet voice of hers. "Did you know that I summoned the same spirit that lives in you right now?"

What the…

"I did. And it was supposed to come to me, but instead it somehow found you." And she smiled brightly, showing me all of her yellowed teeth. "It's because nature has a way of making better decisions for us, even when we don't know it. I thought it was best to get you out of here for this, which is why I had Jones send you out there, but it's okay. I see your purpose now. There's always a purpose to everything—we just have to keep our eyes and minds open to see it."

My gods, she meant every word.

This woman was responsible for the spirit that lives inside me? Was she fucking kidding me?

"You know—Jacob told me about people like you and I honestly didn't believe him because who in the world is that stupid?" Summoning spirits and trying to actually *use* them? Had she no idea about the kind of power she was trying to play with?

"I've sacrificed my life for this," the sorceress said. "I've given up everything to stand here tonight. It was my purpose since the day I was born. I'll admit it took me much longer than I'd have liked, but everything is falling into place now." And she leaned her head to the side as she smiled at me. "I'm sorry, dear. But it's all clear to me now. You're here because you needed to be. Because to finish this, it seems..." she smiled so wickedly, my knees shook. "I will need that spirit, after all." And she raised her both her hands at me.

My heart skipped a long beat. Ax grabbed my arm and pulled me behind him. Jacob moved, too.

And I jumped back, my instincts taking over. The spirit taking over.

But...it wasn't fast enough.

The white cloud of magic expanded as it came for me. I stepped to the side, determined to get all around them, but the more I moved, the bigger the cloud became, and when it was close enough, it sort of wrapped all around me in a way I'd *never* seen magic do before. It *chased* me like it had a mind of its own, and when I jumped to get out of the circle of smoke that was closing in around me, it *grabbed* me by my feet. The moment it touched me, my entire body froze in place, and I fell on the ground like a sack of potatoes.

My spirit lost it. The screams in my head became so loud they hurt me physically. Gritting my teeth, I squeezed my eyes shut to push the pain away and gave every ounce of control up so the spirit could take over. It was perfectly clear to me that I couldn't win against that woman on my own. I needed the spirit. I needed the magic it could give me, the strength, the endurance.

And the spirit came forth.

Except...something was wrong. The pain was there, I

felt it in my bones, a different kind from what the white magic was causing me, but it was also not the same as the pain I always felt when I shifted. I'd done it so many times these past few months that I recognized it perfectly—and *this* wasn't it.

A howl somewhere close to me made my eyes pop open, but I couldn't see anything through the white smoke that was spinning around me. I heard my name being called, recognized Ax's voice, but no matter how hard I tried to move, my body refused to obey my commands.

My body refused to obey my spirit's commands, too.

A screeching cry exploded in my mind, and it felt like it ran a knife right through my brain, cut my skull in half. My limbs were locked, my senses barely working, and something kept digging into my chest, trying to pull my heart right out of my ribcage.

Not—*not* my heart. Something else. Something...more.

The spirit's cry took over my mind again, and I felt its fear. I felt its panic. I felt *all* of it as if it were mine. In those moments, it *was* mine, except it didn't last. Because something inside me snapped, and the magic, way too powerful to even try to stop it, pulled.

The spirit cut off from me.

It felt like having a knife inside your body. The object is foreign at first, but in time you get used to the blade. It becomes a part of you, even if you don't realize it. And then all of a sudden, something pulls it out of you all at once.

And you realize that that fucking blade was the only thing keeping your body together, keeping you from falling apart.

Without it, you're just going to break to pieces.

That's what it felt like I was doing—breaking to pieces. Every cell in my body had caught fire. I was burning and I was frozen at the same time. Ax's voice reached my ears again as if from another world, but I couldn't respond. I couldn't hold onto it. I was coming apart because the spirit was being ripped right out of me.

And in that last moment that I was conscious...that I was *alive*, what Jacob said to me made perfect sense—I would not survive being separated from my spirit. Fuck ten percent—I would die without a doubt.

That hadn't been what had changed my mind about it, though. Being unable to keep Ax safe on my own had made me give up on that idea, and now look at me. It hadn't even been my choice. That sorceress had simply taken my life from me, and now I wouldn't be here at all to make sure Ax made it.

Ironically, my ending made perfect sense with the way I'd lived—just a bunch of fucked up things thrown together with no rhyme or reason. Tragedy. Horror. A fucking comedy, too. I'd always been powerless against everything that life had thrown at me. It had never been my choice—not to be turned, not to be touched, not to be thrust out there into the world again.

This wasn't my choice, either, but I had no more fight left in me. Not when I knew how little it would matter if I tried.

The only thing I could do was pray and let go.

CHAPTER
TWENTY-SIX

Ax Creed

THE MAGIC SLIPPED into my nostrils, into my pores, invading my body within seconds. I pushed forward anyway, even though I couldn't see anything, until I slammed onto something and hit the ground on my side hard.

My mind buzzed, heart almost beating out of my chest. It all happened too fucking fast. I always thought I was good enough at reading people so that I could never truly be caught off guard. I'd been dead wrong because Alida Morgans had pulled my string like a master, and I'd be a liar if I said I saw it coming. The siblings, too. Fuck, Marie and even Marcus had known exactly how to talk to me. Exactly how to make me believe what they needed me to believe. I'd had them in my house. Had fed them. Had protected them. Damsel had almost given her life for them...and for what?

I blinked and the magic moving past me was a shock in

its bright red color. A wolf howled, and people chanted spells, the air growing heavier by the second.

But...Damsel was right there. I looked up and she was on the ground on her back, eyes closed, arms spread to the sides, no more of that white smoke that had wrapped around her.

She hadn't shifted. My gods, she hadn't fucking shifted.

Why? Her heart was beating but only barely. She was breathing way too slowly.

Shift! I wanted to shout, but I just pushed myself up on all fours instead. And when I did...I saw. Through the corner of my eye, I saw the shape in the air, being pulled closer to the circle that surrounded Alida and the siblings. It was yellow and glowy, an outline of something like a cross between a feline beast and a person. Something that looked almost identical to Damsel when her spirit took over her and shifted her physical body.

The world shut down completely for me in that second. I watched the spirit floating closer and closer to Alida as she chanted, pulling it to her, and I knew exactly what had happened.

She'd taken the spirit out of Damsel.

She'd fucking pulled it right out of her, and what did Damsel say? That there was a ninety percent chance she'd die if she got separated from her spirit?

I moved before I even realized it. Her face was in my hands, and I was calling her name, though reality had taken on a different quality. Not exactly like a dream, but not *real*, either. It felt like I was on the brink of exploding into a million pieces. Damsel, dead. *Again.* Not something I wanted to acknowledge, feel, live with.

No.

"Damsel!" I called, slapping her pale cheeks, shaking her shoulders.

And by some miracle, her eyes opened.

Shouts around me. Screams and howls—hisses of magic launching in the air, but none of it mattered.

"Look at me," I told her, bringing my face right in front of hers. My gods, she was barely breathing.

"Ax…"

"Bite me, baby," I said, bringing my face to her neck, and hers to mine. "Bite me!"

"No, I—"

"You no longer have the spirit in you. You will be stronger if we're mated. *Please*, bite me!" I begged like I had never done before in my life.

And I didn't wait. I sank my fangs into her neck the next second, screw everything else. She cried weakly, and her entire body jerked in my arms. Her blood in my mouth was different from anything I'd ever tasted before. It wasn't just blood—it was *life*. It was her, her essence, her very soul running down my throat, filling up my veins, rushing all over me. The power that came with it was like a blinding white light going off in the center of my mind, and I didn't even realize that she'd bitten me, too, until I felt her sucking my blood.

Her hold on my arms became stronger, fingers digging into me as we took from one another, both of us wide open, just as we had been months ago. It had come naturally to want to share my body, my mind, my strength with her since that night, and to resist it had been torture.

Not anymore. I felt her growing in my mind's eye. I felt her heart beating faster, her lungs expanding same as mine. I felt every inch of her body as if she lived inside me…

And that's why I felt it the second her heart skipped a beat, too.

She let go of me and fell back on the ground, eyes squeezed shut, my blood in her mouth, coating her fangs, dripping down her chin. Her heart slowed down to a crawl all over again, and she lost control of her fingers. She lost control of her mind, too.

"Damsel," I called, so full of what *she* was feeling, what her body was going through, it was easy to forget that I had a body of my own, too. Right now, all that mattered was her heart, barely pumping blood. Her lungs, barely filling up. Her mind, a black void. Her life slipping right out of her limp fingers.

She wasn't going to make it.

No amount of my calling out her name, shaking her, was making a difference. Fuck—she'd bitten me. My blood was in her veins, hers in mine. We'd mated. I *felt* all of her like I'd never felt anyone before. We were one.

Wasn't that supposed to make us both *stronger*? Wasn't that supposed to make her open her eyes, get up, fucking talk to me?

I think I shouted, but I wasn't sure. It was all very chaotic in my mind. It felt like nothing reached me as I held Damsel against my chest, willing her to hold on with all my being, even though I knew it wouldn't work.

It was already done.

But the glow behind my closed eyelids faded out of existence in an instant, drenching the world in darkness again. My eyes snapped open, and I saw Alida Morgans with her head thrown back, screaming her guts out at the sky, falling to her knees as her body shook.

Her skin turned a couple of shades paler within seconds, and black veins appeared, like someone was spilling ink all over her. Her eyes changed, became black, and her fingernails turned to black claws, too.

She stopped screaming, chest rising and falling fast as she struggled to make it to her feet. She hadn't quite transformed like Damsel did—she wasn't hunched over—but the eyes and the skin and the claws were the same. That fucking sorceress had taken Damsel's spirit right into herself.

And now she smiled, looking at Jacob and the others who were throwing magic her way, never managing to break through the magic protecting her. They were no match for her at all. She'd done a fucking great job convincing Robert and Jones and even *me* that she was weak, merely a seer.

A small reason why she needed to die now, but a reason, nonetheless.

"Hold on, baby," I whispered to Damsel, kissing her forehead. She wasn't conscious, she couldn't hear me, and she was slowly fading away, but I couldn't help her if I stayed here. I couldn't do shit if I didn't get up. "I'll be right back. Just hold on for me," I begged, then put her on the ground slowly. Fuck, she looked so breathtaking like that. Like she was simply sleeping.

The sky was turning grey with daylight. Not that it mattered. I ran too fast for anyone to see and slammed my fists onto the magic. It burned my skin and threw me back just as fast. I didn't lose my balance, though, and I saw everything in perfect clarity. I had no idea if it was the mating instinct or just the fact that I was about to lose Damsel again and the monster in me was more focused than ever before, but I saw the small currents that went through the shield of magic, and I saw where they were weakest, too.

I *saw* the fabric of magic, and it felt like the blood in my veins suddenly *burned*, too. Like it was infused with it.

Was it possible that it was the residue from the spirit, the same thing that Jacob said would *kill me* when he found us in that cave, a second away from mating?

Was it going to kill me?

If it would, it had to wait until Damsel was okay first.

"Is she alive?!" Jacob said, grabbing my arm as the two men kept on trying to get through the magic—and the wolf slammed against it, too. No luck.

"For now," I told the sorcerer. "She will need that spirit back inside her, Jacob. That woman needs to die."

Jacob shook his head, completely disoriented. "We won't know the spirit will go back inside her."

I grabbed him by the arm and pulled him in front of me. "Then we make sure it does," I hissed. "We lock it in with Damsel until it does."

"It's *a spirit!* We don't know how it will behave and if Nikki isn't even conscious—" But I didn't want to fucking hear it.

"I will show you where to attack. I will kill that sorceress. All you have to do is lock us up together." I pulled him closer until I could clearly see the fear in his wide eyes. "Do it fast, or she dies."

He cared about Damsel. I knew he had feelings for her. He didn't want her dead.

He would fucking help because he *wanted* to, because right now, I couldn't force him to do shit.

"Okay," he finally said, pushing my hand away. "Okay, we'll do that. But Alida needs to be stopped. She's trying to pull out a Vein right here, Ax. If she does that, every vampire in the Realm will die. Nothing will be able to stop those spirits—you saw them in Arizona."

And he thought I gave a shit about other vampires or other spirits?

"If she dies, every vampire *and* every sorcerer in the world will die, too. You have my word on that." If he didn't believe it, that would be on him. "Now, *move.*"

I let go of the sorcerer and started running all around the shield of magic protecting Alida and the siblings. I made it to the other side, following the currents like tiny snakes going up and down the magic. And I saw exactly where the weakest spot was.

"Hey, Ax." I looked to the side, to Marcus standing just inside the shield. "I'm really sorry, man. I am. It's just how it's supposed to be—nothing personal." And he shrugged.

I grinned for his sake. "I was never really a believer in doing things the way they're supposed to be done, kid. I'd rather make my own fucking choices."

He shook his head and watched me like he was *sorry* for me, but it was okay. I knew exactly how to get through to that woman, and Jacob and his friends were already beside me.

"Right there," I told them, pointing up at the magic. I wasn't sure how much they could see, but it shouldn't have been hard to just hit it in that general area or close to it.

"Two seconds!" Jacob called as red smoke gathered in all their hands. I moved, slamming my fists right where the magic shield was weakest, and it pushed me back just in time for the three spells to hit it at the same place, at the same time.

The ground shook, groaning like a monster. It almost knocked me down, too.

"Again!" Jacob shouted, and I could see the way the magic had grown a bit *thinner* right where we'd all hit it. It had lost its glow, too.

It was working, and Alida and Marie knew it. That's why they both turned to us, though they kept on chanting. The asphalt between them had already cracked, and something underneath it was glowing.

But the sorcerers threw their red magic at the shield again. And again.

I waited, fangs ready, the plan clear in my mind. The wolf was beside me, teeth bared as he growled, waiting for the moment to jump, too. I looked at him, at the grey fur, his wide yellow eyes. He was pretty fucking terrifying in his own right, and he would be able to kill at least Marie, if not Marcus, too.

The red magic slammed onto the shield for the fifth time, and finally, we heard the crack. I was counting on that until I was done with Alida.

The wolf howled. When I jumped, he jumped with me, and we slammed onto the shield hard. I thought it would throw me back again at least a couple of more times, but it gave. It felt like it peeled the skin from my flesh, but it let us through. We were on the other side.

Hisses and growls, chanting of spells filled my ears, and the sky was getting lighter by the minute, but my eyes were sharp. My mind was sharp.

And I didn't really need to see much to wrap my arms around Alida Morgan and slam her to the ground on the other side. Claws sank into my chest even before I made it to my feet, but the pain barely registered. I slammed my fist onto her face, and she hissed, black eyes rolling in her skull for a moment.

The wolf and the other sorcerers were already onto Marie and Marcus. Marcus, whom I thought *couldn't* fight, didn't have enough magic or knowledge. Turns out, he could take care of himself just fine. Both of them could.

Not that it mattered. It took me a good minute to be able to grab Alida by the neck, then drag her all the way to where Damsel was lying on the ground. She thrashed and clawed at my forearms, trying to get away, but she wasn't as strong as Damsel had been. Maybe it was her age, or maybe it was because Damsel's spirit had barely been in her minutes, but I was able to drag her without dying.

"Jacob!" I shouted and saw him approaching from the corner of my eye, but I couldn't look away from Alida.

"Do you realize what you're dealing with here?" she said, and though her voice was transformed, it wasn't as robotic as Damsel's had been those few times I'd heard her speak through the spirit. "You can't stop this. It's the fate of this world. *Nobody* can. It's already set in motion!"

I slammed my forehead to her nose. Blood exploded as I held her down to the ground, pushing my knee on her chest. She laughed like a maniac as she tried to push me away.

"You should have never existed! You bloodsucking parasites, you should have never existed!"

"I need more blood," Jacob hissed from behind me, and I turned to see him drawing fucking symbols on the asphalt with the blood from his hands.

I let go of Alida just for a second, then ran my fangs through my forearm deep enough so that the wound wouldn't close for at least a few minutes.

Then, I let my blood drip to the ground next to me. Jacob moved, picking up the thick blood from the asphalt with his fingers, and drawing his symbols all around Damsel, Alida, and me.

"You're a traitor," Alida was saying. "Going behind your own kind's back? You're a traitor, boy! There's a special place in hell for the likes of you!" And she laughed some more.

To his credit, Jacob ignored her perfectly. When he finally drew all around us, he raised his hands and began to whisper words.

It was now or never.

I grabbed Alida's hair with one hand, held back her arms with the other, then I bit into her neck, intending to tear through her flesh until her head was completely cut off.

Except it didn't go as I planned.

I thought I had her. I thought she wouldn't be able to move me, but she did. She pushed me up and slammed me to the ground before I could blink. A greenish yellow shimmer was spreading to our sides, growing and growing until it met a few feet in the air, locking us up.

"Ax!" Jacob shouted, but I couldn't see him because Alida was trying to sink her claws in my face, in my neck, and she wouldn't stop moving for a second.

The sun was already peeking through the horizon, too, and half my vision went with it. Half my strength.

Screams reached my ears from the distance. Jacob stated running back to the others.

"Your time has already come," Alida told me, smiling widely as she sank her claws in my gut then twisted her hand. The pain took my breath away, but if she thought I was going to give up, she was in for the surprise of her life.

I didn't care if she cut me to fucking pieces—she was giving that spirit back to Damsel. It belonged to her. She was going to *live,* even if none of us made it.

The monster already had full control of my body. The thirst from the bloodlust helped, so that when I grabbed her hand and pushed it back, I did it with enough strength that her bone broke instantly. The pain didn't affect her that much—all she did was hiss. But it distracted her long enough for me to push her to the side, and she fell right on top of Damsel's chest on her back.

I didn't think, didn't allow myself to try to make sense of any of it, or even formulate a plan. I just let the monster do what it needed to do, so that it even surprised *me* when I jumped to my feet and slammed the heel of my boot to Alida's chin with all my strength.

Her jaw broke. She screamed and growled and hissed as I grabbed her by the ankle and pulled her off Damsel's chest. She tried to move away when I kicked her again, but there was no place to go. The magic Jacob had locked us in was right there. But she still tried to get out, so when I grabbed her hair and pushed her head to the side, then bit her neck hard, she was too distracted to stop me.

It only took me one second to bite half of her neck off. The taste of her blood in my mouth was foul, especially after I'd tasted Damsel's. I spit it out when I stood up, but my legs gave. The sun fell on my face, and I barely saw, but I could hear just fine. I could hear that Alida's heart no longer beat.

Damsel's was even slower than it had been five minutes ago.

And...Alida's dead body transformed yet again. The veins disappeared from her skin, and the claws retreated, becoming fingernails again. Her eyes turned back to blue, too, as she stared at the sky but didn't see anything, half her face broken, her neck almost completely torn apart.

The spirit that was inside her slowly slipped out of her —right out of her mouth. I watched it, mesmerized as the yellow light expanded and began to take shape. It fucking hypnotized me to watch its eyes, its ears, its claws that looked even sharper made out of light like that.

I thought I heard my name being called, but I couldn't move. Couldn't stop staring at it as it floated in the air, its small yellow eyes locked on me. My heart skipped a long beat when it moved slowly, *toward* me. I wanted to talk, to tell it to get to Damsel—she was lying right there!

But the spirit kept coming, locking me in place with every movement, and—

"For fuck's sake—move!"

A hand grabbed the back of my shirt and pulled me hard.

I slipped through the magic that set every cell in my body on fire, then hit the asphalt on my back.

"What the fuck were you waiting for?!" Jacob shouted, slowly making it back to his feet. I did, too, but I had no answer for him.

The sun was up in the sky, and the spirit was right there, separated by that shield, locked inside with only Damsel and the dead body of Alida to get to. But it still watched me, like it wanted to fucking tell me something.

Bile rose up my throat. If Jacob hadn't taken me out, would that spirit have come inside *me*? Would it have let Damsel to die?

Don't think, I urged myself.

"C'mon, c'mon, c'mon," Jacob chanted at himself, arms at the ready as he watched the spirit slowly float around the magic shield, as if testing it, as if searching for a breaking point.

But it never really attacked. The next second, it moved lower, closer to Damsel's body. Her chest barely rose as she breathed, halfway dead already. But the spirit was there. It would get inside her—what other choice did it have? If

Damsel died, Jacob would banish it. It wouldn't be here on Earth anymore.

Did it know that? Did it care?

It felt like an eternity until it began to slip inside Damsel's slightly parted lips and through her nostrils. The yellow light of it disappeared completely, and Damsel's heart stopped beating. She stopped breathing, too.

I moved closer, the heat of the magic searing my skin, but I didn't care. I needed to see. I needed to know that she would make it. Then, I could let go. Anybody could do anything with me—I just needed to know that she would make it.

The moment her eyes snapped open, and she took in a sharp breath like she'd been drowning until now, my legs gave up on me.

"Nikki?" Jacob called from my side. "Nikki, is that you?"

Damsel turned her eyes toward him. Toward me.

My gods, she looked like she was seeing ghosts. She was shocked, her pale cheeks hollow, barely any color in her eyes still. I laughed, my shoulders shaking as Jacob asked her again if it was *her*. Of course, it was—did he not have eyes? It was Damsel. It was my Damsel.

And she was alive.

All my lights went off.

Chapter
TWENTY-SEVEN

Nikki Arella

BLOOD. That was it—he'd just lost a lot of blood and had been exposed to a shitload of magic, too, so that's why he was sleeping. Yeah, he didn't do that, not even when the sun was up, but this time it was different. Like that time when I slept with him. Just...*different.*

Because Ax's heart still beat. And he was breathing. He was there—just not awake yet. But he would be.

"How are you feeling?" Jacob asked, though he was in *much* worse shape than me, wounded in several places. He'd lost a lot of blood, too.

At least he was alive. So were Ethan and Ray. Dylan didn't make it, though. Marie killed him.

But she and her brother didn't make it, either.

"Like I came back from the dead." Which was funny because I'd truly believed that I'd died.

Until the spirit somehow slipped back into me and forced my mind to turn *on* with all that screaming. It was still trying to scream right now, locked up in my head like always, but it was so ridiculously easy to ignore, it made me smile.

"You did, technically," Jacob said. "What a fucking mess."

I turned around to look at the center of the square, at the large grey wolf walking around the cracked asphalt, sniffing as he went. No vampire was up yet, but it was daylight, so that was a given. It wasn't all that difficult for me to be up right now, which I suspect had everything to do with the fact that Ax wasn't waking up yet, but soon, he would. And soon, I'd lay right there on the sidewalk with him, hidden in the shade of a three-story building, and sleep, too.

"So, she literally was trying to bring up a Vein? Right here?" And I thought *I* had problems.

"Turns out, she created the Realm for that. Which is funny because, technically speaking, this place is sort of like a limbo. Like a portal. A backdoor straight into the Ley lines," Jacob said, shaking his head.

"So, why didn't anybody see it?" Vampires, other sorcerers?

"Because it fit us all. You guys were free from us and spirits, and we were free of you. Nobody cared to dig deeper. It just worked, so we all took it."

I nodded. "It still works...right?"

"Should work, yes. Though I'll still need to do some tests, some extra spells here." And he flinched. "She brought up that Vein almost completely. I was able to put a lock on it, but I'm not sure how long it will hold. I wasn't exactly at my strongest when I cast that spell." He looked at me almost like he was sorry. "You think your rulers will let me come back here? Because I need to speak to others out there, tell them what happened. I'm pretty sure they will want to make sure that nothing like this ever happens again, too."

I grinned. "I'd love to see any of them try to stop you." They'd have to go through me first.

I was pretty sure Ax would get in their way, too.

"Good," Jacob said, nodding, before he smiled sadly at me. "I'm sorry, Nikki."

"I'm sorry, too. I'm sorry I wasn't here to help you guys out. I'm sorry I just made it harder for you instead." The guilt had settled on my shoulders, but it wasn't as suffocating as I thought it would be. It wouldn't be until Ax woke up.

Jacob chuckled. "Trust me, the best thing that could have happened was for you to almost die."

"That wasn't very nice for a *good guy*, asshole," I teased.

"No—I mean it. This man really doesn't like it when people come after you." He nodded at Ax, lying next to me on the asphalt. "I'm pretty sure if Alida hadn't taken your spirit, he wouldn't have killed her the way he did. She would have killed all of us instead."

I grinned, my heart fucking swelling in my chest as I laced my fingers with Ax's. He was still asleep, so he didn't squeeze back, but it was okay. His heart was still beating.

"He really is something." He was *everything*.

"He's still a bad man, you know," Jacob muttered.

"I know." I always did. "But he can do better." And right now, as I watched him sleeping so peacefully, I really believed that.

"You want to *change* him?" Jacob asked, brows raised at me.

"Ugh—gods, no. Of course not. He's perfect," I said, way too soon, and he rolled his eyes. "No, I just mean I can *guide* him. I can…I don't know, just give him something to do." Like *me*, for example. All day, every day.

Fuck, I couldn't believe I almost lost him. And he almost lost me.

"What a mess," Jacob repeated, shaking his head. "But right now, I need a bed. Ray and Ethan do, too. It'll just be a few hours, and hopefully we'll be able to reinforce that spell before nightfall so we can get the hell out of here. We'll still need to come back, but that will be a problem for another day."

I smiled. "Of course. And I wouldn't worry about that at all. I owe you my life. So much more than that." I owed him Ax's life, too. "You'll always be safe when I'm around, Jacob. Pinkie swear." And I offered him my pinkie.

Smiling, he linked his to mine. "We make a good team, don't we?"

"We make a hell of a team, actually. No more Vein. No more trouble with my spirit. We did everything we made that deal to do, didn't we?" It hadn't exactly worked out the way we thought, but it *had* worked out.

"Yes, we did," Jacob said, longing written in his amber eyes as he watched me.

It was safe to say that I loved the bastard now. I loved him enough to give my life for his. I'd just have to make sure it didn't come to that. Not too soon, at least.

But for now, I took him to the nearest empty room I could find. We didn't have inns or motels in the Realm—everybody had their own places around here. But I doubted anybody would mind when they woke up and found out what happened.

Once they were safely inside, I went back to Ax.

I didn't bother trying to carry him inside, either—I

wouldn't be able to. I was too weak. Though...not half as weak as I should have been, considering the sun was up.

We'd mated. My gods, just the thought of it made shivers run down my back. We'd actually mated in that short time when the spirit had left me.

I'd experienced what it meant to be *free* of it—for a minute only, but I had.

And it was...*horrible*. My chest had been so empty. My mind —completely blank. No whispers. No screams. No demands.

It was like there was no *me* inside me in those moments, either.

Fuck, I never thought I'd actually say this, but I couldn't live without that spirit inside me anymore. I didn't want to.

So, I lay on the ground next to Ax and looked at the square in front of me, the blood on the asphalt, the bodies of Marie and Marcus and Alida Morgans on one side, and Dylan on the other. Four lives lost.

My mind wandered and sleep almost took me. I don't know how long we stayed like that, but eventually, the sun no longer shone because big clouds took over the sky.

And Ax finally squeezed my fingers.

My eyes popped open, and I moved, climbing over his chest, grabbing his face in my hands.

His eyes were barely open, but I could see the brilliant blue of them. I could hear his heartbeat accelerating, the blood in his veins rushing at the sight of me.

Tears pricked the back of my eyes as I kissed him, wrapping my arms around his neck as he wrapped his around my waist. He was here. He was awake. He was alive.

We both were.

Fuck, that had been so close.

"Let's go to Paris," I whispered against his lips, as two

tears slipped down my cheeks. But they were happy tears this time—actually *happy*. Because I was happy. So happy I could fucking burst right now.

Ax chuckled, his body vibrating under mine—*alive*. "Sure thing. Just let me pack a bag."

"You're not really gonna need clothes."

"We might be in public at some point," he mumbled.

"We can just run super fast, get all the way to the top of the Eiffel Tower, then stay there."

"That's actually a great idea," he said, kissing my chin.

"That's a terrible idea."

"I was gonna fuck you on the Eiffel Tower, anyway."

I raised my head. "But it's dangerous."

The grin that stretched his lips had my heart tripping all over itself. "Even better."

I brought my lips to his again. "So long as there's no crazy sorcerers who want to wipe us off the face of the earth up there."

Ax's hold on me tightened. "Are they all dead?"

"Yep. Dylan, too."

"Marcus?"

I nodded. "Ethan killed them both."

He sighed, relieved. "She almost got us."

"Jacob tells me you went fucking crazy." Which I completely understood. I'd gone fucking crazy when he was in danger, too.

"I *am* fucking crazy, Damsel," he said, closing his eyes. "I think I've had enough of magic for at least a couple of lifetimes."

I laughed. "Yep. Same."

"Let's just keep away from it at all costs."

"We will."

"Let's keep away from the Realm, too," he said, and my stomach twisted. That's exactly what I wanted, too.

"I'll have to talk to Jones, first."

"You really don't."

"I want to."

"What if he asks you to stay?"

"Oh, I won't stay. Of course not," I reassured him. "I've spent my whole life doing things for other people. Because of my spirit. For Jones. For Ezra. For Anya. For *everyone*—or because of everyone—but never for me. It's time I changed that, don't you think?"

"Fuck, yeah," he whispered, pulling my lip between his teeth. "It's time you do whatever the fuck you want, baby."

"And I just want to go everywhere with you." I wanted to see places, meet people, do ordinary things that seemed so extraordinary to my eyes.

"I want to go everywhere with you."

"What if the rulers have a problem with us leaving, though?" Jones would probably be against it.

"If they do, they can talk about it all night, every night, while we're out there living our lives. Maybe they'll bond over it," Ax said, making me laugh.

"I'm pretty sure Jacob will keep sorcerers off our back, too." Though one couldn't be too sure. He didn't control sorcerers, not the way the rulers of our covens controlled vampires.

"He's actually...a good guy," Ax whispered. "Not that I'd ever tell him, but he's decent."

"Hate to say it, baby, but I fucking told you so." I kissed the breath out of him. "Also—we're *mated* now. I think that's why I have so little trouble staying awake."

"Yep. I don't. You shouldn't, either."

"Is that how that works?" I wondered. Nobody really

knew what mating felt like without actually trying it. Those who were mated always said *you'll know when you're mated*. Like it's some big fucking secret they didn't want to share with anyone.

"Not sure, but they do say you become *one*. I'm pretty sure I have a bit more resistance to magic, too, though that could have just been the moment," Ax said. "I could also feel it perfectly when you were unconscious. When you were...*dying*." His voice turned down a notch at that. Shivers rushed down his back, making me kiss him harder.

"I'm right here," I reassured him.

"I know, baby. We made it." And he sounded just as much in awe as I felt.

We'd made it, even with the Veins, and the spirits, and the crazy old sorceress, and even Will Thorne...which reminded me.

"But you have to promise me you won't kill people like that again." Especially not poison them to death while they slept, the way he'd done with Thorne.

Ax didn't hesitate. "Okay. I won't kill people behind your back." I raised a brow, and he added: "I won't kill people *unless* you're awake and watching?"

I sighed. "That's not the point, you asshole!"

"Baby, no man or creature that hurts you is going to live. You can't ask that of me," he said.

"But I—"

"It's my job to make the world a safer place for you."

"No, it's not."

But he wouldn't hear it. "I've *made* it my job. Arguing about it is pointless."

Didn't I know. Fuck, as much as I hated that he was so *violent,* I fucking loved it, too. I'd be a damn liar if I said that I didn't.

"So, you're just gonna take care of me now?" I whispered, kissing his chest.

He barely shrugged. "Beats torturing people all day."

"So, technically, I'm saving people, aren't I? Simply by keeping you busy."

He grinned. "You're a real hero, baby," he said, kissing my hair. "Let's just leave this fucked up place behind for good, okay? Let's just go."

"We will. I just need tonight." To talk to Jones—and to hang out with Anya for a bit. I couldn't wait to see her face.

"Then let's go to my house until sundown."

"Why? What do you want to do there?" We were *not* gonna have sex. We were both completely spent!

"I just want to lay with you on my bed," he said, pushing me to the side so he could get up. He did, but barely.

"Aww, baby, you're such a romantic," I teased.

But he stood up and pulled me up with him. "You're my mate. That's where you belong now."

I rolled my eyes. "How come *you* don't belong in *my* bed?"

He put his arm around my shoulders and started walking—slowly, barely holding himself up. Fuck, he really needed to lie down.

"I do. Except you live in a dorm, so..."

"Asshole," I muttered, only because it was true.

"It's a nice bed. It's comfortable," he said as he led me closer to the dead bodies so he could see them better. The sun was at our back and even though there were clouds in the sky, the heat of it still made it hard for me to breathe. Yeah—I would rather just be asleep when the sun was up, even though I technically *could* stay up now.

"Yeah? How many women have you had in that thing?"

Not that I cared—the past was the past. We both had them. Right now was all that mattered, but...

"None. Nobody else has ever laid in my bed except me."

I looked at him. "Liar."

"Nope."

"So, you *never* had sex in your house?" Because I wasn't going to believe that.

"Of course, I did. I just took them to the guest room, never in my bedroom."

"Really? Why?"

"Because I don't like other people's scent on my sheets."

"But you want *my* scent there?" He nodded. "Aww, the savage is *really* a hopeless romantic. Who knew?" And I kissed his cheek.

We stopped a few feet away from Marie's and Marcus's dead bodies. It still sucked to see them like that, though I didn't really regret that they died. It was better them than *all* of us.

"You cared about them," I said to Ax because I recognized the way his heart beat, and...I just *felt* how heavy he felt at the moment. It was very subtle, very *natural,* like the feeling had always been there, though it hadn't. It wasn't invading my privacy or making me uncomfortable.

This mating bond just might be much better than I thought.

"A little bit," he admitted, but what he meant was *a lot*. Which was understandable, since he'd lived with them for a while.

"The savage is also a real gentle giant. The list keeps growing," I teased, trying to make him feel better.

He pulled me to his chest and kissed me until my toes curled. "And you'll keep pretending like you're tough and cold and don't give a shit about anything or anyone. Got it."

"I *am* tough and cold. I don't give a shit about anything or anyone!"

He grinned. "Yep. That's what I said."

"No—you said *pretend*."

"Yep. That's exactly what I said."

"You—" But he kissed me again before I could say anything else.

"Take me home, baby. Since you're so tough, take me home because I'm gonna collapse." He was smiling when he said it—he couldn't care less that he was weak right now. Barely standing.

Because he trusted me to take care of him, to make sure he was safe.

Warmth spilled all over me as I guided him away from the dead bodies, toward the Sangria castle. A lot waited for me with nightfall. Anya would be the first person I'd find. Then Jones. I was going to have some difficult conversations, no doubt, but I wasn't half as worried as I thought I'd be before we came into the Realm this morning. I knew that whatever was coming my way, I'd handle it.

I'd come a long way since I left my comfort zone three months ago. And, yeah, it had been hard to get here, but Jones was absolutely right. Every second was absolutely worth it.

CHAPTER
TWENTY-EIGHT

Two years later

I HEARD him coming up behind me, but I pretended I didn't. He knew I was pretending, too, but he kept hoping he'd be able to sneak up on me one day. I kept hoping he'd stop hoping.

So far, it hadn't worked for either of us.

But when he grabbed me, spun me around and wrapped his arms around me, I still pretended to be surprised.

"I didn't even hear you coming," I told Ax, batting my lashes at him.

"That's okay, Damsel. I'll get you next time," he said, then stuck his tongue in my mouth, pressing me against the tree trunk to my right. He was so deliciously hard, it was impossible to keep my body in check. Not that I wanted to, but I kept getting curious to see how long *this* would last.

How long would he simply have to *look* at me for me to

start begging for him? Because it had been a long time now, and the need just kept getting stronger.

"We're mated, Savage. You *can't* sneak up on me. It's been two years. You should know that by now."

"I don't care. I'll still get you eventually."

"It's *impossible.*"

"And I make impossible things happen. *Watch* me," he said, pressing me harder against the tree trunk, making me moan when he pressed his hard cock against my throbbing center. I was wearing shorts, which had seemed like a good idea when I woke up, but fuck, nothing beat skirts. They were just so easy.

"Oh, I do believe it. I mean, you've settled down," I said, kissing his cheek. "In a house in the middle of nowhere." I bit the tip of his nose a bit. "And we have a fucking *garden,* too."

"We do have a garden. So what?" he teased, because he knew exactly how *I* felt about it. "I like the house. I like the garden. I like that nobody ever bothers us here."

He most definitely didn't.

"Me, too," I lied, too. "I finally found my peace here."

He leaned his head back, grinning because he could smell my bullshit perfectly. "It's been five days."

Well, yeah, but it felt like five fucking years to me.

When I suggested we buy a house near a mountain and try to *set roots* somewhere, I thought, why the fuck not? We went back to the Hidden Realm to visit sometimes, but mostly we just stayed out here in the world, traveling. Eating. Fucking. Just living life. Why not have a permanent place we could call home? We could still have that good life —and it was a *great* life. It was so amazing to just be able to wake up and be with him, go wherever I wanted, do whatever I wanted, and...

Lose my fucking mind about it.

Ugh, so boring I wanted to claw my eyes out when we weren't fucking. We couldn't just be fucking every waking second, could we? And we couldn't stay in the Realm, though Jones and Anya would have loved that. That place was way too small for us now—we just needed more space. And it suited the covens to have us out here, too—I'd helped Jones with human affairs at least five times, and Ax had helped Robert Sangria, too. Win-win.

Going back was not an option, but staying out here was proving to be…difficult, too.

"I know it's been five days. And it's going great. It's going perfect," I mumbled.

"You can't fucking stand this place, baby."

"But I'll get used to it," I insisted.

"Or we can go out there. Do a little something." His hands moved down my thighs, under my shorts, squeezing my ass.

"Something like what?"

"Something a little bad. Something a little evil. Something—"

"No—we're done with that, remember? We're living *peacefully* now. We got this!"

"Except we really don't. This isn't us. We'll stay here, do whatever you want for as long as you want, but you know as well as I do, we won't last here when there's a whole world of trouble out there for us to get into."

The more he talked, the more I wanted to say *yes*.

It was his voice—he could get me to do anything by just talking to me. Paired with the brilliant blue of his eyes and that spark of madness in them, he really could make the impossible happen, at least with me. I was already a lost cause.

"We're not killing people. We don't need to steal. We don't need to be doing *anything*," I insisted, trying to convince *myself* more than him.

"Yes, but—"

Ax stopped speaking abruptly.

The mating bond was so fucking incredible that when he heard something, I heard it, too. I heard it *through* him in a way, and he could hear everything through me, too.

We both froze at the sound of the car coming closer by the second, and then Ax let me go. The whispers in my head got curious, too. They were a bit louder, but it was nothing I couldn't handle. In fact, ever since that old sorceress had separated me from my spirit and I'd seen what it was like without it, it had changed my perspective about sharing my body with it completely. I wasn't even close to controlling the spirit a hundred percent yet, but I was *sharing* with it. I was learning day by day that we did not have to be enemies. In fact, if anything, we could be sort of *friends*, since we lived in the same body.

Some days were great, some were still a struggle, but it was getting better. And I was never afraid of losing it like I used to be. I was much stronger than I gave myself credit for, not to mention Ax was by my side all the time.

"Maybe they got the wrong address?" I suggested as we both walked down the pathway of our freaking *garden* and to the fence gate to see the main road that went by our house.

"Maybe they just want trouble," Ax said with a grin. "This could be a sign, Damsel."

"We are *not* killing anyone."

He'd killed plenty of times during the two years we'd been together—bad people, like it was his damn job to get rid of them. Whenever we heard stories about rapists or kidnappers or murderers, he just went after them, no matter how much I begged him to just drop it. They were *human,* for fuck's sake. The police would handle them just fine. We shouldn't have intervened.

But I was starting to think that that was his *thing*. And I was pretty sure by now that all those people he killed and tortured in the Hidden Realm that sparked all those rumors about him had been evil motherfuckers, too.

"Unless they want to kill us first. That would make it fair," Ax said, his eyes vibrant. He came alive at the idea of trouble like a fucking teenager, and I loved that about him.

"Do not attack, Savage," I warned him, just as the car turned the corner, and we finally saw the headlights.

The next second, I burst out laughing because I recognized the truck coming our way. The red paint of it, the sound of the engine, and the man sitting in the driver's seat, slowly coming to us.

"I'll be fucking damned," Ax said, shaking his head in disbelief.

A minute later, the truck stopped, the driver's door opened, and none other than Jacob Thorne stepped out, cowboy hat and boots included.

I ran to him and jumped in his arms, laughing still. We'd seen him about a year and a half ago, completely by accident. He'd been on a job and we couldn't even hang out for long, but I'd missed the asshole. I hugged him tightly until I made sure he couldn't breathe for a few seconds, then I let him go.

"I think it's time someone told you to ditch that hat, Thorne," I said, grinning as I took him in. "It's *really* time to ditch the hat." There were a couple wrinkles around his eyes when he laughed, but nothing major. He still looked almost exactly like he used to—except his eyes. Every new

DEADLY MATCH

time I saw him, they looked *sharper*, the color in them deeper. Much more similar to his uncle Will's, which shouldn't have been so surprising to me.

"You've got no style, Arella," Jacob said, shaking his head.

"Thorne, long time no see," Ax said, and he actually offered Jacob his hand *willingly*. If you knew Ax, you'd know that that was a big deal—he didn't really shake anybody's hand.

But Jacob was different, and they were kind-of, sort-of friends. *Almost*. Not that I'd say it out loud to Ax.

"It's good to see you guys," Jacob said, finally taking that hat off. "I see you've settled down." And he looked behind us at the two-story house we had been living in for the past five days.

"How'd you even know?" I asked.

"Jones told me," Jacob said.

"Could have just called us directly." He had our numbers, and we had his. Just in case.

"I wasn't actually looking for you when I called him and he told me about...um...*this*." He was trying to keep from laughing.

I rolled my eyes. "It's a nice house. We're setting up roots." His cheeks turned redder. I crossed my arms in front of me. "Don't be a dick, sorcerer."

But he couldn't help himself, and Ax joined in the laughter, too. Whatever.

"She's not gonna last another twenty-four hours," Ax said to Jacob.

"I'm betting less," the sorcerer said.

"Fuck you both," I muttered. I was going to last twenty *years* in this place. It was home! Maybe not right now, but it would be. I'd fucking *make* it home.

"Don't be rude, baby," Ax said, putting his arm around my shoulder. "Let's invite our guest in. We've got refreshments...don't we?"

I flinched. "We've got blood." Shit. "I'm sorry, Jacob. We've been meaning to go grocery shopping." Except it was too boring to even think about it.

"That's okay, I'm not here for refreshments. I'm actually here to ask for some help."

On the outside, my face was perfectly composed, but on the inside, it almost felt like I had an orgasm.

My gods. I hadn't heard better words in ages. "You are?"

"We're in," Ax said without missing a beat.

I slapped him on the chest, though I wanted nothing more than to tell Jacob to get back in his trunk and take us to...*where*, exactly?

"We don't know what it is yet," I said, already impatient.

"We don't have to. It will beat your garden. We're in, Jacob," he repeated. "Otherwise, I'm gonna lose my mind for real and then you'll be sent out here to hunt me again."

Jacob smiled, but it didn't quite reach his eyes. It was okay. We all knew what he really thought about Ax.

"What is it? What do you need help for?"

"Vampires—and sorcerers. A sort of cult that's been forming the past year. I thought I had it covered, but turns out, there's more of them than I anticipated," he said, and fuck, I was about to come *for real* from all that talk. "I could hire other sorcerers, but I somehow feel like you two would be—"

"We're in."

Yeah, fuck setting up roots. And gardening. And everything. I wanted to fight. Kill something. *Do* something useful! It's been two long, *long* years.

"You sure? Because it might take a couple weeks to track them down. Round them up. And there will be no killing, either," Jacob said.

I looked at Ax as he tried to stifle a smile. "You heard that? No killing."

He cleared his throat. "Yes. Yep. Absolutely. No killing." He was lying through his fucking teeth.

I smiled. "No killing."

Jacob squinted his eyes at me. "You're lying, aren't you." It wasn't really a question.

"Of course not. We're friends, Jacob. We wouldn't lie to you."

"Exactly," Ax said. "I'm a changed man now, Jacob. I do not kill people anymore." He put his hands on my hips and pulled me back. I could feel his excitement rushing in his veins same as mine. And he got turned on by it, same as me. "So, just sit there tight in your car and give us a minute to go, erm…pack some things."

Suddenly, Jacob looked like he'd seen a ghost.

"No, no, no, no," he said because he probably remembered our meeting at Ax's cabin two years ago. "I know what you're going to do. You're not going in there to pack—you're going to have sex!"

Well…

Both Ax and I looked at the ground. It would just be a couple minutes…a few, at most.

Jacob laughed bitterly. "I will not sit here and wait around for you two to start screaming!"

"Don't be ridiculous. We're not! We're just packing a bag!" I said, waving him off as Ax and I moved backward. But Ax was already impatient.

"We'll be back in no time, man," he said, then grabbed

me and threw me over his shoulder, before he ran to the house.

"You two are *sick*!" Jacob called, and we heard him get in his car and drive in reverse—and fast. It just made us laugh.

But it was okay. He wouldn't be too far. All we really needed was like half an hour. Maybe *one*, tops.

"You heard that? We're going to get into trouble," Ax said, tearing the shirt off my body. I was used to it by now, so I didn't waste breath complaining. I just tore *his* shirt off him, too, and I'll be damned if I didn't enjoy it. Why did it even feel amazing to rip clothes off? It made no sense still.

"Fuck yeah, baby." *Trouble* had never sounded sexier than it did right now.

"We'll spill blood. We'll fight. We'll kill," he said, tearing my shorts off as he pressed me against the wall.

"We might be on the run, too. Maybe someone will chase us."

He growled. "Maybe someone will insult you."

I laughed. "Maybe we should work with Jacob for a little while. You know. Until we're *really* ready to settle down."

He moved his head back for a second. "Or we can just work on our own—because we're *never* gonna settle down, Damsel. It's just not us."

Just not us.

And maybe he was right. I still wanted to hope, though. I still wanted to think there'd come a time when I'd enjoy a quiet, peaceful life.

That time just wasn't right now.

"You're worried," he said, planting gentle kisses on my cheek as his fingers teased my entrance, making my back arch. "Stop worrying, baby. No matter what happens, we'll still be us."

I nodded, hanging onto his wide shoulders for dear life. "We'll still be us," I whispered.

He continued circling his thumb over my clit until I cried out. And when he had me trembling, exactly like he wanted me, he held me up and brought the tip of his cock to my wet folds.

Fuck, I still loved the feel of it just as much as I did the first time. Everything about him was the right amount of intense without being too overwhelming. It kept me wanting more and never getting bored at the same time.

"Whatever it takes, Damsel," he whispered, looking into my eyes as he slowly lowered me down onto him.

I held my breath until he filled every inch inside of me. When we were like that, connected physically, too, the world just made so much more sense. Everything looked more beautiful, had more color, more meaning. I knew by now that that was *never* going to change.

"Whatever it takes, Savage," I promised him, too. And I meant it.

No matter where tonight—or the next or the one after that—took us, we'd always be us. We'd always have this. And we'd go back to it over and over again, no matter what we had to do.

The future didn't scare me. My spirit didn't, either—it made me feel stronger instead. Fear no longer dictated my life, and that was how I finally set myself free.

—THE END

Thank you for reading the final book in The Hidden Realm

*series! I hope you enjoyed reading **Deadly Match** as much as I enjoyed writing it.*

For more books, turn the page, or you can follow me on Amazon, social media, or visit www.dnhoxa.com

*Sincerely,
Dori Hoxa*

More by D.N. Hoxa: The Reign of Dragons Series

King of Air (Reign of Dragons, Book 1)

Being stuck in a time loop sucks, especially when I die on the same day, at the hands of the same man, over and over again. But in Life Number Seven, I'm determined to change my fate.

You'd think being the princess of all shifters would come with benefits and glamour and *freedom*--it doesn't. It comes with isolation, constant fear, and a fabric over my head the whole damn time.

Nobody will believe me or lift a finger to help me figure out why I'm stuck in this loop, not even my father, the dragon king. If I dare to even mention it to him, I end up with a bloody lip. Yeah, he's a very hard man to talk to. That's why I have no other choice but to switch places with my maid and run away.

But things don't exactly go as planned when I'm kidnapped and find myself a captive of my father's sworn enemy. *Just my luck.*

Lucien Di Laurier is a cocky bastard who thinks I'm an object to be owned. It doesn't help that he's impossibly beautiful and can literally control the air in my lungs with a wave of his hand. He wants to get his revenge on the king, and that's why he's after the princess...never realizing that I'm right there, in his home, pretending to be my maid. He vows to break me until I tell him all of my secrets, but...

That still doesn't stop me.

He'll kill me if he finds out my real name. He'll probably do worse things before that, but I can't help myself. He's everything I was never allowed to have. He's blinding light and passion and *life*, the perfect mistake wrapped up in a pretty ribbon, just for me.

So I take what I can get even knowing how it will all end... until it does.

PIXIE PINK SERIES

Werewolves Like Pink Too (Pixie Pink, Book 1)

What's worse than a pink pixie living all alone in the Big City, eight thousand miles away from home?

A pink pixie who's stuck behind a desk all day, taking calls and managing monster-fighting crews without ever seeing the light of day herself. *That's* what.

For two years, I worked my ass off to prove myself to my boss, and prayed for a chance to do the work I left my family behind for.

And I'm finally about to catch my break. I've got an undercover mission with my name on it, and it's everything I've been dreaming of since I got here.

Until I find out that Dominic Dane will be my partner. That self absorbed, narcissistic werewolf who humiliated me in front of all my coworkers on day one, and loves to pretend that I don't even exist.

It's bad enough that he tried to kick me out of my mission. It's even worse that he's sinfully hot and fries braincells with a single look of those gorgeous green eyes.

Now, on top of having to kick ass on my first mission, I have to pretend to be his *girlfriend* for three days, and keep my ridiculous attraction to him under control, too. So much for catching a break.

Lucky for me, I've got a secret weapon that's going to help me handle Dominic Dane, and it's God's best gift to mankind: chocolate. Armed with as many bars as my purse can fit, and with my wits about me, I'm going to survive the gorgeous wolf-ass one way or the other—and *win*.

THE NEW YORK SHADE SERIES

Magic Thief (The New York Shade, Book 1)

Welcome to the New York Shade!

My name is Sin Montero--hellbeast mercenary, professional liar, and I'll happily be your guide.

Supernaturals are free to be who they are in the Shade. That's the point of its existence--just not for me. I've spent my whole life lying about what I am, until it all comes crashing down on me with a single bite. Turns out, my blood can't tell lies, not to a vampire.

Damian Reed is achingly beautiful the way a lion is breathtaking--right until he rips your throat out. He claims my baby brother is in trouble...

THE NEW ORLEANS SHADE SERIES

Pain Seeker (The New Orleans Shade, Book 1)

Betrayed. Defeated. Chained.

I used to be a sister, a friend, a ruler of the elflands that belonged to my family's House. Now, I am a prisoner of the fae, my kind's sworn enemy since the beginning of time.

They put chains around me, thinking they can keep me from breaking free and taking their lives. They can't.

The only reason I stay is because I no longer need a life. My home, my family, my dignity were all taken away from me.

But I have the fae. My captor. He is every bit the man I was taught to hate long before I knew how to love...

THE DARK SHADE SERIES

Shadow Born (The Dark Shade, Book 1)

They call me Kallista Nix, but that is not my real name. *My past was taken from me, and though I search for it every day for the past five years, all I find are dead ends.*

Though I search for the Dark Shade, everyone keeps telling me that it doesn't exist. The darkness, the monsters, the fear—they're all in my head. I'm tempted to believe them. The Shades are magical safe havens where everyone can be who they truly are without having to hide. Supernaturals of all kinds love them. They're not supposed to be *dark*. But how can I argue with my own memories? Everything changes when I steal a magical artifact...

SMOKE & ASHES SERIES

Firestorm (Smoke & Ashes, Book 1)

Having no soul definitely has its perks.

After all, I can kill as many magical beasts as I want and not have to worry about the blood on my hands. But no matter how hard I try to run, I can never escape where I came from: the pits of Hell. Now Hell's elite have a job for me, a job I can't refuse. A nocturnal witch is on the loose and those are never up to anything good. She's hiding in my city, so they've decided I'm the best person for the job—together with Lexar Dagon'an. He's Hell's very own Golden Boy, my archnemesis, and he's sexy as the sins he makes me want to commit when I look at him. Like *murder*, obviously...

ALSO BY D.N. HOXA

Winter Wayne Series (Completed)

Bone Witch

Bone Coven

Bone Magic

Bone Spell

Bone Prison

Bone Fairy

Scarlet Jones Series (Completed)

Storm Witch

Storm Power

Storm Legacy

Storm Secrets

Storm Vengeance

Storm Dragon

Victoria Brigham Series (Completed)

Wolf Witch

Wolf Uncovered

Wolf Unleashed

Wolf's Rise

The Marked Series (Completed)

Blood and Fire

Deadly Secrets

Death Marked

Starlight Series (Completed)

Assassin

Villain

Sinner

Savior

Morta Fox Series (Completed)

Heartbeat

Reclaimed

Unchanged